THE
HOUSE
GUEST

ALSO BY MARK EDWARDS

The Magpies

Kissing Games

What You Wish For

Because She Loves Me

Follow You Home

The Devil's Work

The Lucky Ones

The Retreat

A Murder of Magpies

In Her Shadow

Here to Stay

Last of the Magpies

WITH LOUISE VOSS

Forward Slash

Killing Cupid

Catch Your Death

All Fall Down

From the Cradle

The Blissfully Dead

THE
HOUSE
GUEST

MARK
EDWARDS

THOMAS & MERCER

Text copyright © 2020 by Mark Edwards
All rights reserved.

Published by Thomas & Mercer, Seattle

www.apub.com

Amazon, the Amazon logo, and Thomas & Mercer are trademarks of Amazon.com, Inc., or its affiliates.

ISBN-13: 9781542094030
ISBN-10: 1542094038

Cover design by Tom Sanderson

Printed in the United States of America

THE
HOUSE
GUEST

PART ONE

Chapter 1

The woman standing on the front stoop looked like she'd crawled straight out of the Hudson. Water dripped from the hem of her little summer dress and pooled around her boots. Her hair, blonde but darkened by rain, stuck to her forehead.

Seeing me, she did a double take and glanced at the number on the mailbox beside the door.

'Um . . . are Mona or Jack home?' she asked. 'Have I got the right address?'

'They're away,' I replied.

'Away?'

'Yeah, afraid so. I'm the house-sitter.'

'Oh. Damn it.' Water clung to her eyelashes like teardrops. 'I *knew* I should have called ahead.'

Night had not yet fallen, but the sun, which had burned brightly all day, was nowhere to be seen – though the air, and the rain, retained their warmth. It wasn't like England, where the rain falls cold throughout the year. New York summers are different.

'Damn,' the young woman said again. 'When will they be back?'

'Next Sunday.'

'Next Sunday?' She sighed and pushed her wet hair out of her face, peering past me into the house. Behind her, someone ran along the street, seeking shelter, and a car went past slowly, wipers on maximum, spraying water on to the steps below where the young woman stood. The Bedford Avenue subway was a few minutes away, and I guessed that was where she had come from.

'Sorry to have disturbed you,' she said, but she hesitated, looking over her shoulder, past the backpack she was wearing. Then she laughed. 'Why am I being such a wimp? I can't get any wetter, can I?'

I laughed too.

'I don't suppose I could come in for a moment and write a note for Mona and Jack?'

This wasn't my house. I didn't feel comfortable inviting a stranger in. But she knew Jack and Mona's names, didn't she? And she looked so pathetic standing there on the stoop while rain pummelled the pavement behind her. What harm could it do?

'Of course,' I said. 'Come in.'

She rewarded me with a broad smile. 'Thank you.'

The woman stepped into the hallway and glanced at herself in the mirror that hung by the front door. She laughed. 'Whoa. I look even wetter then I feel.'

We both looked down at the puddle that was forming on the floorboards. 'Wait there, I'll fetch you a towel.'

I hurried to the downstairs bathroom, which was at the back of the house beside the kitchen. As I approached the door, Ruth came out.

'What's going on?' she asked.

'There's a woman, a friend of the Cunninghams. She's drenched.'

I grabbed a towel from the rail in the bathroom and headed back to the front door, Ruth at my heels. The young woman was crouching, fishing in her backpack for something. As she stood, I handed her the towel and she wiped at her face and arms, rubbing her hair before tying it back in a scrunchie she'd pulled out of her bag. She tugged at the shoulder straps of her dress and pulled herself up to her full height. She was around five-six or five-seven, and I guessed she was about twenty-five. A few years younger than Ruth and me, anyway. She was pretty, with a gently sloped nose and hazel eyes.

'I'm Eden,' she said.

'Adam.'

She turned to Ruth. 'Please tell me your name is Eve.'

All three of us laughed at that.

'I'm afraid not. It's Ruth.'

'Oh well. I guess that would have been too weird. Adam, Eve, Eden. We'd have to start watching out for serpents and whatnot.'

We all laughed again, a little awkwardly.

'So Mona and Jack have gone away?' Eden said.

'Yeah,' I replied. 'They're on a retreat in New Mexico.'

'You mean like one of those things where people go into the desert and . . . find themselves?'

'Something like that.'

'Ha. That sounds like them. I mean, if I want to find myself, I go to a bar, but different strokes, right?'

Ruth rolled her eyes slightly. If she wasn't committed to being in New York, the retreat would have been the kind of thing she'd have loved to go to.

'Did you say they get back next Sunday?'

'That's right.'

Eden tapped her forehead with her palm, fingers splayed. 'I'm such a doofus. I thought, *Hey, I'll surprise them*. I had this vision of Mona opening the door with this big look of shocked delight on her face, like, "What are you doing here? Come on in!"'

5

'And instead you found us,' said Ruth.

We had all moved further into the house during this conversation, so I was adjacent to the door to the living room. From here I could see through the front window, with its view of the street. The sky was growing blacker, the rain even heavier. Eden followed my gaze.

'I don't suppose you guys have an umbrella I could borrow? Or should I say a brolly? That's what you Brits call it, right?'

'You detected our accents,' I said.

'They're difficult to miss.' She grinned. 'I used to be obsessed with Harry Potter. I still am, a little.'

'Eden asked if she could leave a note for Jack and Mona,' I said. 'Any idea where—'

Ruth cut me off. 'We can't send her back out into that rain.' She exchanged a 'typical men' look with Eden. 'What is he like? Why don't you have a drink with us, wait for the rain to stop?'

'Are you sure you don't mind?'

'Of course not.'

'That would be so kind. But can I use your bathroom to get changed into some dry clothes?'

'I'll show you where it is,' I said.

'And I'll open some wine,' said Ruth. 'Red okay?'

'Whatever you've got. I'm easy.'

The downstairs bathroom was a bit of a mess, so I led Eden up the creaky staircase to the upper floor, where there was a second bathroom.

'Your girlfriend's lovely,' she said.

'I know. And I'm sorry. I wasn't going to send you back into the rain.'

She smiled and touched my shoulder, leaving a damp handprint on my T-shirt. 'It's cool. I get it. You don't know me from

Adam.' She realised what she'd said. 'I guess that expression doesn't work with you, does it?'

She took her backpack into the bathroom and shut the door behind her.

Back downstairs, I found Ruth pouring red wine into three glasses.

'It's nice to have a guest, isn't it?' I said.

She raised an eyebrow. 'Especially one who's hot.'

'What? I don't think—'

'I'm teasing you, Adam. She is cute, though. Your type.'

I pulled her into my arms and kissed the top of her head. 'You're my type. The most typical of my type.'

She squirmed away, laughing. 'Oh my God, you're so corny.'

It was good to see her laugh; to joke around with her like this. Since arriving in New York a few weeks ago she'd been busy and distracted, and everything had been so intense that there had been very little time for us and the way we used to be. I'd been worrying about it.

'Ruth—' I began.

But I didn't get to finish the sentence. Eden had reappeared already, dressed in a pair of jeans and a T-shirt. Her feet were bare and she'd wrapped the towel I'd given her around her head. She had come down the stairs as quietly as a cat.

She took the glass of wine Ruth offered her and looked from Ruth to me then back again. Ruth was right – Eden was pretty. But she had nothing on my girlfriend.

'Cheers!' Eden said, raising her glass. 'Thank you for inviting me in.'

Chapter 2

'Where have you come from?' Ruth asked as we went into the living room and sat down. The two women took the sofa, and I sat in the armchair that looked and smelled like it should have been condemned years ago, but which was, apparently, Jack's favourite.

'California,' Eden said. 'Bakersfield? But the last couple of years I've been living in LA.' She shifted in her seat as she said this, and a frown flitted across her face as if she'd been reminded of something unpleasant. Maybe she didn't like thinking about home.

'LA? Are you an actress?' I asked.

'God, no.' She laughed. 'I couldn't act to save my life. I'm not in the entertainment industry at all, which I guess makes me pretty rare for someone who moved to LA, right? Except I went there for a guy.'

'Uh-oh,' said Ruth.

'Yeah. And guess what? He turned out to be a loser. The latest in a long line of them. And that's why I decided I needed to get away for a while. I figured New York was just about far enough.' She got up and began looking around the room. 'This place is awesome. I mean, a whole house in Williamsburg? I knew Mona and Jack were loaded but this is ridiculous. Though I'm kind of surprised, to be honest. I thought they'd live somewhere totally minimalist. All, like, polished surfaces and pebbles.'

'Pebbles?'

'Yeah, you know. A smooth granite counter with just a polished grey pebble sitting on it. Maybe a fancy-schmancy candle? I wasn't expecting clutter and old books with broken spines and peeling paint and *this*.' She lay her hand on the vintage jukebox that was the focal point of the room. 'This is, like, the sickest thing I've ever seen. Does it actually work?'

'It does.' I got up to show her. 'What do you want to listen to?'

She bent forward to read the names of the seven-inch singles that were stored inside the jukebox.

'How about the Eagles?' she said.

I pressed a couple of buttons, and the jukebox, which according to Jack and Mona had been here since the mid-seventies, whirred into life. The needle dropped and 'Witchy Woman' began to play.

'Oh my God, I love this,' Eden said. 'My mom used to play it all the time.' She nodded her head along to the song, one bare foot tapping on the wooden floor. I found myself grinning, and turned to see Ruth smiling too. It was hard not to be swept up in Eden's enthusiasm.

'Want me to put something on for you, Ruth?' Eden asked as the Eagles track ended. 'What's your jam? Wait, let me guess.'

A moment later, Bob Dylan started singing 'Subterranean Homesick Blues' and Ruth said, 'How did you know?'

'You've got that look about you,' Eden said. 'A poetic soul.'

'She is,' I said. 'Ruth's an actress. That's the main reason we're in New York. She's got a role in a new play on Broadway called *Dare*. The female lead.'

'That's amazing.'

'It's her big break. Well, that and this film she made last year.'

'Oh, wow. What's it called? Will I have seen it?'

Ruth waved a hand self-deprecatingly. 'It's doubtful. It had a very limited release. A couple of festivals and a few movie theatres but that's all.'

'It's on streaming though,' I said.

'Really? What's it called? I've got to look it up.'

Ruth was being typically modest so I told Eden about the film. 'It's called *The Immaculate* and it's about this woman, a virgin, who gets pregnant and gives birth to this super-evolved girl and—'

'It's kind of embarrassing,' said Ruth.

'No, it's great,' I said. 'Low-budget but really well written and creepy. And all the reviewers said Ruth is the best thing in it. And now she has this play plus a ton of auditions lined up for more movies. Bigger movies.'

'That's amazing,' Eden said. 'So I'm meeting you just before you become famous?'

'I don't know about that,' Ruth responded.

'No, I can feel it. You're going to be a star. This time next year you'll refuse to talk to any of us little people.'

Ruth stared into her lap and Eden must have seen something in my face that made her stop gushing about Ruth's impending celebrity.

'What about you, Adam? What do you do?'

'I'm a writer. A playwright.'

'You wrote Ruth's play?'

'Oh, no, I'm not at that level. But I've just finished something. I've got a meeting about it tomorrow, actually.'

'Wow. This is so cool. You're both going to be famous.'

'This is why I love Americans,' I said. 'Your optimism.'

'That's us.'

'Also, Cinnabon.'

Ruth rolled her eyes. 'Adam is obsessed with Cinnabon.'

'How could anyone not be?' said Eden.

'So, how do you know Jack and Mona?' Ruth asked.

'Remember the guy I was telling you about? The loser? He went to college with Jack. They came out to LA to see him a few times. Stayed at my boyfriend's place. They were always really nice to me. Mona actually told me I was too good for him – for the jerk. She was right.'

The mood in the room had darkened and, now that the music had stopped and the conversation had halted, the house felt very quiet. Eden slapped her own legs and laughed. 'Listen to me, bumming everyone out. You didn't tell me how you guys met Jack and Mona. Or did you organise this on a house-sitting website or something?'

'We actually met them on a cruise,' Ruth said, sipping her wine.

'Oh! The cruise they took to the Caribbean? That sounded awesome.'

'It was,' I said.

Earlier this year, Ruth had got a gig playing Miranda in *The Tempest* on a cruise from the UK to the Bahamas via New York. The cruise company were trying to put on more upscale enter-tainment, presumably to draw a more cultured crowd, and had hired the director Sally Klay, presumably paying her an enormous sum. It said something about Sally's dark sense of humour that she had chosen a play about a shipwreck, though the audiences that crowded in twice a day didn't seem bothered.

I had gone along as a paying passenger, partly because I didn't want to be apart from Ruth for so long, but also because I thought it would give me the perfect opportunity to work on my new play. Lots of empty hours, intermittent internet access, nowhere to go. As it turned out, I had been right. I completed the script halfway through the journey and, shortly after that, I met Jack and Mona

Cunningham in the lounge. They had boarded the ship in New York.

They were in their early forties, which made them more than a decade older than Ruth and me, and I was instantly charmed by them. Jack was a professor of psychology at Columbia and Mona was something called a 'domestic wellness coach', which meant she told rich people how to rearrange their homes to make themselves feel less stressed out. As far as I could tell it mostly involved chucking stuff away and folding your clothes neatly. But they drank Martinis and talked about summers in the Hamptons, all mixed in with yoga and mindfulness and veganism. If F. Scott Fitzgerald were alive today, I imagine he'd be writing about people like Jack and Mona.

Ruth got along well with them too. She was as passionate about spirituality and meditation and all the rest as they were, and they had been fascinated to hear about her acting career. Jack and Mona came to see her performance two or three times – and when she told them Sally Klay had offered her the lead role in her new Broadway play, and that we would be coming to New York for the summer and beyond, they had exchanged a look of delight.

'You should stay at our place in Brooklyn,' Mona said.

'That's right,' agreed Jack. 'We're going away for the summer, to this retreat in New Mexico. We were going to look for house-sitters anyway. What do you think?'

We had agreed on the spot. And now here we were, coming towards the end of our stay. It hadn't been as idyllic as I'd hoped, but it had still been better than staying in a hotel. Or remaining in London while Ruth took on the world alone.

'So, what are you planning to do when Jack and Mona get back?' Eden asked.

'I'm not sure,' I replied.

'I'm sure they'd be cool with you staying,' she said. 'They're such nice people. So welcoming. That's why I'm here. Last time I saw them Mona said I could come and stay with them any time I want.'

'That sounds like them,' I said.

Eden smiled but there was a hint of sadness in her eyes. 'It's stopped raining,' she said, wandering over to the window. 'I should get out of your hair.'

'Where are you going to go?' I asked. 'Do you know anyone else in the city?'

'Not really.' She stared out at the wet street. I could see her frown reflected in the glass. 'But don't worry about me. I'll be fine.'

I got the feeling she didn't have much money, that any room she could afford would be a fleapit. And she had come all this way, clearly needing to get away from the wreckage of her relationship, only to find a couple of strangers inhabiting the place where she thought she'd be able to stay. I felt bad for her.

I glanced at Ruth to see if she was thinking the same as me. Back in London, we had a cat called Willow who we had taken in as a stray. The cat was vicious and peed everywhere, but Ruth always forgave her, saying she'd had a hard start in life, that we just needed to be patient. This was a very different situation, but I could tell from Ruth's expression that we were on a similar wavelength.

'Why don't you stay here?' I said.

Eden turned from the window. 'I couldn't. I don't want to get in your way.'

'You wouldn't, would she, Ruth?'

'No. Not at all.'

'There's a second spare bedroom that we aren't using. I'm sure Jack and Mona wouldn't want us to turn you away.'

Eden brought her thumb to her mouth and chewed on the nail. 'Maybe you should call them, check it's okay.'

'We can't get hold of them while they're at the retreat. They're not allowed phones there.'

Eden took a step towards us. 'Are you sure?'

I looked at Ruth, who nodded. 'We're sure.'

'Oh my God, that's so kind of you.' Her mood changed like a switch had been flicked. She bounded over and wrapped me in a hug – she smelled of rain and, faintly, of cigarettes – then bent down and embraced Ruth, who smiled at me over Eden's shoulder.

Eden stood up straight and said, 'Wait here. Let me buy you dinner. What are you in the mood for?'

'There's no need,' Ruth began, but I had already started to say, 'There's a taco truck on the corner.'

'Tacos coming right up. Let me grab some cash.' She ran up the stairs.

'Do you think we've done the right thing?' I asked.

'Yeah, I like her. And it'll be nice for you to have company while I'm at work.'

'It will,' I said.

Ruth went back to the kitchen to pour herself more wine. Eden was still upstairs, and I went over to the front window.

There was a man standing across the street, holding an umbrella which obscured most of his face, but I could see that he had a grey beard. He appeared to be staring straight at the house. Straight at me. And as soon as our eyes met he put his head down, pulled the umbrella lower and hurried away.

Weird, I thought. But when Eden came running back down the stairs, clutching a fistful of cash, I didn't say anything to her about it.

Chapter 3

I emerged on to Eighth Avenue wondering if there was a manhole I could jump into. Sam Mendoza, the producer I'd just met, hated my play. He hadn't used those words, but it was obvious. He had said it had 'some potential'. And then he'd turned the conversation to Ruth, asking me how rehearsals for *Dare* were going. If I knew what kind of role she was looking for next. That, I realised, was why he'd wanted to see me. Not because he was interested in me or my writing, but because my girlfriend was a hot up-and-coming actor.

I was used to rejection and lack of interest. It went with the territory. After all, writers are as commonplace as rats. The world needs another one like it needs an extra hole in the ozone layer. I hadn't been expecting miracles from this meeting.

But it still stung.

I got out of the Theater District as quickly as I could and walked towards Central Park. The city was as hot as hell, and crowded with tourists. In desperate need of a break from the heat, I popped into a Starbucks and bought an iced latte.

As I came out, I saw a familiar figure going into a jewellery store.

'Cara?' I called.

She stopped, looked around, then spotted me. 'Adam?'

I reached her and we exchanged a quick hug. 'This is a coincidence,' I said.

'Small world,' she replied with her customary smile. It was the first time I'd seen her since we'd been in New York.

Cara had been on the cruise, the only other actress in the company. Miranda is the only female part in *The Tempest*, and Cara, an Australian who had something of the young Nicole Kidman about her, with strawberry-blonde hair and a cute smattering of freckles across her nose, had been Ruth's understudy.

'Why aren't you in rehearsals?' I asked.

'I'm not needed today. Sally keeps reworking the script and my part has shrunk from tiny to infinitesimal.'

'Oh dear.'

She shrugged. 'That's showbiz.'

'But you're still Ruth's understudy, right?'

'Yeah. Again. But unless she gets struck down by a mystery virus . . .' She sighed. 'Anyway, I've gotta run. I need to buy a birthday present for my sister. She's sent me a wish list full of words like Tiffany's and Saks. But why don't I give you my number? We could go for a drink or something.'

'That would be . . .' I wasn't sure how Ruth would feel about me going for a drink with Cara. But I took the phone she offered me and tapped my number into it.

'I'll call you,' she said, and she disappeared into the store, turning at the last moment to give me a little wave.

By the time I reached Central Park I was coated in sweat, but it was a little cooler and quieter beneath the trees, away from the sunbathers and children clutching helium balloons. I sat on a bench and flicked through my script. Sam hadn't even made any notes on it. I doubted he'd looked at it.

I got up and put it in a bin, laughing at myself even as I did it. I mean, it wasn't as if I didn't have a copy saved on my laptop.

As I sat back down I tried to ignore the whisper of panic, the voice that told me I was wasting my time, that I wasn't good enough. I had been writing for years, since I was at college, and apart from a couple of amateur plays put on with friends, I had got nowhere. And there were no signs that I was going anywhere, either. I didn't even enjoy the act of writing anymore. Maybe it was time—

I stood up. This was ridiculous. I was in New York, the greatest city in the world. It was a beautiful day. I was young. Sam Mendoza was a dickhead who wouldn't recognise talent if it sank its teeth into his behind. And I had Ruth. I still had Ruth.

As five o'clock approached, I headed towards Tavern on the Green, where she and I had arranged to meet. There were a lot of people around: joggers, dog-walkers, families with kids. Walking past the lake, I got the peculiar sensation of eyes crawling over my skin, but when I turned there was no one looking at me, just a pair of young women in Lycra, running slowly in tandem. Behind them, an elderly man had a stall set up beside the path, selling paintings. He blinked at me with milky eyes and I took a closer look at his work, expecting to see portraits of tourists or etchings of local landmarks. Instead, the paintings depicted crowds fleeing down Manhattan's avenues, pursued by screaming flocks of mutant seagulls; children weeping as their parents were led away by faceless figures in black uniforms; boiling seas and dying mermaids and scorched landscapes littered with bones and plastic Coke bottles.

'See anything you like?' he asked.

I hurried away.

I took a seat outside the Tavern and waited for Ruth, keen to tell her about my meeting with Sam – figuring out how I could put a comical spin on it – and the man with the frightening paintings.

Here she came, walking coolly down the path towards me. She had headphones in and a little bag over her shoulder. A plain white T-shirt and a knee-length skirt. Shoulder-length blonde hair. No different to the hundreds of other young women who were roaming Central Park right now.

But as she passed, people stopped mid-conversation. They turned their heads, men and women alike, to watch her. To stare. Why? Because there was an energy coming off her. Something invisible; something that crackled silently, shifting the molecules in the air around her. No one recognised her – her movie had been a small critical success, seen mostly by hardcore horror buffs and industry insiders – but they recognised *something*. A sun that shone from within her. The sense that here was someone on the cusp; someone who had been sprinkled with magic dust but hadn't yet learned to stretch her wings. Like Marilyn Monroe in 1951, Madonna in 1982, Beyoncé right before she joined Destiny's Child. I watched the faces of the people she passed and I knew that soon she would belong among the stars.

'Hey,' she said, kissing me lightly on the lips. A waiter appeared almost immediately and took her drinks order. Her beer arrived quickly and she held the icy bottle against her cheek for a moment. 'Oh my God, I need this. What a day. I have to keep reminding myself I'm living the dream.'

'You are.'

She told me about the rehearsal, about how Sally had made her and the lead actor, a guy named Alex, act out the same scene over and over until they'd got it 'almost' right.

'It's so hard, Adam. Sally is such a . . .'

'Bitch?'

'No!' She grinned. 'I was going to say "visionary". A perfectionist too.'

'She's a tyrant. I saw the way she talked to you and the other actors on the cruise.'

'I know she can be a little tough – but, well, it's tough love. She's making us into better actors. Creating better art. I feel like . . .

you know, it's often like being part of a family, being with the cast and the crew, and then at the end you all disperse and you never see half of them again, but this time, I don't know, it feels different.'

I didn't point out that she always said this.

'Sally hasn't said so but I really think she values me. And Alex is so good, it's ridiculous. I was struggling so much to capture the agony of the scene, to truly feel it, you know? But he helped me. We did this exercise that . . .' She stopped herself. 'How was your meeting?'

I hesitated. I really didn't want to stick a pin in her mood. 'It was great. He liked it.'

'Really?'

'Don't sound so shocked.'

'I'm not! I know it's a great play. So . . . what's going to happen next?'

I tried to keep my voice light. 'Oh, I'm not sure. He wants me to work on some revisions.'

'But he sounded keen? Like something might happen?' She sounded almost as desperate as I felt.

'Yeah. Definitely.'

I couldn't look her in the eye.

'Oh, that's brilliant.' She sat back. 'I can't believe it. It's actually happening for us, isn't it?' She raised her beer bottle. 'To success.'

I clinked my bottle against hers, forcing myself to smile. 'To success.'

ϖ

We left the Tavern and walked towards the edge of the park. I was dreading the subway ride home. It was rush hour and I didn't know if I'd be able to bear the crush of bodies. The sweat.

Ruth must have been thinking the same thing. 'Let's get an Uber,' she said.

'That's a bit extravagant, isn't it?'

'It's fine. We'll both have money soon.' She had barely earned anything from the movie and was being paid a weekly wage for *Dare*, though her agent had yet to pass on any of the money. 'Anyway, I'll pay. My treat.'

She took her phone out of her bag and opened the Uber app. At the exact same moment, somebody shot past us on a bicycle, almost colliding with Ruth.

She stared at her empty hand. 'My phone!'

I broke into a run, shouting out something ineffectual like, 'Hey, stop!' Ahead of us on the path, a man looked over his shoulder and saw me running towards him, just as the bike passed him. He must have figured out what was going on, as he gave chase too. But it was no good. The cyclist was way too fast, and was out of sight within seconds.

It had all happened so quickly, in a blur of movement and colour, that I hadn't got a proper look at the mugger. I recalled something red on his head, a baseball cap or similar. All around us, people stared.

The man who had chased the cyclist came up to us. He was out of breath. He took off his sunglasses for a second and wiped his brow. 'Sorry, I tried.'

'Thank you,' said Ruth. She looked close to tears.

'What did he get?' asked the man. 'Your purse?'

'My phone.' I saw her make an effort to get hold of herself. 'It's just the shock.'

'And the inconvenience, right? Hey, there's a cop over there. You should go report it. Anyway, sorry I couldn't catch him. I'm not as young as I used to be.' He smiled sympathetically and walked away.

'He's right,' I said.

Ruth stared towards the police officer. He was standing near the edge of the park. 'What's the point?'

'You'll need a crime number for the insurance.'

'It's not insured.'

'But—'

'My insurance only covers medical and legal costs, not gadgets. I went for the cheap option. Anyway, it's not the phone itself I'm worried about.'

'What is it then?'

She had gone pale. She dropped her voice to a whisper. 'There are pictures on the phone. You know. The ones I sent you. If they get out . . .'

'It wouldn't be a disaster.'

'It might not damage my career but it would be *embarrassing*.'

'Try not to worry. They won't be able to unlock it without—'

'Adam, I was using it. It was already unlocked.'

'Shit. Okay, in that case, we can remotely delete the contents.' I took my own phone out and opened the Find My iPhone app. 'Just give me the login to your iCloud account and I can do it now.'

We sat down together on a bench and Ruth typed her login details into the app. Her hand was shaking and she kept mistyping them. Gently, I took the phone from her and she told me the password.

'There,' I said, a minute later. 'It's done. Should take five minutes or so to erase everything.'

What I didn't mention was that if the thief had done the sensible thing and switched the phone into offline mode, this remote erase wouldn't work. I quickly checked Find My iPhone and discovered this was exactly what they had done.

I didn't tell Ruth. I didn't want to worry her.

'Let's go home,' I said.

Chapter 4

Back at the house, I thought Eden had gone out. But heading through to the kitchen to get a glass of water, I saw her through the back window, in the garden.

It was one of the amazing things about this place. When we told New Yorkers we were staying in a house in the centre of Williamsburg, right next to the L train, and that we had a decent-sized garden, their jaws dropped open. This house must have been worth a fortune. Okay, it was shabby and needed modernising. The paint was peeling from the walls, the plumbing and electrics both needed attention, the A/C was constantly on the blink and there were damp patches in the basement. But this was a townhouse with three bedrooms in one of the most desirable neighbourhoods in not just New York but the whole country. When we first came here I had, out of interest, checked the local real estate listings. There was a similar property a few streets away that was on the market for an eye-watering $3 million.

Jack and Mona were rich. I didn't know if they had earned this money themselves or if it was inherited wealth, but I had to assume it was mostly the latter. College professors don't earn big bucks, and even though Mona had told me her business was lucrative, I found it hard to believe it was *that* lucrative.

'We only bought this place last year and we've both been so busy we haven't had time to fix it up,' Mona had explained when they showed us around.

'Plus we kinda like it as it is,' Jack added. 'It's got character.'

'I don't even know how we're going to fit all our stuff in here when we finally unpack,' Mona said. 'There are, like, thirty boxes full of stuff in the basement.'

'Which is supposed to be the office,' said Jack.

The basement apartment, the Cunninghams explained, had originally been part of the house, but at some point in the building's history it had been turned into a separate dwelling with its own front and back doors, accessed via steps that led down from the front yard and the garden. Jack and Mona had bought the apartment too, and were planning to eventually reintegrate it. They told Ruth and me there was no need for us ever to go down there.

The house was tidier now than it had been when Ruth and I left this morning. The dirty dishes had been washed and stacked neatly on the draining board. The whole place appeared to have been vacuumed, and the previously overflowing recycling bin was empty.

Eden was seated on the rope swing, sunglasses on, reading a book. She was wearing shorts and her bare legs were stretched out in front of her. She pushed her hair – now it was fully dry, it looked much blonder, the colour of California sunshine – out of her face and must have felt me watching because she smiled at me and waved. 'Hi,' she mouthed.

I waved back then went out to see her.

'Thanks for tidying the house. You really didn't have to.'

'Hey, you guys are letting me stay here.' She closed the book she'd been reading. It was a battered copy of *The Collector*. 'Plus I was bored.'

'You didn't go out?'

'Hmm. Not really. The heat here – it's different from out west.' She got off the swing. Again, I was struck by the oasis-like qualities of this place. It was a long way from where I'd grown up in suburban Kent. I momentarily drifted off, picturing my own back garden – the square, scruffy lawn, the tall wooden fences that boxed us all in on the estate where I'd grown up.

'How was your day?' Eden asked, bringing me back to the present.

'It was good. Great, in fact. Until Ruth got mugged in Central Park.'

'Wait, what? You're kidding.'

I told her what had happened.

'That's awful. I thought Central Park was meant to be totally safe these days.'

'Yeah. Well, I guess nowhere's totally safe, is it? The whole thing is going to be a massive pain in the arse . . .'

Eden smiled. 'Sorry, it's just I love the way you say that. Not "ass". *Arse*.' She impersonated my accent. 'Somehow you manage to sound cultured even when you swear.'

'And you sound glamorous even when you're talking about housework.'

'We're even then. But I love your accent. It's super-cute.'

Was she flirting with me? I suddenly became aware that Ruth was in the kitchen, watching us, a neutral expression on her face. Eden spotted her too and immediately hurried inside. I followed, feeling guilty and not quite knowing why.

'Adam told me about your phone,' Eden said to Ruth. 'I'm so sorry.'

Ruth had calmed down in the Uber home. 'It's fine. It's inconvenient, that's all. I need to get a new one, right away, and then let everyone know my new number, and getting a contract over here will be impossible, I think, and I don't have enough cash to buy a phone outright.'

She paused for breath and Eden jumped in. 'I have a spare phone.'

We both looked at her. 'Really?' Ruth said.

'Yeah. I got a new iPhone last month and the old one is still in my bag. I was going to sell it but it's got a couple of little cracks in the screen so it's hardly worth anything. You can have it if you like.'

Before Ruth could respond, Eden found her bag, rummaged through it and handed the phone to Ruth.

'It's hardly damaged at all,' Ruth said. There were a few tiny cracks in the bottom corner.

'Yeah, but it's enough to wipe out its resale value. It's yours, anyway. If you want it. Then you'll just have to get a new SIM.'

'I can't take it from you. Can I just borrow it until I get a new one?'

'Sure. I'm easy.'

'Thanks, Eden.'

'You're welcome. You guys are doing me a big favour, so it's the least I can do.'

She went back out into the garden, leaving Ruth and me alone in the kitchen.

'I think there's a place down the street where you can get a SIM,' I said. 'You should probably do that now.'

'Yeah. Okay.' She headed out.

In the garden, Eden was back on the swing, nose buried in her book. I went out to join her.

'Mona told me about this place last time I saw her,' Eden said, closing the novel. 'She said a record producer used to own it. I guess that explains the jukebox. He must have left it behind.' She shook her head. 'Jack doesn't even like music. He told me it does nothing for him. Can you believe that?'

'It's hard to imagine.'

'Right?' She sighed. 'You know, if this was my house I'd stay here all the time. I wouldn't go off on a retreat or a cruise or anywhere. I'd never want to go out. Some people just don't realise how lucky they are.' She tapped the book. 'Have you read this?'

'No.'

'You should. It's about this guy who inherits loads of money and buys a big house in the middle of nowhere with a basement. Then he abducts this woman and keeps her locked up there. You know what I keep thinking when I read it? If some rich guy abducted me and kept me in a place like this, I wouldn't mind. It would still be better than where I came from.'

She smiled at me but there was a slyness to it. Like there was something she wanted to say.

I waited. But she opened the novel and said, 'I can't wait to find out what happens.'

ϖ

Ruth got her new SIM card and spent the evening messaging her friends and contacts, giving them her new number. Then she went up for an early night while I had a bath, needing to wash away the grime of the day. I sat in the tub and thought about my miserable meeting with Sam and wondered what I was going to do with my life. It would be easy to wriggle out of the lie I'd told Ruth – the industry was full of flaky people whose enthusiasm waned faster than it waxed – but I still felt guilty about it. And I knew that admitting the lie, telling her why I'd done it, would be opening a can of worms. Giant worms with teeth.

I got out of the bath, dressed, and looked in on Ruth. She was asleep but I was wired. I went downstairs and found Eden staring at moving images on her iPad. Familiar images.

Eden reacted like I'd caught her masturbating. She slammed the cover of the iPad shut and her face turned pink with embarrassment. For a moment I wondered if I was mistaken and she had in fact been looking at porn.

'Oh my God, did you see what I was watching?'

'It was *The Immaculate*, wasn't it?' I sat in the armchair opposite.

'Yeah. You caught me.'

It was a strange reaction, but I guessed she was worried I would think she was being deeply uncool. Or something. 'What do you reckon?'

'I love it,' she responded. 'It actually made me cry.'

'Really? Which part?'

'The part where her dad calls her a slut and throws her out – you know, after she tells her parents she's pregnant. And then she realises she's all alone.'

It was a powerful scene, beautifully played by Ruth, but I was surprised it would make anyone cry.

'And now everyone's after her. The government. The cops. That weird priest. It's so clever, isn't it? The way that reality shifts and cracks around her . . . like, all these signs that the world is falling apart and everyone just keeps going about their business. It's giving me chills.'

'It's a great film,' I said.

'And Ruth is incredible,' Eden said, eyes wide. 'When she's on-screen it's like . . . you can't look away. Do you want to watch the rest of it with me?'

I had already watched *The Immaculate* a dozen times but I nodded. 'Sure.'

To make space for the iPad, I moved a pile of books to the edge of the coffee table. They were all self-help books with titles like *The Power of Now* and *Belonging: Remembering Ourselves Home*; then

27

there was a book by the Dalai Lama and another about kundalini yoga.

'Are these all Ruth's?' Eden asked.

'Yeah. She's a seeker.'

Eden raised an eyebrow.

'I mean she's always looking for something. Something to believe in. To belong to. Like, when we were first together she decided she was going to start going to church. She took me along a few times then said it wasn't for her and moved on to the next thing. She flits from group to group. And she buys a lot of these books but never finishes them.' I smiled. 'She says she's still looking; that she'll find the right fit eventually.'

Eden nodded like she understood.

'I guess you must be used to that kind of thing, living in LA.'

'Oh yeah,' she said. 'Totally.'

She placed the iPad on the coffee table and hit 'Play'. I snuck glances at Eden as she watched the film. She was enrapt. When the character known as the Saviour appeared and took Ruth's heroine in, giving her shelter from the hunters and the collapsing world, Eden exhaled like a young girl watching the most beautiful wedding scene. During the climax, I was as gripped as Eden, marvelling at the special effects that had been achieved on a tiny budget: the sky the colour of a blood orange; black clouds like cancer; the screaming hordes fleeing the fires and floods and quakes that tore the world apart while Ruth and the Saviour sheltered in a cave and she gave birth to her miracle child. It was overblown and clichéd in parts, but the rawness of Ruth's performance made it seem so real.

When I tore my eyes away from the screen I saw that Eden was crying again.

She wiped the tears away. 'I'm such a loser.'

'Join the club,' I said.

She gave me a quizzical look.

'Forget I said that.' I left her tapping at the iPad, skipping back through the film to watch part of it again, and went to bed. At the top of the stairs, I glanced out the window.

The man with the grey beard was standing across the street again, watching the house. I ran back down.

'What is it?' Eden asked, jumping up.

'There's someone over the street, watching us.'

She joined me at the front window, staring out at the night.

'Where?' she said.

But the man had gone.

Chapter 5

It was Wednesday night, three days after Eden had arrived, and she and I were in a bar called Alison's Starting To Happen, just around the corner from the house. Ruth had a bunch of new lines to learn following a rewrite of some scenes in her play, so I had suggested to Eden that we get out of her way.

Alison's was busy and loud, full of young men with impressive beards, and cool women drinking craft beer. Eden and I had managed to find a table at the back and were on our third drink of the evening – or was it the fourth? The beer had been going down too easily and I didn't realise how tipsy I was until I stood up and went to the bathroom.

'Have you seen our stalker again?' Eden asked with a smirk.

'No, I haven't. But it's probably just some guy who lives or works locally. Maybe someone who likes the house.'

'Or a fan of Ruth's.'

'Oh God, don't say that. And definitely don't say it to her. She'd freak out.'

Eden had been fiddling with her phone, which she now slipped into the bag that hung on the back of her chair. 'She's going to have to get used to it, though, when she becomes super-famous. Stalkers and superfans. All the big stars have them. You'll end up living in some mansion in Beverly Hills, hiding behind high walls and security cameras.'

'The dream.'

She laughed. 'It must be weird, though. Dating someone who's on the verge of becoming famous. I'd be sick with worry, wondering what it was going to do to our relationship.'

It was as if Eden had poked me right in my most sensitive spot.

'The loser I told you about, back in LA. That was one of the reasons why we broke up. He's in a band. Did I tell you that? They were going nowhere until one of their songs got featured on a Netflix show and suddenly I was in the way.'

'Ruth's not like that.'

'Oh yeah, I know. She's not a dude. But also you're going to be famous too, right? A big writer.'

I almost didn't respond. But I'd had four beers. And I had been longing for someone to talk to about this. I couldn't hold back.

'I'm not going to be a big writer.'

'Don't say that.'

'But it's true. And you're right.' I took a long swig of my drink. 'We used to be equals. We were going to take on the world together. I was going to write the plays and the movies and she was going to star in them. Then she got that role in *The Immaculate*. I thought it was just going to be a crappy low-budget horror flick, but it turned out to be brilliant. And now everyone wants her. That meeting I had on Monday? He only wanted to see me as a way to get to Ruth.'

'What? That sucks.'

'Yeah, it sucks.'

'People are such assholes. I bet you're just as talented as Ruth. Just as deserving of success.'

'I'm not.' I experienced a rush of emotion, mainly self-pity. I couldn't help it, not with the way Eden was looking at me, her eyes liquid and full of sympathy. She reached across the table and

31

squeezed my hand and I confessed. 'I'm scared. Scared that she's going to leave me behind, that she won't want me anymore. I'm happy for her, thrilled for her, of course I am. She deserves everything that's coming her way. But there's a part of me that . . . I wish it could be the way it was. Just me and her, on our own, against the world.'

'Losers together.'

'Ha! Yeah, two losers together.' I shook my head. 'God, when you put it like that, of course it's not what I want. I love her. I think she still loves me. And I don't want to do anything to stop her being successful. I don't want to stand in her way. But this fear . . . I can't help it.'

There was a long silence.

'I hate myself for feeling like this,' I said.

'Don't. It's totally natural. But listen, Adam. You don't need to worry. I've seen the way Ruth looks at you. She's not going to leave you behind. She's going to take you along for the ride.'

'I hope so.'

'I know so.'

She patted my hand and I sniffed, realising that I believed it. I felt better. Did it matter if my writing career didn't take off? I didn't even enjoy it that much anyway; not anymore. I'd find something else to do. Something I was really good at.

'Thanks, Eden.'

'You're welcome.' She smiled and I felt a rush of warmth towards her. I was so glad she'd turned up on our doorstep.

I went to the bar and bought more drinks. Eden went to the bathroom. When she got back I said, 'I feel like I've been a real idiot, worrying so much. It's stupid. I'm not the one with abandonment issues.'

'What do you mean?'

It had come out too bluntly. Something else I could blame on the beer. 'I mean . . . Ruth never had a family when she was growing up. Not a proper one.' I wouldn't normally talk about Ruth's private life, her upbringing, but much of it was in the public domain, and Ruth had talked about it with Jack and Mona on the cruise. She was open about her childhood. And Eden was a friend now. 'Ruth's mum gave her up when she was a toddler. She never knew who her dad was.'

'Gave her up? You mean she grew up in care?'

'Yeah. A children's home. She was in and out of foster care for years.'

'That must have been rough.'

Eden stared into the middle distance and I wondered if she had a similar story herself, and if she would share it with me. I waited. But she didn't say anything. After a minute, we changed the subject.

We finished our drinks and I said, 'We'd better get going. I can't drink another drop.'

'Me either. But it's been nice, Adam.' Her eyes were glazed and I guessed I looked similar. 'Come on, let's take a photo.'

She picked up my phone from the table and gestured for me to get up. I obliged, taking the phone from her and inputting the code to unlock it. I stood beside her, bending forward with an arm around her shoulders.

'Say cheese,' she said, and together we smiled into the camera.

Chapter 6

'Fancy going out and doing something?' I asked.

It was Friday morning. Eden was lying on the couch in the living room, reading.

'Like what?' she asked, eyes still on the page. Again, she reminded me of a cat, stretched out and immobile, seemingly happy to lie around for hours doing nothing.

'I don't know. We could go to the park? Hey, why don't we go for a swim?'

She put her book down and sat up. 'I really don't know if I've got the energy, Adam. I had a late night.'

'Talking to Ruth?' I had heard them when I was in bed, chatting while I drifted off. 'What was it about?'

Eden laughed. 'Nosy, aren't you?'

'All right. Sorry.' I paused. 'Come on, let's go for a swim. It'll be fun. Do you have a bathing suit with you?'

'Yeah, I do.' She hesitated then rolled her eyes. 'Okay, okay. Just to get you off my back.'

'Great.' I grinned.

Fifteen minutes later, after finding my trunks and checking the pool rules on Google, Eden and I were walking up Bedford Avenue.

I popped into a store to buy a gym padlock, and came out to find Eden frowning at her phone.

'I haven't been swimming in ages,' I said. 'I bet in LA you were always—'

I stopped. Her phone had beeped and she was looking at it again, the space between her eyebrows creased with stress or concern.

'Everything all right?' I asked.

She stuck her phone in the pocket of her cut-offs and it immediately beeped again. She left it where it was, but she was clearly not happy.

'Is someone bothering you?' I asked.

'You could say that.' She rummaged in her bag, found her shades and put them on, then started walking again, so fast that I had to hurry to keep up.

'Is it your ex?'

She didn't respond and I thought I'd better not push it.

We didn't speak again until we got to the park. Through the fence, the pool looked like human soup, and the line to get in – mainly consisting of teenagers, and weary-looking parents with their kids – was dispiritingly long.

'I think half of Brooklyn is here today,' I said.

'Hmm.'

'Maybe this wasn't a great idea. There's not going to be any room to swim. Maybe—'

'Oh my God, Adam, we're here now,' she snapped. 'I'm not going anywhere else.'

A tall guy in his early twenties, wearing a blue Mets cap, turned and smirked at us. His eyes lingered on Eden, flicking up and down her body. He whispered something to his friend, who had the physique of someone who spent all his free time lifting weights, and they snickered together. Eden ignored them. I guessed she was used to unwelcome male attention.

Twenty minutes later, I had changed into my trunks and smothered myself with sunscreen. As per the pool's instructions, my phone and other possessions were secured in a locker. I looked for Eden as I came out of the changing room but couldn't see her. Maybe she was already in the water.

I jumped in and immediately started swimming. Even though I had to weave around people and at one point collided with a hairy middle-aged man, before getting in the middle of a group of kids chucking an inflatable ball back and forth, I felt better than I had in days.

I dived beneath the water and practised holding my breath, the sun a shimmering white disc above me, all the noises of the world dim and subdued.

When I grew bored of this and emerged, I remembered Eden. Where was she? I got out of the pool and grabbed my towel, drying myself off as I walked back towards the changing rooms, looking around for her.

It didn't take me long to spot her. She was standing over in the corner, close to a spot where dozens of people were stretched out on towels, sunbathing. She was wearing a turquoise bathing suit, her shades up on her forehead, and was talking to two men. As I got a little closer, I recognised them as the young guys who'd been in front of us in the queue. The one who had looked Eden up and down was still wearing his Mets cap.

Eden had her back to the fence and the two men were standing very close to her. She was completely dry and I realised she couldn't have gone in the water. As I approached, the one in the Mets cap reached out a hand to touch her, and she backed away. The man's shoulders shook with laughter but now I could see Eden's face. She wasn't smiling. She looked pissed off and uncomfortable.

She spotted me as I got close enough to be within earshot. I heard Eden say, 'It's my boyfriend', and the two young men turned to glare at me.

'Hey, sweetheart,' I said, taking hold of her hand. Her palm was damp with sweat. 'You coming in?'

Mets sneered at me, while I could see Muscles appraising my physique. I wasn't in bad shape, but compared to him I looked like a twig.

'*This* guy is your boyfriend?' said Mets.

'Come on, Eden,' I said, ignoring him.

I tried to lead her away but Mets stepped into my path. My heart was beating fast, remembering encounters with bullies and meatheads during my teenage years. We were out of the eyeline of the lifeguards, and no one else appeared to be paying us any attention.

I tried to move around him, but Muscles blocked me. Meanwhile, Mets smiled at Eden. 'Why don't you ditch the loser and hang with us?'

'He's not a loser,' Eden said. She sounded angry now.

'Come on, guys,' I said, trying to cool the situation. 'She's not interested. Stop harassing her.'

Muscles made a noise in his throat, somewhere between a grunt and a laugh. Mets stepped closer, so his face was inches from mine. I could smell beer on his breath. I didn't think he'd get violent in a public place like this, but with a drink inside him, who knew? And where the hell were the security guys?

'Listen, boys, just leave us alone,' Eden said. 'We really don't want any trouble.'

Mets glared at her.

'Come on,' she said. 'Let's all chill out. Okay?'

Mets let his eyes roam up and down her body again, lingering on her breasts.

'Suck my dick,' said Muscles.

'Fuck you,' said Eden very quietly, and Muscles took a step closer to her. Mets had retreated a step, but had a smile on his face. It was as if he had been the warm-up man, and now here was the main act.

'You think you're so fucking special,' Muscles said. 'Too special to fuck someone like me, huh?'

'What the hell?' I said, attempting to step between Eden and Muscles, who held up an arm to hold me back. Mets watched on, a smirk on his face.

Before I could say anything else, Eden jabbed Muscles in the chest with a finger and said, 'You're fucking with the wrong bitch.'

All of a sudden, she looked calm, almost smug, like she knew something these idiots didn't. Mets and Muscles must have seen it too, because they exchanged a look – confusion with a hint of fear. She pointed at them and said, 'Dead. Men. Walking.'

'Screw you,' said Muscles, but there was doubt in his voice now.

'Dead men walking,' Eden repeated, as though speaking to herself.

And then someone else appeared beside us, dressed all in green with 'Parks Security' emblazoned across the front of his T-shirt. 'Everything okay here?' he asked.

'Yeah, we're cool,' said Mets, acting like a kid who'd just been caught out by a strict teacher. He looked at me. 'Isn't that right?'

'We were just leaving,' I said, and before anyone else could say anything, I took hold of Eden's hand again and we hurried away. I could feel the eyes of the two men burning into my back, and looking over my shoulder I saw them watching us. For a moment I thought they might try to follow, but the security guy flapped a hand at them, clearly telling them he wasn't going to stand for any trouble. They drifted away.

'Are you all right?' I asked Eden.

She was breathing heavily, pupils dilated, anger swirling in her blood. 'They're dead,' she said.

I tried to make light of it. 'Er, you're scaring me.'

She seemed to remember where she was and who she was with. She smiled, though it appeared as more of a grimace.

'Let's get out of here,' I said.

We both headed towards the changing room. As I reached the door of the men's, I looked back. She was standing still, staring across at where Mets and Muscles were chatting, oblivious to her glare. It was as if she were filming them with her eyes, fixing them in her memory.

Finally, she turned away and went in to get changed.

Chapter 7

Ruth came into the house, letting the door bang shut behind her, threw her bag on to the dining table and herself on to the sofa. She let out a long, dramatic groan.

'What happened?' I asked. A few hours had passed since we'd got back from the pool, but I was still a little shaken. Eden hadn't wanted to talk about it much and had gone up to her room for a nap.

'Oh, just . . . intense rehearsals again. Sally's really putting us through it.' She closed her eyes and her chest rose as she took a long, deep breath. When she opened them again, she said, 'It's all worth it, though. This play . . . You're going to love it, Adam. I can't wait for opening night.'

'You're not nervous?'

'Of course I am. To actually step on to a Broadway stage.' She clutched her stomach dramatically. 'I'll probably be sick.'

'Well, that will be some debut.'

She smiled but didn't seem particularly amused. 'I actually do feel scared, Adam.'

'You'll be great. I'm—'

She didn't let me finish. 'I don't just mean about the play. I'm sure first-night nerves are similar whatever stage you're on. I almost vomited the first time I did that play above that pub.'

'I remember.' Her first lead role, in a tiny production in one of London's smallest venues. We'd only been together a few months and it was the first time I realised she might actually make it; that one day she could be famous.

'I'm talking about everything that comes after,' she said. 'As soon as this run's over, we'll be off to LA. I just got another new script to look at from Jayne.' That was her agent, who was based in the UK. 'It's like I'm standing at this junction, with a dozen different paths to choose between and not a clue which one to take.'

Something or someone had clearly got her riled up today. For weeks she had been saying she only wanted to concentrate on the play and not think about anything else. Maybe it had been Sally, or one of the other actors, or perhaps something she'd seen on social media.

'What does Jayne say?' I asked.

'Oh, well, she's just going to want me to take whatever pays the most, isn't she? She sent me a terrible script for this ridiculous action movie. A girlfriend role. But the money is insane.' She narrowed her eyes. 'Jayne's great for British theatre and TV but I'm starting to wonder if she's the right person for me now.'

I was taken aback. She hadn't mentioned any of this before.

'I was talking to Eden about it and she thinks I should do more indie films. Build a cult following . . .'

'Wait. Is Eden an expert?'

'Did I hear my name?'

Eden had come silently down the stairs.

'Oh, we were just talking about the future,' Ruth said. 'Adam thinks I should take the dumb action role.'

'What? No, I don't!'

Ruth sat up and put her head in her hands. 'Oh God, I don't know what to do. If I make the wrong move . . .'

Eden sat beside her and put a hand on her shoulder. 'Take a deep breath. I'm sure whatever you do—'

'No, you're wrong. It would be so easy to fuck it up now. It happens all the time. People make promises, tell you something is going to happen, and then they let you down.'

I went over. 'Ruth, come on.'

'Don't "come on" me.' She paused, then laughed. 'Oh God, that sounded really rude.' She kept laughing, and Eden and I joined in. It broke the tension. 'I'm sorry,' Ruth said. 'It's been a long day. Sometimes I let everything get to me.' She stood up and gave me a hug. 'It's going to be all right, isn't it? Whatever happens.'

'Of course it is. But we should talk about this.'

'I know. But not tonight, eh?'

It was half seven but it seemed less bright than normal outside. I went over to the window. The sky had clouded over. 'Looks like it's going to rain again.'

'There's going to be a storm. Can't you feel it?'

I could. The air was heavy, oppressive, and the A/C was struggling to keep the house cool. Apparently, updating this ancient air conditioning system was high on Jack and Mona's to-do list.

Which reminded me: 'Jack and Mona will be back the day after tomorrow.'

'I know. So soon,' Ruth said. 'What happened to the last few weeks?'

'I bet you can't wait,' I said to Eden.

'What's that?' She had been doing something on her phone.

'Jack and Mona. I imagine they'll be surprised to see you.'

She put the phone away and smiled. 'Yeah. I'm picturing their faces. They'll be like, "What are *you* doing here?"'

ℳ

Eden went out to get dinner from the Japanese place round the corner. While she was gone, I tried to continue the conversation with Ruth. I thought this would be the perfect opportunity to reassure her because, since the chat with Eden the other night, I'd been feeling a lot better. I knew from a couple of remarks she'd made that Ruth must have been worried about her career and its potential impact on our relationship. I wanted her to know that, whatever happened, I would support her, and I was sure she would do the same for me.

But then Ruth got a call from Jayne and disappeared into the kitchen to take it. At the same time, the A/C unit made a shuddering noise before falling silent. I was still prodding at the buttons, trying to resuscitate it, when Eden returned.

'Dinner,' she said, holding up a pair of bags. The smell of noodles and hot, spicy sauce filled the room. She was holding a third bag too, which she placed on the table with a thump. 'Look what I got,' she said, pulling out one bottle then another. 'Tequila! I got limes and salt too.'

The last time I'd drunk tequila I had spent half the night vomiting.

'I'm really not sure—' I began.

But Ruth interrupted me. 'I'll get the shot glasses. This is exactly what I need tonight. To get wasted.'

ω

The storm broke sometime around ten, with a boom of thunder that seemed like it was right there in the room with us. Lightning followed a split second later, and then came the rain, pounding the roof and the windows and the door, like the Big Bad Wolf banging to be let in.

'Maybe it'll cool down now,' I said, going over to watch people running for cover outside, a sheet of water already forming on the surface of the road and rushing towards the drains. For a moment I wondered what would happen if the rain didn't stop, if it filled the sewers beneath us and the river overflowed and the streets flooded. I pictured a world washed clean of its sins, and thought I might welcome it.

Then I turned back to reality.

Ruth was slumped on the sofa, Eden beside her, the remains of our meal spilling from cartons on the coffee table in front of them. Noodles and lumps of tofu that had fallen on to the floor; chopsticks standing rigid in the unfinished rice. A Japanese friend had once told me that a bowl of rice with the chopsticks stuck upright is a symbol of death. But I had drunk too much tequila to do anything about it. With the broken A/C, the room was as hot as a restaurant kitchen, like sitting in a cloud of steam. My hair was plastered to my forehead with sweat and my T-shirt clung to my chest. My armpits and the backs of my knees were wet. Ruth and Eden were in a similar state. Ruth's hair had gone frizzy and kind of wild, and Eden's cheeks were pink. She had produced a little portable fan which we had been passing between us like stoners handing round a spliff, grateful for the tiniest breath of relief.

I sat back down on the wooden chair I'd pulled over from the table.

I was sure Ruth was about to fall asleep. I didn't know how many shots of tequila she'd had before she moved on to beer. Her eyes were half open, her chin dipped low towards her chest.

'Ruth, are you okay?' I asked. The tequila was heavy in my bloodstream too. I could feel it in my brain, like fingers stroking the inside of my head. I shifted forward to pick up my own bottle of beer. 'Do you need to go to bed?'

'No.' Ruth pushed herself upright and lifted her head. 'I'm fine. I'm hunky-dory.'

Another clap of thunder filled the air, and she suddenly got to her feet and headed towards the back door.

'What are you doing?' I asked.

'I'm going to wake myself up, Adam.'

Ruth ran outside, laughing as she went, and I jumped up – my head whirled; maybe I was even drunker than I thought – and watched through the kitchen window as she danced in the rain, spinning in a slow circle, face raised to the sky, barefoot on the grass.

'It feels so good!' Ruth called, and Eden hesitated for a moment before running outside to join her. They held each other's hands and jumped up and down like excited children.

More thunder boomed, and lightning flashed overhead, revealing, just for a moment, a flotilla of black clouds. My booze-addled brain was thrown into that scene in *The Immaculate*. The apocalypse. The end of the world. I blinked and rubbed my eyes and lightning flashed again, so close I thought I could smell it: a singed electric scent. The sky had turned the colour of dried blood and the trees in the garden swayed and seemed to be calling to me. I stared at the ground and imagined worms wriggling in the soil; watched as fat raindrops bounced in slow motion off the surface of the swing, which moved back and forth as if an invisible child were playing there.

Jesus, this tequila was strong.

Then Ruth and Eden were running back inside, dripping wet, just like the first time I'd seen Eden. They grabbed towels from the bathroom.

'I feel so much better,' said Ruth, casting the towel aside and going back into the living room. She sat back on the sofa, still wet and not seeming to care. Eden said something about getting changed and ran up the stairs.

Ruth reached for the bottle of tequila. One was already empty. I didn't feel better at all, but I saw my own arm pick up a shot glass, waiting for Ruth to pour.

We both knocked back a shot, not bothering with the salt or lime. I banged my glass down, refilled it and did it again. Ruth did the same. I closed my eyes and felt the chill creep through my bones. When I opened them again the room seemed both darker and lighter, objects glinting and shining in the shadows. Ruth shone too, like her skin was luminescent.

Oh God, she was beautiful. I wanted to kiss her. She looked like she wanted to kiss me too. But then Eden came back down wearing a dry shirt and pair of shorts. She flopped on to the sofa and smiled at me, showing off her perfect white teeth. Thunder sounded again, but from further away.

'Hey, Adam, are you still with us?'

I blinked at Eden, who was clicking her fingers in front of my face. I must have spaced out for a second. Or was it a minute? Nothing seemed to make much sense anymore. I had a jagged pain in my stomach and I clutched it, leaning forward, telling myself not to be sick. Ruth was holding her hand in front of her face and studying it like she'd never seen it before. Eden got up and left the room and I don't know how much time passed before she came back, but when she sat back down her expression was serious. Sad.

'I've got to tell you guys how grateful I am,' she said. 'For letting me stay here. A complete stranger. I could have been anyone.'

'You're a friend of Jack and Mona's,' I said, as the pain in my belly abated a little.

'Yeah,' added Ruth, in what sounded like a slowed-down version of her regular voice. 'Any friend of theirs is a friend of ours.'

Eden's eyes were damp. 'Thank you. But you both . . . You showed trust. And kindness. I can't tell you what that means after . . . after everything that's happened to me.'

'What do you mean?' I asked.

Eden's gaze was fixed on a point on the floor by my feet. 'It doesn't matter.'

I exchanged a quick glance with Ruth. She appeared as woozy as I felt. 'Come on, you can tell us,' I said to Eden.

'No, I can't. Please, leave it.'

'We love you,' said Ruth, leaning over to give Eden a hug.

'Hey, you're getting me wet!'

All I could hear, in the moment that followed, was the patter of rain against glass. The storm had eased but the noise of that rain was sharp and clear, and the room was bathed in a sickly, mustardy light. My mouth felt like a hole where a spider might go to die.

I was never going to drink tequila again.

We stood up, all three of us, and hugged in a circle. I tried to speak but my lips and tongue wouldn't work properly. I remember staring at Eden and jolting as she morphed, just for a second, into someone else. I recall that my heart beat so fast I thought I might die. I remember the growing pain in my stomach, the heaviness in my limbs, the dryness of my mouth. Finally, I remember that hug, my chin on Eden's shoulder, Ruth's arm around my back, the dampness of her clothes against me, and Eden looking up at me with a faint, sly smile.

Then a blank space where the memories should be.

Chapter 8

I woke up in a puddle of sweat, naked, sun pouring into the room. I'd left the curtains open overnight. My body felt like a strip of salted beef jerky, and there was what felt like a laser piercing my skull.

I had the vaguest memory of myself in the bathroom at some point during the night. The porcelain of the toilet. The stink of tequila and vomit.

I groped blindly for the glass of water I always kept beside the bed. It wasn't there. Neither was the bedside cabinet. My brain tried to make sense of what was happening. Where was I? Where was my bed?

Sleep sucked me back under before I could find the answers.

I have no idea how much time passed before I woke again. This time, on top of the pounding in my head and the cold nausea that shuddered through me, I became aware of an ache in my back, a hardness beneath me. I was on the floor of my and Ruth's bedroom.

And I was going to be sick again.

I tried to stand but the room spun so violently that I fell on to my knees then crawled to the bathroom and vomited into the toilet. The stench of tequila hit me and I threw up again. Every part of my body, inside and out, hurt like I was being jabbed by a million tiny needles. Once I was sure I wasn't going to be sick again, I was overcome by the need to get the foul taste out of my mouth. I found the bathtub and heaved myself into it, reaching up to turn on the cold tap. Then I lay there, naked, shivering and sweating, with my mouth open beneath the life-saving trickle of water.

I don't remember getting out of the tub. When I woke again, I was lying on our bed, alone. There was no sign of Ruth. I felt wretched, feverish and sick, but I no longer felt like I was going to die. I reached out to find my phone, to see what time it was, but it wasn't there. With enormous effort, I got up again and, this time, was able to walk – well, stagger – to the bathroom, where I found some Advil in the cabinet. I wrapped a towel around my waist and went back out into the hallway. There was no sound of movement in the house, though I could hear the usual hubbub outside, and Eden's door was shut.

I paused outside her door, a claw of unease squeezing my insides. Something had happened last night.

Something I couldn't remember and didn't want to face.

I went back into my room, shut the door behind me and closed the curtains. I cranked up the A/C – it was still working upstairs, thank God – and stripped the damp sheets off my bed before lying down on the bare mattress. Where was Ruth? Asleep downstairs? Already got up and gone to her rehearsal? I knew I ought to go down and check on her, but I couldn't move.

Like a snail crawling into its shell, I retreated into sleep.

ω

I was awoken by the blaring horn of a van or truck outside, an end-less honking that made me pull my pillow over my head. I had been dreaming about the cruise. In the dream, I was running through the corridors, shouting for help. The ship had struck an iceberg and was filling with water, but it seemed I was all alone because everyone else had already boarded the lifeboats and escaped.

The honking stopped. I still had no idea what time it was, but I felt a little better than when I'd woken earlier. Well enough to sit up without feeling like I was going to be sick. The A/C had chilled the room, though the room still stank of sweat and stale alcohol. I could taste tequila and, once again, I swore my relationship with that drink, perhaps all alcohol, was over for good. Groaning, I put on a T-shirt and yesterday's jeans, then left the bedroom. I needed to find my phone so I could at least see what time it was.

Eden's door was still shut. I assumed Ruth had gone to her rehearsal; I couldn't imagine her missing it. No matter how hungover she was – and I hoped for her sake she didn't feel anything like me – she wouldn't risk incurring Sally's wrath.

The walk down the stairs made me realise my hangover was far from gone – every step made my brain shake – and when I saw the state of the living room, I wanted to go straight back up to bed. The remains of our Japanese meal were congealing where we'd left them, with a bunch of flies buzzing above the cartons. Noodles hung off the edge of the table, a little pile of them gathered on the wooden floor like worms having a party. A container of dark-coloured sauce had tipped over on the sofa, as had the unfinished second tequila bottle. Books had been pulled from the shelves and scattered across the floor, and there were orange smears on the vintage jukebox, as if someone had sprayed sauce over it. On top of the mess, the room was stiflingly hot and fetid, filled with the stench of last night's food and booze.

The kitchen was almost as bad. There were muddy footprints on the floor – presumably from when Ruth and Eden had come in from dancing in the garden – and the bins were overflowing. The sink was full of dishes. The food cupboards were open and looked like they'd been ransacked by sugar-crazed kids. To my horror, I saw that the freezer door had been left ajar and a tub of ice cream had melted and oozed out on to the floor beneath.

I was ashamed. This wasn't our place and we had no right to treat it like this. What would Jack and Mona—

Oh Jesus. Assuming I hadn't been asleep for more than twenty-four hours, today was Saturday. The Cunninghams were due home tomorrow.

I couldn't think about that. Not yet. I finally found my phone, lying on the kitchen counter, and was stunned to see it was seven fifteen in the evening.

I'd been asleep all day.

My phone was nearly dead, so I plugged it into its charger and, after filling a glass with water, sat down on one of the kitchen stools.

Something had happened last night. Something I couldn't remember. I held on to the breakfast bar and waited for it to hit me, in that way that embarrassing memories always do after a drunken night.

Nothing came. Just a chilling sense of disquiet.

I tried to peer back through the fog in my brain. I remembered sitting on the chair, the two women on the sofa. I remembered Eden telling us something. A story.

A spasm of nausea hit me and I doubled over, just managing to stop myself from throwing up.

Eden had told us something last night. A secret.

Something about a friend of hers . . . a girl who had died. Or disappeared? It was unclear. I remembered Eden getting upset. We had all hugged, hadn't we? I had a vague recollection that my stomach had hurt.

And then nothing.

I had no memory of going upstairs or getting undressed. As I thought this, I saw that the clothes I'd been wearing the night before were in a bundle on the living room floor. So I'd gone upstairs naked?

Oh God, what had happened?

The sight of the mess made me remember Jack and Mona's impending return again. I got up and checked the noticeboard, where details of their flight home were pinned up. They were scheduled to leave Albuquerque airport at midnight. The plane would land at 6 a.m., New York time. I figured it would take them another hour or two to get through JFK and back here. That gave us twelve hours to clean up.

With three of us, that would be fine.

It was seven thirty. Ruth would usually be home by now. Had she been planning to go out tonight with the cast? I couldn't remember. Maybe Eden would know. Eden who, I assumed, was still sleeping off her hangover.

I got up, still a little wobbly, and went upstairs. I knocked lightly on Eden's door. There was no response so I knocked harder.

'Eden,' I called through the door. 'I'm coming in.'

The room was empty.

Chapter 9

Unlike mine, Eden's room smelled fresh, no stink of sweat or second-hand alcohol. The bed was unmade.

Be rational, I thought. Eden and Ruth had gone out – Ruth to her rehearsal. And Eden could have gone anywhere. To the park. Shopping. Anywhere.

So why did I feel so uneasy?

I went back downstairs and picked up my phone. I tried to call Ruth.

It went straight to voicemail.

I should call Eden, I thought. But as I scrolled through my contacts, I realised I didn't even have her number. We had never had the need to exchange them.

I took in the wreckage of my surroundings again, and my anxiety about the whereabouts of the two women was replaced by a more pressing, practical worry. I was going to have to clean this place up. That was urgent. If Jack and Mona got home and found it in this state . . .

I opened the cupboard under the sink. We were out of garbage bags and low on cleaning products. There was nothing to eat in the house either. I was going to have to go to the store.

It was muggy outside, the streets of Williamsburg full of young people heading out to have fun. I should have been one of them. Instead, I carried a basket around the insanely expensive grocery store, and bought all the supplies I would need to deal with the mess and keep myself going.

On the way back, I saw a pair of young blonde women turn the corner into the next street. Ruth and Eden! Thank God. I ran after them, the bags slowing me down, but I'd only taken a couple of steps around the corner when I realised it wasn't them. And now my nerves were jangling.

Back at the house, I tried to phone Ruth again. Once more, she didn't reply, so I tapped out a message. *Just want to check you're OK. How much did we drink last night??* I wrote. *Can you call me as soon as you can?*

I stared at my phone. The message had been delivered, but the status didn't change to read. There were no dots to indicate a reply was forthcoming.

I checked the time. Somehow, two hours had passed since I'd first looked at my phone, and it was just after nine. Jack and Mona would be home in ten hours or less and I hadn't done a thing to clean up yet. At least dealing with the mess would give me something to focus on while I waited for Ruth to appear or call me back.

I filled a bucket with hot water, emptied my shopping bags and made a start. I filled the garbage bags with leftover food and separated out the recycling to go outside.

While I cleaned, I tried to remember more details of what had happened, but there was nothing there but a hole. It frightened me; I had rarely been so drunk that I couldn't remember any of the events of the previous night. I usually stopped drinking when I started to feel sick, an in-built safety mechanism that had served me well over the years. But last night had been different, even though I didn't think I'd drunk *that* much. Had the tequila been extra-strong? I found one of the bottles and checked it. It seemed standard. And it wasn't as if I'd drunk on an empty stomach either.

It didn't make sense. And Ruth and Eden, who I was sure had drunk more than me and who were smaller and lighter, had apparently been less affected than me.

I scrubbed at the sofa and fought back the urge to be sick. With every passing minute, my sense of dread and anxiety increased. Something had happened last night, after Eden had told her story. Something that hovered at the edge of memory, like a presence behind a door. I thought about my clothes, piled up here on the living room floor. The women's absence. The state I'd been in when I woke up. I was no longer sure if I'd really crawled naked into the bathtub or if I'd dreamt it.

I tried to concentrate on the task at hand, but I kept getting up and going over to the front window, looking out. A group of teenagers were gathered outside the frozen yoghurt place opposite. A heavily muscled man walked a tiny dog. Life went on as normal. There was no sign of the man with the grey beard.

And the minutes ticked by. Sixty of them. Another hour.

Soon, it was almost midnight and neither Ruth nor Eden had appeared. Ruth still wasn't answering her phone. The message I'd sent her hadn't been read.

Where were they?

What had happened last night?

I finished cleaning the house at three in the morning, jumping at every noise outside, compulsively checking my phone. I even scoured the local news websites, seeing if there were any reports of accidents, or, worse, involving two young women.

Finally, exhausted by worry and still feeling the effects of the night before, I collapsed on the sofa and closed my eyes.

ω

I woke up to hear a car door slamming outside.

I jumped up from the sofa and rushed over to the front window. It was already sunny and a cab had pulled up to the kerb. The driver was lifting bags out of the boot, setting them on the pavement, and then the back door of the cab opened on my side and Jack got out. On the other side, Mona emerged. She saw me watching them through the window and looked startled for a moment – clearly not expecting me to be up, waiting for them – before she smiled and waved. She said something to Jack, and he turned and smiled at me too.

I opened the front door and ran down the front steps to greet them. I hugged Mona and shook Jack's hand. I was already on the pavement before I realised my feet were bare.

'You two look great,' I said. It was true. They were both tanned – actually, a little sun-scorched – and Jack had grown a beard, which suited him. He looked like he'd lost a little weight too. Mona looked exactly as she had on the last days of the cruise: relaxed and healthy, with her hair tied back in a loose ponytail.

'You look a little green,' said Mona. 'Are you okay?'

I touched my face. I actually felt okay. Sleepy but much better than yesterday. Better, that was, until a lurch in my belly reminded me that Ruth and Eden hadn't come home.

Had they?

Jack paid the cabbie and I helped him carry the bags up into the house.

'Ruth still in bed?' Jack asked.

I opened my mouth to answer, then thought I'd better check, just in case she and Eden had snuck in while I was asleep. I'd look daft if I told Jack and Mona that Ruth had vanished and the next second she came sauntering down the stairs wondering what all the fuss was about.

'Hang on a second,' I said, before running up the stairs. I prayed that I would find both women in their beds.

But they weren't there. Both rooms remained empty.

I went back down. Jack and Mona had gone into the living room, and Jack had picked up the pile of post that had arrived while they were away and was sorting through it, muttering about bills and junk mail.

'Anything?' Mona asked.

He shook his head and tossed the pile of envelopes aside. 'Is it me or does this place feel smaller?' he asked.

'It's you,' Mona responded. She winked at me. 'Be prepared for him to go on and on about the wide-open spaces of New Mexico. Thanks for keeping the place so clean and tidy.'

'Yeah,' Jack said. 'Though it smells like you had a party last night. Ruth hungover, is she?'

Mona laughed. 'That explains why Adam is so pale.'

'And why isn't the A/C on? It's almost as hot as the desert in here.'

I needed to stop this banter.

'The unit's broken,' I said. 'And I don't know where Ruth is.'

Mona and Jack exchanged a look. 'What?' Mona said.

'I haven't seen her since Friday night. When I got up yesterday, she wasn't here and neither was Eden and—'

I stopped. They were both staring at me blankly.

'Oh, sorry, you didn't know. Your friend Eden has been staying here for the past week. She just turned up and we weren't sure what to do, and we couldn't get hold of you, so . . .'

They were looking at me like I was talking in a foreign language.

'Eden?' said Jack.

'Yes. She said you'd told her she could come and stay with you whenever she was in New York. She didn't have anywhere else to go and we didn't want to turf her out. I hope that was okay.'

57

'Eden?' asked Mona after a beat. 'Like the Garden of . . . ?'

Now it was my turn to be confused. 'Yes.'

Jack looked at Mona and Mona looked at Jack. They both shook their heads at the same time, before turning their attention back to me.

My insides had gone cold.

'Who the hell,' Jack said, 'is Eden?'

PART TWO

Chapter 10

Silence filled the room. I stared at Jack and Mona. They stared back.

'Wait,' Jack said, a hopeful smile appearing at one corner of his mouth. 'You're pranking us, right?'

'No. Why would I be?'

Mona had taken a seat on the sofa. Her hands twisted together in her lap. 'Tell us everything,' she said.

So I did. I told them how Eden had turned up on a rainy night a week ago. I recounted the story she'd told us about how her ex was a friend of theirs.

'Which friend?' Jack asked, interrupting me.

'She never told us his name. She said she couldn't bear to say it. But she said he was an old college friend of yours who lives in LA.'

'I don't have a college friend in LA,' Jack said. 'No one I've been in touch with for years, anyway.'

I went on with the story until I reached Friday night. 'She went out to buy us dinner and came back with two bottles of tequila. Ruth was having a crisis about her career and . . . well, we both drank a lot more than we would normally. I was wasted. I didn't wake up until about seven yesterday evening, and they weren't here.'

Neither Jack nor Mona seemed particularly bothered about Ruth's absence yet. They were focused purely on Eden.

'And she definitely told you she knew us?' Mona asked.

'Yes. She made out that you were great friends. She said you told her she could come and stay if she was ever in New York.'

'And you believed her?' Jack said.

'Yes. I mean, you invited us to stay. It seemed like the kind of thing you'd do. And the way she talked about you. She was so convincing. Are you certain you don't know her?'

Blank looks.

I groped for an explanation. 'Maybe she exaggerated how well she knows you. It could have been a brief encounter. One you've both forgotten.' I was aware how unlikely this sounded. Eden had told us that Jack and Mona had stayed with her and her boyfriend in Los Angeles. She'd clearly said the Cunninghams had told her she could come and stay anytime she was in New York.

'Whoever she was,' Jack said, 'she told you a pack of lies.'

Mona hugged herself. 'This is creeping me out.'

'Me too,' said Jack. 'It's like, I don't know, finding out you've got a stalker. I mean, how did she know we live here? How does she know us?'

'Do you have any photos of her?' Mona asked.

'Yes! Yes, I do.'

My phone was charging in the kitchen. I rushed to grab it and brought it back to the living room. I sat beside Mona on the sofa and Jack perched on the other side of her, both of them leaning over to peer at the screen as I unlocked the phone and opened the photos app. I flicked the screen with my thumb and watched pictures from the last few days float downwards. There were lots of shots of random things I'd seen wandering around New York. A few selfies in front of landmarks. Photos of Ruth in the house.

Then I found myself looking at photos from London, before we'd come to America.

I scrolled back up. Then down again.

'What is it?' Mona asked.

'The photos I took of her. They're gone.'

We had taken selfies in the bar on Wednesday night. I knew that for a fact.

'They've been deleted,' I said, no doubt sounding as stunned as I felt. 'How . . . Oh God.'

'What is it?' asked Jack.

'She saw me enter my passcode. She must have memorised it.'

'You are kidding me. I mean, what the fuck, Adam?'

My cheeks burned with embarrassment. I checked the deleted items folder on my phone, just in case she'd forgotten to remove the pictures entirely, but it was empty.

Mona had got up and was looking around the room, inspecting shelves, opening drawers.

'What are you doing?' Jack asked.

'What do you think? I'm checking to see if anything is missing.'

He jumped up like he'd been bitten. He ran up the stairs and I could hear doors opening and closing while I sat there, dumbfounded. This could not be happening.

For want of something to do, anything, I called Ruth's number again. Once more, it went straight to voicemail. But then I saw the last messages I'd sent her had been read. That was a good sign. Wasn't it? Except, why hadn't she replied?

Jack came back downstairs. 'I can't see anything missing up there. But you should check your jewellery, honey, just in case.'

Mona nodded. 'I will. I can't see anything missing down here either. Did you check the laptops? What if she managed to get on to those? I have all my banking details saved on mine . . .'

Jack swore and ran back upstairs to find their laptops, which they had apparently left behind while they went on their retreat. Mona thumbed her phone, and I guessed she was checking her bank balance.

I stared at my phone, at the unanswered texts. 'Where are you?' I said in a whisper.

Mona lifted her face from her screen. 'What?'

It felt as if someone had removed my bones and replaced them with jelly. 'Ruth,' I said. 'Where is she?'

Jack came back downstairs with a pair of laptops under his arms. 'They need charging,' he said. 'We'll have to wait—'

Mona shushed him with a gesture, then sat beside me. 'Remind us when you last saw her.'

'Friday night, like I said.' I tried to keep the impatience out of my voice. 'I slept through most of Saturday but she wasn't here when I woke up. She's not answering her phone or responding to messages. And now it's Sunday morning and she's still not back.'

'Did she have any plans yesterday?'

'Yeah, rehearsals.'

'On a Saturday?'

'Yeah. They do six days a week. Sally Klay would have them working seven if she could.'

'And do you know if she turned up for the rehearsal? Can you find out?'

I thought about it. I didn't have Sally Klay's contact details. And when I'd bumped into Cara a few days ago I had given her my number but hadn't taken hers. I wasn't friends with any of the actors on Facebook.

'No,' I said, explaining the situation.

'I take it her phone isn't here?' Jack asked. 'Or does she have a laptop or tablet with Sally's contact info?'

'Her phone's not here.' I had kept an eye out for it while clean-ing the house. 'She doesn't have a tablet. But her MacBook should be in our room.'

I ran upstairs and checked the bedroom. I knew the password for her computer and knew that if she had stayed logged in to social media I would be able to message Cara and some of the other cast members using Ruth's accounts. Sally's contact details would be on there too.

But there was no sign of her computer. I searched the obvious spots, looked under the pillows, even got down on my hands and knees and peered beneath the bed. I opened the drawers where she kept her clothes and searched the wardrobe. I checked inside her empty suitcase. It wasn't there.

While I was in the room, I had a look round, trying to ascertain if anything else was missing. A thought struck me, and I rummaged through the wardrobe again and checked the laundry basket.

I went back downstairs.

'There's no sign of her MacBook. I also think the clothes she was wearing on Friday night are missing too.' I could picture her clearly; she'd been wearing a black playsuit with a scoop neck and buttons up the front. I described it.

'I can't believe she'd have gone to her rehearsal in the same outfit she'd worn the day before. She would never go near Sally if she wasn't wearing clean clothes. It had got wet in the rain and she must have reeked of alcohol and Japanese food. There's no way she would have gone out without showering and getting changed.'

Jack tried to suppress a yawn. 'Sorry. I'm not bored. Far fuck-ing from it. I've just been awake since yesterday morning. And I was expecting to be able to go for a nap when we got back. I wasn't expecting any of this. Some woman turning up and staying here, pretending to know us.' Almost as an afterthought, he added, 'And Ruth going AWOL, of course.'

'Maybe we should call Dennis,' Mona said.

'Who's Dennis?' I asked.

'He's a detective,' Mona replied. 'Brooklyn PD. He lives nearby.'

'You're friends with a detective?'

'We met him through the local residents' association.' She turned to Jack. 'We should definitely call him.'

The room was beginning to spin. It wasn't just the stress. My body was still recovering from the hangover that had wiped me out yesterday. I had barely eaten all day, my sleep pattern was seriously screwed up and I was dehydrated. It must have shown, because Mona said, 'Perhaps you should lie down.'

'I can't. I need to find out what's going on. And what if Ruth calls?'

'One of us will answer the phone.'

I really didn't want to. But my body had other ideas. Mona moved aside and let me lie down. I closed my eyes and heard her say something about a glass of water.

ϖ

I didn't wake up till lunchtime.

As soon as I opened my eyes, seeing Jack sitting at the table in the window with his laptop in front of him, I said, 'Is she back? Is Ruth back?'

'Afraid not. Mona's upstairs, taking a nap. I said I'd keep watch till you woke up.'

I sat up. My headache was back and I took a long drink from the glass Mona had left beside me on the coffee table.

Jack studied me. 'You need some Advil?'

'Yes. Please.'

He went into the kitchen and came back with a couple of pills, which he handed to me. He sat back down at the table and watched as I swallowed the tablets.

'This is a messed-up situation, huh?' he said.

'That's one way of putting it.'

'I've been racking my brains, trying to remember if I ever met anyone called Eden. Apparently it can be a girl or boy's name, but I'm sure I've never met anyone called that. It just seems so crazy. Someone turning up and saying they know us. I'm hoping it's all a mix-up or misunderstanding. That we do know her but can't remember her.'

'Except she deleted the photos I took of her.'

'Yeah. Although Mona often deletes photos I take of her if she thinks they make her look old or fat or whatever. Hell, I do it too.'

I frowned. 'You sound like you're trying to make excuses for her. For Eden, I mean.'

'I'm trying to come up with a scenario that makes sense. One in which Ruth comes walking through that door with some girl in tow who Mona and I suddenly remember.' He shrugged. 'There's usually a simple explanation for everything. Did you and Ruth have a fight while you were drunk?'

'No. I don't think so.'

'But maybe you forgot. Maybe you said something that upset her. Perhaps you flirted with this Eden chick and Ruth got jealous.'

I remembered the three of us hugging. The warmth that had spread through me. But it hadn't been sexual; not that I recalled anyway. It was like trying to remember a dream, or something that had happened twenty years ago. Everything beyond that point was blank.

'I bet you fought, maybe one of you said something when you were drunk, something you can't remember, and she's gone off to stay somewhere else. That totally makes sense, doesn't it?'

I had to admit that it did. But even when we had fought badly in the past, Ruth had never avoided talking to me. She'd certainly never gone missing. And in the three years we'd been a couple, I could count the number of major arguments on one hand.

'What did your friend say?' I asked. 'The detective. Did you tell him about Ruth being missing?'

'Missing? That's a strong word. But yeah, I told him everything you said about Eden and of course I told him that you – *we* – are concerned about Ruth's whereabouts. He's busy today but he said he'll call round tomorrow afternoon. He'll want to talk to you.'

'Of course.'

Jack yawned, showing off his perfect, filling-free teeth.

'Try not to worry,' he said. 'Has Ruth got a rehearsal tomorrow morning?'

'She has.'

'Well, there you go. Assuming she doesn't come home tonight, that's where you'll find her.' He smiled. 'Just don't cause a scene, okay?'

Chapter 11

I travelled into Manhattan with the Monday-morning commuters and waited outside the rehearsal studios on Eighth Street. This was where Ruth had spent most of her days since arriving in New York. Rehearsals usually didn't start till mid-morning but I wanted to ensure I didn't miss Sally when she arrived – or that I didn't miss Ruth. I was praying that Jack was right. That we'd had some kind of argument I couldn't remember and she was either too upset to see me or was punishing me by staying away. At least that would be a problem I could understand and attempt to fix.

But was she with Eden? And did she know that Eden had been lying about her friendship with Jack and Mona?

I was trying not to think about the next, obvious, questions. Like, who the hell was Eden? And what did she want?

Had she done something to Ruth?

Ever since Jack and Mona had told me they didn't know Eden, I had been thinking about the other day in the park; the way Eden had reacted to those two meatheads. The threats she'd made. I suddenly realised that I didn't really know her at all.

I waited for an hour, the city heating up as I paced around on the asphalt. I kept checking my phone, just in case Ruth texted me or I got a message from the Cunninghams to say she'd turned up. Neither Jack nor Mona were due to start work again until next month, when the Columbia students came back for the new semester, and the rich people came back to the city and Mona got her business up and running again. I didn't know where I would be then. Mona and Jack had told Ruth and me we could continue to stay at theirs if we wanted to, but we had been planning to look for somewhere else where we'd have privacy until the play ended its run.

I couldn't think about any of that at the moment. None of it was important. All that mattered was finding Ruth.

I was so deep in thought that I almost didn't see the familiar figure of Sally Klay get out of a taxi and stride towards the building. She was wearing all black – one of her trademarks – and wraparound shades. Her hair was piled crookedly on her head like a bird's nest teetering on a cliff-edge. She held what looked like a USB stick between finger and thumb: an e-cigarette, which she lifted to her lips, expelling a great cloud of vapour.

She was almost at the door by the time I stepped into her path.

She recoiled, clearly not recognising me in this different environment, or not remembering me at all, though we had met a couple of times on the cruise. She had always been rude and dismissive, the kind of person who would only speak to people she considered her intellectual and economic equal. She had looked at me the way one might look at a puddle of sick on the street.

She gave me the same look now, then reached into her bag. I wondered what she had in there. Mace? A gun? I knew, from interviews, that she was a keen supporter of the Second Amendment.

'Ms Klay,' I said hurriedly. 'I'm Adam—'

She took off her sunglasses and narrowed her eyes at me. 'You're Ruth's boyfriend.'

'Yes, Adam, and I was—'

She waved a hand at me. 'What are you doing here? Did she send you here to make sure her message got through?'

She was angry, her words curdling the air between us.

'What . . . message?' I had gone cold. 'I came here to talk to her.'

Shooting me a look of contempt, she turned towards the door and banged on it with her curled fist. Instantaneously, an unseen person opened it from within. Sally went to step through.

'Wait,' I said. 'What message did she send you?'

She stared at me and dipped her hand back into her bag. I flinched. But she was only retrieving her e-cigarette again. She took a deep drag, and exhaled sweet-scented vapour into my face.

'Tell her my lawyers will be in touch,' she said, before vanishing into the building. I tried to follow her, to ask her more questions, but the doorman shut the door in my face.

'Ms Klay,' I shouted. 'Please. What message did she send you?'

The doorman came back out and said, 'Fuck off or I'm calling the cops.' He looked over my shoulder. 'Oh, hey, Ms Baker. Don't be alarmed. This gentleman is leaving.'

I turned and found Cara, Ruth's understudy, staring at me.

'I'm so happy to see you,' I said.

'And I'm happy to see you too?' she said with a smile, her Aussie accent making it sound like a question.

'You know this guy?' said the doorman.

He shut the door and Cara studied me. 'What are you doing here? Has Ruth changed her mind?'

Changed her mind? I didn't know where to start. There was a bagel shop across the street. 'Do you have time to grab a coffee?'

She checked her phone. 'I've got fifteen minutes before Sally needs me.'

We hurried across the road and I ordered the drinks, taking a seat at the counter in the window. Cara perched on the stool beside me.

I spoke rapidly. 'This is possibly going to sound nuts, but I haven't seen Ruth since Friday night. She's not answering her phone. And Sally said something about getting a message from her. I don't know what's going on.'

Cara's eyes were wide. 'You haven't seen her since Friday?'

'No. Did she come to rehearsals on Saturday?'

She shook her head. 'She was a no-show, which was totally weird because she's never been a second late before. Sally's assistant kept trying to ring Ruth and Sally was *not* happy.' She paused to build the drama. 'And then someone called, saying that Ruth wasn't going to be able to make it.'

'What? Who?

'I don't know. A woman, I think.'

'Eden?'

Cara looked blankly at me. 'I have no idea who that is.'

'It doesn't matter. What did this woman say?'

'That Ruth wasn't feeling well and that she was going to take a couple of days off. And Sally went nuts and told this woman that if Ruth didn't drag herself out of her sickbed and get to the studio, like, right now, she would be fired. I didn't hear exactly what Sally said but Brian – that's Sally's assistant – heard it and he said Sally was spitting blood.'

I could imagine.

'And then, according to Brian, the caller said that she was sorry but Ruth definitely wouldn't be in and Sally said that was it, she was sacked. Brian loves a bit of drama so he was very excited about it.'

It must have been Eden who had called.

'This woman. Did she say where she was calling from?'

'Sorry, Adam, but I don't know any more. You should know more than me. Was she sick? She seemed fine on Friday.'

'She would have had a hangover. But I can't believe it would have been bad enough for her to risk getting fired.'

Cara laughed. 'Jesus. We've all been to rehearsals with hangovers. I've been on stage with a hangover!'

'And even if she did have the hangover from hell and couldn't face going in, that doesn't explain why she's not at home. It doesn't tell me where she and Eden have gone.'

'Who is this Eden?'

I laughed humourlessly. 'I don't know.'

Cara blinked at me. 'Well, anyway. If I were Ruth I wouldn't show my face around here again. I didn't hear the call but I saw Sally afterwards. She was *fuming*. She marched over to the wall where we had a poster up – one of the posters advertising the play, with a photo of Ruth on it – tore it down and ripped it up. Brian tried to calm her down and I thought she was going to punch him in the face. Then she marched off, sucking on her vape, and we didn't see her for hours.'

It seemed impossible to believe. Ruth's entire adult life had been leading up to this moment. No matter how stressed she was, I couldn't picture her ever being so hungover she would risk angering Sally Klay, or walking out on this play. Sure, she had drunk a lot of tequila on Friday night. But then again, I had slept through the whole of Saturday. Maybe Ruth, wherever the hell she was, had done the same, and Eden had taken it upon herself to call Sally, not realising what an unforgiving dragon she could be. I could picture Ruth waking up to the news that she had been fired.

'Did Ruth try to call again? Or her agent?'

'Not that I know of.'

'Jesus.' I stared into my coffee cup and muttered, 'Where the hell are you, Ruth?'

As we were leaving the bagel shop, Cara said, 'If Ruth gets in touch, let me know, okay? Although I'm going to be insanely busy making sure I know all my new lines.'

'New lines?'

'Yeah. I'm not the understudy any more. I'm taking her place.'

Of course. Why hadn't I realised that?

'I'm totally stressing out about it. I mean, it's exciting, of course, but I'd be hugely relieved if Ruth came back so I didn't have to do it.'

We said goodbye. Before we parted, Cara said, 'Try not to worry, Adam. I'm sure Ruth's fine. Sometimes when people get close to what they want, they realise it's too much, too scary. Some people just aren't cut out for the spotlight. Maybe this is all an elaborate way of her quitting without actually having to quit.'

I watched her cross the road. What she said made a kind of sense, but she didn't know about Eden. And besides, Ruth lived for the spotlight – not because she wanted fame and fortune, but because acting was what she was good at. It was what she loved. I thought Cara would have understood that.

And I didn't believe Cara was right. Ruth wasn't fine. If she was, she would have called me. I could feel it, beneath my flesh, in my bones. Something was very wrong; something beyond Ruth getting drunk and being fired. Firstly, there was the question of where she was and why she wasn't answering her phone or letting me know where she was. That was out of character. But what was really making me sick with worry was this whole question of who Eden really was.

She was a liar. A stranger. And we had let her into our lives.

Chapter 12

Detective Dennis Krugman was younger than I expected, in his late thirties. He was tall, around six-five, and stood in the Cunninghams' living room like Gulliver freshly arrived in Lilliput, speaking in a rumbling tone. *Bear's breath*, my mum would say. Jack and Mona hung around the edges of the room while I told the detective everything I knew, up to and including what I'd just learned from Cara.

'Hmm,' Krugman said.

I waited for him to elaborate.

'So she called the theatre to say she was sick? Hungover, you think?'

'She didn't call. Someone else did. Eden, I expect. Whoever she is really.'

'Yes. Eden. The problem we have here is that all indications are that Ms Armstrong left of her own accord. She's an adult, she's not a vulnerable person. You said she's not on any medication that you know of . . .'

'She's not on any medication.'

'And she has no history of attempting to harm herself?'

'No.'

'Hmmmm.'

I wished he'd stop doing that. Although, apart from the hmming, I liked him. The way he spoke was soothing, the bass frequency of his voice helping to calm me down. I could imagine he'd be the kind of person you'd want to rely on in a crisis. The fact he looked like he could crush a man's head with his bare hands was a bonus.

'I can register her as a missing person, but I have to warn you, this is not going to be high-priority. You know how many people go missing in this country every month?'

'How many?'

He smiled. 'A lot.'

Later, I looked it up. There were almost 100,000 active missing-persons cases in the US at any given time.

He wrote something in the tiny notepad he cradled in his massive hand. 'What was Ms Armstrong's visa situation?'

'She has a working visa.'

'Hmm. And she's been fired from her job. I'm guessing Immigration Services would be interested to hear about that.'

'Wait, you're going to report her to Immigration?'

He tilted his head. 'If you want me to file an official report – which you'd have to come to the station house to do – then Immigration Services will need to be informed.'

'Uh-oh,' said Jack.

Krugman smiled without opening his mouth. 'What about her folks? Her friends? Have you spoken to any of them?'

'She doesn't have any family. And she doesn't really have any close friends either. She's been so focused on her career . . .'

'Hmm. I assume you've checked her social media?'

'Yes. She's not on Twitter but I've checked Facebook and Instagram. She hasn't updated either of them since I saw her.'

'You said she has an iPhone. Does she have the Find My iPhone app? Not that I'm suggesting you should log in to her account . . .'

'I've already thought of that. I don't know her new password and her MacBook is missing.' Ruth had changed her iCloud password after her phone was stolen.

'I see.' He paused. 'What about your relationship? Had you had an argument? Any reason why she might not want to contact you?'

'No.'

'Not that he can remember, anyway,' said Jack.

I shot him an irritated look. He really wasn't helping. Mona looked annoyed with him too. She seemed to be the only other person who was taking Ruth's disappearance seriously.

'You have to understand that this is all completely out of character,' I said. 'Firstly, not contacting me. We usually text each other all the time.'

I didn't want to admit that, recently, she hadn't texted me as often as I did her. She was too busy.

'More importantly, I can't see her risking her part in the play like that. She's reliable. Almost pathologically so. She's never late for anything.'

'But she did drink a lot on Friday night?' Krugman said. 'About a third of a bottle of tequila? Maybe half? From your description, her body weight is about half mine and I'd struggle to get out of bed after that.'

'I know, but . . .'

I trailed off. This was intensely frustrating. I didn't think Ruth would be a high priority for the police. I didn't, however, expect them to do nothing.

'So, what you're saying is that we need to keep our fingers crossed and hope she comes back?' I said.

He didn't like that. For the first time, I saw a hint that Krugman, while looking and sounding like a friendly bear, was not someone to be fucked with. The atmosphere in the room cooled rapidly and he pointed a huge index finger at me.

Mona interceded before he could give me a piece of his mind. She spoke gently. 'What about this girl, Eden? She came into our home, pretending that she knew us. Isn't that . . . trespassing or something? Shouldn't you be looking for her?'

Krugman shook his head. 'It's not a crime, as far as I can make out. She didn't take anything, did she?'

'Except for Ruth,' I said.

He turned his attention back to me. 'Do you think Eden would be physically capable of dragging Ms Armstrong out of here?'

I pictured Eden, with her slight frame and slender limbs. Ruth wasn't exactly Lara Croft, but I thought she could beat Eden in a fight. She certainly wouldn't be overpowered by her.

'No,' I replied. 'But Eden could have had a weapon. Or she could have lured Ruth outside, got her in a cab . . . I don't know. Anything could have happened!'

'Exactly,' he said. 'And I'm sorry, but right now we have no evidence that a crime has been committed.' He turned to Mona and Jack. 'That's the way I see it, anyway. And all my experience tells me that your friend will turn up soon.'

'Hopefully not dead,' I said.

They all looked at me. I was having to bite my tongue to prevent myself from telling Krugman that he needed to do more. I thought about threatening to get the press involved. But I knew that would be a bad move. Even if they were doing nothing at the moment, I didn't want to antagonise the NYPD. I was worried, too, about the immigration aspect. Because what if Ruth *had* done all this freely and voluntarily? If she was simply holed up somewhere with Eden, pissed off with me for some reason I couldn't remember. She'd be even more pissed off if I got her kicked out of the country.

'Why don't you give it another forty-eight hours?' Krugman said to me. 'If she still doesn't get in touch with you or anyone else, give me a call and I'll see what I can do. In the meantime, if I were you I'd call her friends, anyone who she might get in touch with. What about her agent? I'm sure she'd need to speak to her if she's just been fired.'

'I'll do that,' I said. Calling Jayne had been next on my list anyway.

I went upstairs to my room. I thumped the mattress with frustration then lay on my back, staring at the cracks in the ceiling.

As I lay there, I became aware of voices outside. I peeked out of the window and saw that Jack, Mona and Krugman had gone into the garden. The men were in the lawn chairs, holding glasses of what looked like lemonade. Mona was on the swing. I could make out the faint sound of their conversation.

I turned off the A/C, which instantly made the room fall quiet, and opened the window as quietly as I could. Their voices drifted up to me through the still summer air.

'. . . a reliable character?' said Krugman.

Jack replied first. 'We *thought* he was.'

'I guess we don't know him that well. We don't know either of them well.' That was Mona.

'Maybe it was a mistake inviting them to house-sit for us,' said Jack. 'You know, there's part of me – and I feel awful admitting this – that wonders if he's making the whole thing up. About this Eden woman, I mean.'

I was in a crouching position on the floor and, hearing this, I almost lost my balance. *Making it up?*

'You think Eden might not actually exist?' Mona said.

'Go on,' said Krugman in his low rumble.

'Well, it's such a bizarre story, isn't it? And there are no photos of her. No one else to corroborate what Adam says. There are no signs that she was actually here. The sheets on the bed Eden supposedly slept in are clean, just as we left them, aren't they, Mona?'

Was that right? I was sure Eden's bed had been unmade when I'd looked in her room.

Jack continued. 'I find it so hard to believe someone would turn up here pretending to know us, especially as there's nothing missing.'

'Except Ruth,' said Mona.

'Who was clearly suffering from the hangover to end all hangovers. Maybe she's still on a bender. Getting wasted in some bar somewhere, drowning her sorrows.'

I could hardly believe what I was hearing. I wanted to run down the stairs and into the garden, shout at them, make them believe me. But I needed to stay here. I needed to hear what they said.

'Tell me about Adam and Ruth. What was the state of their relationship?' Krugman asked.

'Difficult to say,' said Mona. 'I mean, they seemed happy enough when we met them on the cruise, but I think they were having some issues.'

'Like what?' Krugman asked.

'Well, I don't know this for sure but I picked up a few hints from things Ruth said. Her career was taking off and his wasn't going anywhere. That can cause a lot of tension in a relationship, especially when it's the woman who's the successful one. You know what the male ego is like. Deny it all you want, but you guys all want to be the breadwinners. I know so many couples who've broken up because the guy couldn't stand his wife earning more than him.'

'Lucky I'm not like that, isn't it?' Jack laughed.

'Yeah, it is. Anyway, when I spoke to Ruth to make the arrangements for them house-sitting, she told me she was worried about what Adam was going to do all day. She was concerned about him. We had a good chat about it, actually.'

'Do you think she was still into him?'

'I don't know. It was hard to tell. I think she loves him but . . .'

But? To my intense frustration, I couldn't hear what she said next.

'He's a writer, isn't he?' said Krugman.

'Yeah,' said Mona. 'A failed one.'

I flinched. It was one thing thinking it myself, but to hear someone else say it was like being punched in the nuts.

'What are you thinking?' Jack asked.

'Exactly what I said to Adam,' Krugman replied. 'I'm sure she'll turn up. My guess is that she's deeply embarrassed about getting drunk and blowing her chance on Broadway. Who wouldn't be? She probably can't face anyone at the moment, including Adam. She probably thinks he's going to tell her off, especially if she's his meal ticket.'

I was beginning to understand why they say you should never eavesdrop on conversations about yourself.

'But what about Eden?' Jack asked. 'Do you think Adam's telling the truth?'

'I don't know,' said Krugman. 'Why would he make her up? Though it does seem odd that Adam can't tell us her surname. That his photos of her have mysteriously vanished.'

'Oh my God,' Mona said. 'Do you think Adam has done something to Ruth?'

I could hardly breathe. They thought Ruth had vanished because I had harmed her? That I had concocted this elaborate story about Eden to cover my tracks?

'Maybe he was so jealous of her success he murdered her,' Jack said. 'Right here in our house!'

'Don't say that!' said Mona.

81

'Then he got someone to call the theatre saying she was sick. He could have an accomplice. A new girlfriend?'

'You think Eden is his new girlfriend?'

Krugman interrupted them. 'Wait, wait, wait. We're all getting carried away. My job isn't about theories, it's about facts. Evidence. I'm sure Ruth is fine. And, I've got to say, Adam appears genuinely concerned to me. He doesn't seem like he's making it all up. Not all of it, anyway.'

There was a long silence, which Krugman broke. 'What are you going to do about him staying here with you?'

'We don't know yet. We haven't discussed it properly,' said Mona. 'Part of me wants to keep an eye on him, see if he does or says anything else that helps us make sense of all this. The other part of me doesn't feel comfortable having him around.'

'Well, let me know what you decide. And call me if you hear from Ruth.'

'We will,' said Jack.

They fell quiet and I heard the back door open and shut. I rushed over to the bedroom door and strained to hear them as Jack and Mona said goodbye to Krugman. But their voices were too quiet and muffled for me to make out their words. Then the front door banged and I heard a car engine start up. Krugman was gone.

Chapter 13

I needed to get out of the house. I didn't feel welcome there anymore. I grabbed my laptop and notepad, stuffed them into my backpack along with most of my clothes, and ran down the stairs. I didn't want to face Jack and Mona, but she was there in the hallway, turning towards me with concern on her face. Fake concern.

I now knew what she and Jack really thought of me, and it burned. I had built up our friendship in my head, but we were virtually strangers, weren't we? We'd spent a week together on the cruise, and Ruth and I had seen them briefly when they handed over the keys to this house. We didn't really know them, and they didn't know us.

I had thought they would be on my side. But they thought I was a liar. They thought I might be capable of murdering my girlfriend.

'Everything all right?' Mona asked as I reached the foot of the stairs.

I was tempted, for a moment, to tell her I'd heard what she and Jack had said. But I realised that would make me appear even worse: an eavesdropper, desperately trying to defend himself.

'I need some air,' I said, slipping past her to get to the door.

'Wait, Adam,' she said.

I turned.

'I know you must be disappointed by what Dennis said. But I'm sure Ruth is okay. I can feel it. I have every confidence she'll be back.'

'And you're not concerned about this woman who came into your home pretending to know you?' I wanted to see how she would explain her lack of worry without revealing any of her and Jack's theories and suspicions.

She opened her mouth. Shut it again. Finally, she said, 'Of course I am. But nothing is missing. She doesn't seem to have accessed our computers.'

'In other words, you don't care about what she might have done to Ruth.'

'What? Why do you think this Eden person has done something to her?'

'I'm going to look for somewhere else to stay,' I said.

'You don't have to do that.'

'No, I think I should. I don't want to be under your feet.' I didn't want to get drawn into a debate about it so I said, 'I really need to go out.'

'Okay. Well, maybe we can chat later.'

'Maybe.'

I slipped through the door and ran down the steps, not pausing or looking back. Perhaps it had been a rash thing to do, but I didn't want to be under the same roof as these people who didn't trust me.

The police wouldn't do anything. Jack and Mona wouldn't believe the truth.

I was on my own.

ꞷ

I walked up Bedford Avenue, the same route I'd taken just a few days ago with Eden when we'd gone to the swimming pool. That had been Friday afternoon, when I thought all I had to worry about was Ruth outgrowing our relationship. Now I knew she had been concerned about it too, and it made me feel sick to think she might have felt sorry for me. Mona was wrong, though, about this being a male-ego thing, wasn't she? Perhaps not. Perhaps it was something that was hardwired into me.

Still, right now it didn't matter very much. All that mattered was finding Ruth and making sure she was okay. When I found her we could have that talk. Figure out how to go forward. And I was more concerned about her career right now than mine. Hoping Sally didn't have much sway in Hollywood; that casting directors weren't putting a big black mark next to Ruth's name.

As soon as I reached the park I took out my phone and called Jayne, Ruth's agent. It was lunchtime in New York, making it just after 5 p.m. in London. Jayne's phone went to voicemail so I left a message and went and sat on a bench.

I checked Ruth's Facebook page, just in case she had updated it, and did the same with Instagram. I tried to call her again, then sent her another text asking her to call me. Then I spent an hour going down the Google rabbit hole, searching for women named Eden across all the social media sites. I put 'Eden Bakersfield' into the search engine but the only result was a bar that had once existed in that city, also called Eden. I searched my memory, trying to recall something, anything, that Eden might have said, anything that could tell me where she might be. She had said she didn't know anyone else in New York. She certainly didn't have her own place . . . although even as I thought it, I remembered that I couldn't trust anything she had told me. She might have her own house or apartment somewhere in the five boroughs.

Which reminded me: after walking out of the Cunninghams' place, I had nowhere to stay tonight, and very little money in the bank. I only had enough to stay in a hotel for maybe a week, even a cheap one. I didn't know anyone who could put me up. What were the other options? A hostel? The YMCA? Maybe I had been too hasty walking out of Jack and Mona's.

I was pondering this when my phone rang. It was Jayne.

'Hi, Adam?' She had a cut-glass accent, like a minor royal. I had met her a few times and had always found her pleasant, if a little brusque. She wasn't a particularly successful agent and I got the impression she lived in fear of losing Ruth to a hungrier, more powerful Hollywood player. She would have been horrified if she'd overheard what Ruth had said about her on Friday night when she'd talked about the action movie she'd been offered. 'Is Ruth there with you?'

'No. That's what I wanted to talk to you about. I was wondering if you've heard from her.'

'What, since she sabotaged her stage career? I've been beside myself, trying to get hold of her.'

'She hasn't called you?'

I could hear traffic in the background and pictured her standing on the street near her office in Soho. Black cabs and red buses. I was hit by a wave of homesickness.

'No, she hasn't,' Jayne said, half yelling against a chorus of car horns. 'The first I heard of it was a furious phone call from someone at Sally Klay's production company. They're threatening legal action for breach of contract. The whole thing is a total nightmare. What on earth has got into the silly girl? What's been going on over there?'

I didn't know what to say. This was bad news. Ruth hadn't even phoned her agent? At least I now knew this couldn't be happening because she was angry with me.

'Maybe it's the pressure,' Jayne was saying. 'I've seen in happen before. These young actors think they want to be famous and successful and as soon as something starts to happen they freak out and can't handle it. I always thought Ruth was reliable and level-headed, though . . .'

I ended the call with both of us promising to call the other if we heard from her.

As I put my phone back into my pocket I looked up – and saw the man with the grey beard.

He was standing beneath the trees opposite me, towards the centre of the park. I was certain it was the same person I'd spotted standing outside the house. He had hair that matched his beard, cropped short, and looked to be about sixty. He was wearing sunglasses and a T-shirt that showed off a stocky figure. As soon as I lifted my face and he realised I'd seen him, he hurried off in the opposite direction.

'Hey!' I called. 'Wait up!'

He strode away, breaking into a jog and disappearing behind a crowd of teenagers who were walking towards us wearing baseball kit. By the time I got through this fresh-faced crowd, he had vanished.

I swore under my breath. Who was he? Was he involved in whatever the hell was going on? Even if he wasn't, he might have seen something.

I walked around the park for twenty minutes looking for him. I could feel my skin burning, the sun microwaving me and making me hot and miserable. It was obvious that Greybeard was long gone. Next time, I was going to have to be quicker.

I headed towards the exit of the park, thinking I should find a hotel, somewhere cheap nearby – I didn't want to stray too far from where I'd last seen Ruth – and opened an app on my phone to search for a room.

I had my head down as I left the park and began to cross the quiet road, going back towards the centre of Williamsburg.

Two things happened at once. A car engine revved and tyres screeched on the hot asphalt. And somebody yelled.

I looked up from my phone screen.

A car roared towards me.

Chapter 14

Something leapt into my peripheral vision. Bones connected with mine. A solid force, knocking me off my feet. I landed on my back on the unforgiving concrete, something heavy on top of me, pain searing through my flesh, a glimpse of blue sky, the stink of burnt rubber. The car that had tried to floor me revved its engine again and then it was gone, a blur of metal and glass vanishing into a side street.

I pushed at the person on top of me, the man who had saved me, and he lifted himself up, rocking back on to his haunches.

'You okay?' he said.

It was Greybeard.

'Man, you were a deer in the headlights.'

A small group had gathered around us, but Greybeard waved them away, told them everything was fine; I'd stepped into the road without looking, that was all. Somebody muttered something about idiots not watching where they were going, and the crowd dispersed, leaving me pushing myself to my feet. Apart from a scrape on the back of one elbow and a bruised coccyx, I was fine, though my heart was still beating fast and hard.

Greybeard had got to his feet too. He panted and brushed the dust from his jacket, tucking his sunglasses into the front pocket.

Up close, I could see that he was indeed in his sixties, but looking good for it, with crinkles around his blue eyes – a face that suited maturity. His beard was not really grey but salt-and-pepper, as was his hair.

'Who are you?' I asked.

He stuck out a hand. 'Callum Maguire.'

'I'm Adam—'

'I know, son.'

I held his gaze. 'You've been following me. Why? Do you know where Ruth is? Do you know Eden? What's going on?'

He held up both hands, palms out. 'Whoa, whoa. Too many questions. Let me buy you a drink and I'll explain everything.'

I hesitated. This man had been watching the house. Stalking me.

'Come on, I just saved your life. *You* should be buying *me* a drink.'

'That car. Was it trying to hit me deliberately? Do you know who was driving? Did you see them?'

'No, I didn't. It had tinted windows. But I'm going into that bar over there.' He pointed a little way down the street. 'And if you want answers to any of your questions, you'll come with me.'

He walked away. He was limping slightly. I hesitated again, but only for a second. What choice did I have? He might know what had happened to Ruth.

ω

The bar was quiet, but beginning to fill up with the lunch crowd. We found a table in the corner and Callum Maguire waved a menu at me and asked if I was hungry.

'Actually, I'm starving.'

'Good. Me too.'

He went to the bar to order beer and burgers. When he came back he slid a pint towards me and said, 'You'll probably feel light-headed for a little while, as the adrenaline leaves your system, but the food will make you feel better.'

'Thanks. So . . . ?'

'Your questions. Okay. Yes, the car was trying to hit you on purpose. And yes, I do know Eden – or at least, I know of her – but no, I don't know where she and your girlfriend are.'

He took a long swallow from his own pint, and rapped his knuckles on the table then dragged them across the wood. A gesture of frustration.

'I should have stayed outside the house. But I was tired and it was raining again. I thought the three of you were staying put for the night.'

I stared at him. 'You were out there on Friday night? Watching us?'

'Until the storm started, yes.'

'Who the hell are you?'

He picked up his beer mat and tore it in half. 'I'm a man who's lost his daughter.'

I waited.

'What did Eden tell you about herself?' he asked.

'Not much. She said she's from a place called Bakersfield, that she's been living in Los Angeles, that she recently broke up with her boyfriend. A musician.' She had told me more, hadn't she, during that drunken last night, but I could only remember small scraps of the story. Living in a roach-infested apartment. A friend she let down. Something about her mother and drugs? It was like trying to read a message through a full pint glass. 'She told me she knows Jack and Mona – the owners of the house where we've been staying – but they deny it. For all I know, everything she told me was a lie.'

'That's right. You can't trust her. But a couple of the details are true. She is from Bakersfield, as far as I know. And she has been living in LA. The part about the musician, though. That's bullshit.'

Our burgers appeared and Callum took a huge bite, wiping a dribble of ketchup from his beard.

'You said you'd lost your daughter?' I said, prompting him to continue.

'Yeah. Sinead. Eden took her from me.'

'What do you mean?'

He chewed more of his burger and seemed to stare down a gloomy but vivid memory lane. 'I thought everything was fine. Sinead's mother, my wife, died when she was sixteen. Cancer.'

'I'm sorry.'

'It was tough. Tough.' He swallowed. 'But Sinead grew up, went to college, had boyfriends, moved into a shared place in the city. She had some problems holding down a job, seemed to flit from one thing to another, but I thought, *She's still young. She'll figure out what she wants to do.* She still came home for lunch every Sunday. Still had time for her old man. And then she told me she'd made a new friend.'

'Eden?'

'Met her at some convention. Some hippy-dippy thing, out in the desert. A spiritual festival, she called it. Discovering your true inner self. Building inner strength through meditation. Vegan food and yoga.' He laughed. 'I thought it was an excuse to sit around and smoke pot and listen to, shit, I don't even know. In my day it was the Grateful Dead.'

He looked at me like I would know what kind of music modern-day hippies listened to. When I didn't respond, he went on: 'I should have known it was more than that. Ever since her mom passed away, Sinead has been looking for something. Meaning, I guess. I wasn't much help there. I'm a lapsed Catholic myself and we weren't a religious household. Maybe it would have been easier if we had been. She could have gone to church. I would have been cool with that. Instead, she spent years searching for something to make her feel better. One week it was politics, the next she was getting into tarot cards. She even called herself a witch for a little while, when she was in high school. She and her friends formed their own coven. But no matter how much she searched, she could never settle.'

'That sounds familiar.'

He cocked an eyebrow at that.

'That's Ruth, too.'

He nodded. 'And then she met Eden. She came round for dinner after she'd been to this convention, and the way she was talking about her I thought maybe she was a girlfriend or something. You young people, you're all bisexual or pansexual, fluid this and fluid that.'

I smiled.

'Anyway, that didn't bother me at all. I'm not one of these bigots. But Sinead assured me they were just friends. Best friends. It was cool. I met Eden at Sinead's apartment and I liked her. She seemed a little intense, a little full of herself. But she had something about her. A spark. I could understand why my daughter was so besotted.'

I knew what he meant about that spark.

'And then I stopped hearing from Sinead so often. She called but she sounded distracted. She started talking about all this weird shit.'

'Like what?'

'Like the end of the world.'

'What?' I hadn't seen that coming.

'Right. How we were all screaming towards the end times. None of it made much sense to me. I told her she was talking nonsense. She pressed it. We argued about it. We argued about how she still didn't have a job, too. She stopped coming round on Sundays. Until one day, last fall, when she turned up asking if I could loan her some money. She said she needed it to take a course. She was going to train to be a masseuse. Eden was waiting outside in the car and wouldn't come in, and I got the feeling Sinead was lying, that she wanted the money for something else. The way she looked, I thought it might be drugs. But then she laid the whole guilt trip on me, started crying, and I could never resist her tears. I gave her the money and off she went.'

He drained his pint.

'That was the last time I saw or heard from her. She stopped answering her phone. Then I started to get a message saying the number was out of service. I went to her apartment and her room-mates said she hadn't come home one night. She still owed them rent. All her social media accounts were deleted. Of course, the cops were of no use whatsoever.' He stroked his beard. 'You know what I thought? That she and Eden had run into trouble with a gang of drug dealers. That the two of them were probably buried out in the desert. I can't begin to tell you how I felt . . .'

For a moment I thought he was about to start crying.

'I spent months searching for her, going to all the places she used to hang out, talking to all her old friends, but got nowhere. So then I decided to concentrate on Eden. I knew they'd met at this spiritual convention and I found the Facebook page, which was full of comments from people who'd been too. I started messaging them, explaining the story, saying I was trying to find Eden. Most of the people ignored me and I was on the verge of giving up when someone messaged me to say he knew Eden. What he told me, well, it gave me the chills.'

It was busier in the bar now. I had to lean forward to hear what Callum said.

'This guy told me Eden is a recruiter.'

'For what?'

Callum paused. 'I need another drink.'

He went to get up but I grabbed his arm. 'For fuck's sake, you can't leave me hanging like that. What do you mean she's a recruiter? For what?'

'Adam, trust me. You're going to need another drink.'

Chapter 15

The lights were too bright. Ruth opened her eyes and pain seared her retinas, leaving blobs of colour inside her eyelids. She turned over, burying her face in the pillow, and fought the nausea that threatened to overwhelm her. It was like being in a boat in the midst of a storm, and she forced herself to lie perfectly still, barely daring to breathe, until the lurching, roiling motion subsided.

Tequila, she remembered. So much tequila.

But why did her body ache like this? Why did her arms and legs and ribs hurt? Now she had noticed it, every breath caused pain, like there was something sharp digging into her lungs. It was as if she'd been trampled on or run over. But she couldn't remember anything except tequila. Drinking with Adam and Eden. Where was Adam now? She turned her head to see if he was beside her – no, it was just her – and the bed began rocking violently again.

She sucked in air. Lay motionless until sleep dragged her back into oblivion.

ᛟ

'Ruth. Ruth, can you hear me?'

There was a voice coming to her from far away. A female voice, gentle but insistent. She had been having the dream again, the one she'd been having since she was a teenager: of stepping on to a stage, excited, ready to show the world who she was, and the audience turning their backs on her.

'Ruth, you should drink something.'

She opened her eyes and saw Eden leaning over her. The light didn't hurt so much now, though the aches in the rest of her body hadn't subsided.

'What time is it?'

Eden didn't answer. Instead, she slid an arm behind Ruth's shoulders. 'Let me help you sit up.'

'I don't need help.'

Except when she tried to move it was like being kicked in the ribs. She cried out in pain.

'Take it easy,' Eden said in a gentle voice. 'Slow. Here we go.'

With her arm still around Ruth's shoulders, Eden helped her into a sitting position, pulling up the pillow so it was positioned behind Ruth's back. Eden held out a glass of water. 'Drink this.'

Ruth took a sip and was hit by an overwhelming urge to throw up.

'I'm going to be—'

She couldn't finish the sentence. Her stomach convulsed, but Eden had positioned a plastic bowl beneath Ruth's chin. Ruth was sick, then sick again. Every muscle in her body tensed as it rejected the poison in her system. She closed her eyes, finding the room wasn't spinning as much now, though her throat was sore, the taste in her mouth bitter and rank.

Eden passed her a couple of tissues so she could wipe her mouth.

Ruth tried to laugh. 'I'm never drinking again.' It was only then that she took in the room beyond Eden.

This wasn't the bedroom in Williamsburg. This wasn't Mona and Jack's house.

'Where are we?'

Eden didn't answer immediately.

'You're with friends.'

'What? Where? And where's Adam?'

'That doesn't matter right now. You need to rest.'

Ruth stared at her. 'Tell me where I am.'

With each passing moment, she took in more details. The room was white and sparse, like a modern hotel room. The bed she was lying in was soft and large, king-sized. There was very little other furniture, just a bedside table, a wardrobe, and a round table with two chairs either side. There was a single window, covered by closed Venetian blinds, and a plastic panel set on the wall beside it. Behind Eden was a solid-looking wooden door – the exit, she assumed – and there was another door on the other side of the room, most likely a bathroom.

Ruth tried to get out of the bed but pain ripped through her again, pinning her to the mattress. She closed her eyes and waited for the nausea to pass.

'Here,' Eden said. 'Have another drink.'

'No. Not until you tell me where we are. What the hell is going on? Am I in hospital?'

'No. But we're looking after you.'

A beat. 'We?'

'That's right.'

She must mean herself and Adam, Ruth thought. There was no other explanation. 'Is Adam here?'

'Not right now. You really should drink some water. It'll help take the taste out of your mouth.'

'Okay. Thank you.' She took another sip from the proffered glass, then watched as Eden placed it gently on the bedside table. There was something different about Eden. The way she moved, her voice – she seemed softer, more elegant. She was wearing a brightly coloured shift dress, patterned with pink and yellow flowers, with a baggy cardigan over the top. It didn't suit her.

Ruth looked down at herself. She was wearing cotton pyjamas. Like the walls of the room and the bedding, they were white.

She felt herself being pulled back towards sleep. She tried to speak, to ask Eden again what time it was – she had this terrible feeling she was supposed to be somewhere – and where her boyfriend was, but her mouth had stopped working.

She gave in and closed her eyes.

ϖ

When she opened them again, Eden was sitting on a chair beside the bed, watching her.

'You're back,' Eden said, with that soft smile. 'Do you feel any better?'

Ruth tried to push herself upright, and this time she was able to do it without quite as much pain, though her ribs were still sore and she winced as she sat up.

Eden passed her the water and she sipped at it again, worried she would be sick if she drank too much.

And then panic jolted through her.

'What time is it?' she demanded. She looked around for her phone, the one Eden had given her, but there was no sign of it. In fact, there was no sign of any of her stuff.

'It's just after three,' Eden said.

'What? Oh Jesus, I'm missing it. Sally's going to go crazy. She'll fire me.'

She pushed the covers aside and tried to get out of bed. This time the pain made her gasp. It was in her thighs, her ribs, even around her collarbone. Eden jumped to her feet and gently helped her lie down again, pulling the sheets back over her. Sweat had broken out on Ruth's forehead.

Eden dabbed at it with a tissue. 'I told you, you need to rest.'

'But my rehearsal—'

'I think you misunderstood. It's three on Sunday. Your rehearsal was yesterday.'

Ruth stared at her. Sunday? She'd lost an entire day and a half? This couldn't be happening.

'It's okay, Ruth. It's all been taken care of.'

She turned her face towards Eden. She was too weak, in too much pain, to fight. 'I don't understand.'

Eden lay a warm hand on her arm. 'Try not to worry, Ruth. It will all become clear. From this point on, everything's going to be all right.'

Chapter 16

'What do you mean?' Ruth struggled to sit up again, but couldn't manage it.

Eden stroked her forehead. 'You don't remember?'

'No.' Ruth's voice was hoarse; barely more than a whisper. 'I can't remember anything, just you and me and Adam drinking. We went out in the rain. I was wet. I remember talking. Listening to you. Everything else is . . . blank.'

She had never been a big drinker, had never experienced the blackouts her friends boasted of after a big night. Ruth had always hated being out of control, found the very notion terrifying.

'What happened?'

'I think we should talk about it when you feel better. When you're stronger.'

Eden's eyes shone with kindness and Ruth felt a rush of gratitude that she was here, looking after her. She reached out from beneath the covers, found Eden's hand and squeezed it.

'I'm scared,' Ruth said.

'It's okay. There's no need to be.' She squeezed Ruth's hand back. 'Are you hungry? Do you think you could eat some soup?'

The very mention of food made Ruth's stomach clench. 'No. I couldn't.'

'Okay. A little later. In the meantime, you rest. If you need anything, I'll be right here.'

Ruth wanted to ask questions. If she'd missed the rehearsal, she needed to call Sally. Speak to her agent. Find out where Adam was and why he wasn't here with her. She had to get out of here. But exhaustion overwhelmed her. She closed her eyes.

ω

When she woke again, Eden wasn't there, and Ruth badly needed to pee. She sat up, gingerly, tentatively, aware of her bones and skin. She felt weak and helpless, cowed by the fear of pain. She told herself to relax and took deep breaths, practising the technique she sometimes used before going onstage.

When she was as calm as she was going to get, she pushed the sheets aside, wondering where the white pyjamas she was wearing had come from and, again, where the hell she was. But the urgency in her bladder prevented her from thinking about it for too long. She stood up, wobbling for a moment, tiny pinpricks of light swimming before her eyes. The carpet was plush against her bare feet, and though it hurt, she forced herself to walk to the bathroom. She had vague dream-like memories of someone helping her into a bathroom – this one, presumably – during the night. Or nights. It was all too blurry for her to make sense of.

She used the toilet, then reached over to the bathtub and turned on the taps. While she waited for the tub to fill, she removed her pyjamas and inspected her flesh, shocked by what she saw: the dark purple bruises on her shins and the outsides of her thighs; another bruise on her forearm. Her face, thankfully, was unmarked, and there was no visible sign of damage to her ribs. Breathing hurt, though, and when she pressed a hand against her side she let out a gasp.

What happened to me?

She still couldn't remember any of it.

She ran the bath as hot as she could bear, then climbed in, struggling to breathe at first as the water pressed against her ribs. After a minute or two she felt better but she couldn't relax. Wherever this was, she needed to get out. She had to talk to Sally.

There was a rap on the bathroom door.

'Ruth?' It was Eden.

'I'm in the bath. Give me a minute.'

With great effort, and wondering if this was what it would be like when she was a very old woman, Ruth heaved herself out of the tub and dried herself with one of the huge, fluffy towels that were folded neatly on the rack. She found a robe on the back of the door, the kind one finds in a five-star spa. Everything she had seen here was high-end. There were definitely worse places to wake up confused and hurt.

Eden was waiting outside the door. She looked more herself now, dressed in a long-sleeved T-shirt with denim shorts and sneakers. Was Ruth imagining it or was there anxiety on Eden's face? If there was, it vanished in a flash as she showed what Ruth had come to think of as the Eden smile.

'Nice bath?' Eden asked.

Ruth didn't want to discuss the merits of the bathroom. But the bath had soothed her. Given her strength. 'What happened to me? Why I am covered in bruises? And where are we? And what about my rehearsal? What did you mean when—'

Eden laughed.

'Sorry. I've just . . . I don't understand what's going on. I can't remember anything and I feel like I'm going crazy. If you told me right now that we were both dead and this was a waiting room for Heaven, I'd probably believe you.'

'We're not dead. Nobody's dead.'

'So where the hell are we? What happened? What—' She stopped herself before she launched into another series of questions.

'Why don't you sit down? I brought you some soup.'

When she saw the bowl of soup and plate of bread on the round table by the window, which was still covered by closed blinds, Ruth's stomach growled. She sat on the wooden chair and began to eat. Chicken soup.

'Good for the soul,' Eden said, taking the seat opposite. 'I knew you'd be starving. You haven't eaten since Friday.'

'Is it still Sunday?'

'Monday.'

Ruth put the spoon down. She'd slept through another day.

'We thought it was best to let you sleep,' Eden said.

'We?'

Eden nodded but didn't say any more. Did she mean doctors? Was this some kind of private hospital?

'Where am I?'

'Ruth, I don't want you to freak out. I think it's important first that I tell you what happened, fill in the gaps in your memory.'

'You're scaring me.' Ruth looked around the room. It had to be a hotel or a hospital. Oh God, was it some kind of psychiatric hospital? She'd heard about people getting committed to such places and never getting out.

She got to her feet again and staggered over towards the window.

Eden stood too and blocked her way.

'I need some daylight. How do you open these blinds?'

'I can do it. But first, let me explain—'

'Eden, open the blinds!' Gathering what remained of her strength, she shouldered her way past Eden and was about to start jabbing at buttons on the wall panel when Eden gently steered her out of the way and pressed the correct button. The blinds opened.

Ruth was speechless.

She had expected to see the grounds of a hospital, a lawn or a courtyard. She had thought she would see other patients shuffling about, nurses and doctors. At the very least she had expected to see the ground.

Instead, she saw the city. A sea of concrete and glass, stretched out before and below her. Rooftops and spires and skyscrapers. There, in the distance, was the familiar towering shape of the Empire State Building. Water shimmered out of focus on the horizon. A helicopter buzzed past, almost close enough to touch.

Ruth recoiled, and the world around her spun.

'Great view, huh?' Eden said.

Ruth watched as the helicopter retreated into the distance. 'Where the hell are we? In a hotel?'

'Not a hotel.'

'Then what?'

'Think of it as a hideaway.'

Ruth's head was starting to throb. 'None of this makes sense. I need to go.'

She crossed to the wardrobe and opened it. There was nothing inside but another pair of white pyjamas, neatly folded.

'Where are my clothes?'

'Being laundered.' Eden approached her. 'Come on, please, sit down. Let me—'

'I have to get out of here. It's Monday. That means I've missed two days of rehearsals. Sally is going to fire me. Cara is going to be going insane with excitement, thinking she can replace me. Does Adam know where I am? He's going to be worrying about me . . .'

'Ruth, please sit down. I need to tell you something.'

There was, Ruth noticed now, a sheen of sweat on Eden's forehead, even though this room was air-conditioned, almost chilly.

'I'm not going to sit down. I want my clothes, now. I want to get out of here.' She took a step towards Eden and a white bolt of agony shot from her ankle up her leg. She cried out.

'Ruth, please, sit down.'

Ruth had no choice but to obey. She limped over to the bed and sat on it, sucking in a deep breath, concentrating on her relaxation technique. *Breathe it in, exhale it out.*

'I have to talk to Sally,' she said. 'Where's my phone?'

'It broke. When you fell.'

Fell?

Eden went on. 'And I keep trying to tell you. There's no point talking to Sally. She's already made up her mind.' She sat beside Ruth and produced her own phone, navigating to a page on the Playbill website. She showed the screen to Ruth, saying, 'I'm so sorry.'

LAST-MINUTE CHANGE OF LEAD IN KLAY'S *DARE*

Ruth read the short news piece with horror. It said that Sally had decided to replace the female lead in her new play after the actress slated for the role had 'acted unprofessionally'. *British actress Ruth Armstrong is to be replaced by another unknown, 24-year-old Australian Cara Barker.*

'This can't be happening,' Ruth said.

'I'm sorry. I called Sally, told her you weren't well and needed to rest for a few days, but she was, well, a total bitch about it.'

'You spoke to Sally herself?'

Eden hesitated for a split second. 'Yeah. She was scary.'

Ruth was still holding Eden's phone. 'I need to call my agent, sort this out.' She pressed the 'Call' icon and tried to remember Jayne's number. It wouldn't come to her, if she'd ever retained it. 'I need to go online to look up my agent's number. Better than that, I need to get out of here, right now. I need some clothes.'

'You need to rest.'

'Get me my fucking clothes!'

Eden didn't flinch. 'Ruth, don't worry about your agent. She's not the right person for you anyway.'

'What?'

'You have a lot of questions. And you'll get answers . . . to everything. But first, I need you to come with me.' She paused. 'I want you to meet my friends.'

Chapter 17

'I was going to wait until your clothes were ready, but . . .'

Eden went over to the door in the corner and took a key out of her pocket.

'Wait,' said Ruth. 'Was I locked in here?'

'Only because we didn't want you wandering out in a confused state, maybe hurting yourself.'

Eden unlocked the door and Ruth stood up. She was beginning to wonder if she was in a dream, a complex, feature-length nightmare which would bring tears of relief when it finally ended. She pulled the robe tightly around herself and looked down at the cracked nail polish on her toes.

Eden opened the heavy door and gestured for Ruth to go through.

Ruth found herself in a short, empty corridor. Halfway along, on the left, was a lift. Diagonally opposite was another solid-looking, unmarked door. At the end of the corridor, another door. Again, Ruth thought of a hotel. Or an apartment block. Eden took hold of Ruth's elbow and guided her along.

Just before they reached the door at the end of the corridor, Eden stopped and whispered in Ruth's ear, 'I'm on your side. Don't forget that.'

Before Ruth could ask what that meant, Eden opened the door to reveal a large room, four or five times the size of the one in which Ruth was staying, decorated in white and cobalt blue. It looked like a brand-new, high-end apartment, complete with designer sofas, a gleaming kitchen area at one end, abstract art on the walls, and not a speck of dust or mess in sight. As Eden guided Ruth into this space, Ruth noticed two more things: firstly, there were two people inside the room, a man and a woman, seated on the sofas; secondly, the entire back wall, which had to be thirty feet long, was made of glass, giving a sweeping, panoramic view of the city.

'Hello, Ruth,' said the man, getting up from the sofa. He was in his early thirties, with dark hair and smart clothes, a blazer over a polo shirt. 'Welcome,' he said, with a broad smile that showed off a set of perfect teeth. 'I'm Emilio.' He was extremely good-looking, like something out of a perfume advert. Ruth was finding it hard not to stare at him.

'What do you reckon?' said the woman who had been sitting next to him, coming over and nodding towards the city outside. 'A view to die for, eh?'

She was British, with red hair. She appeared to be in her mid-thirties, maybe a little older. She wore a cream cashmere sweater and soft-looking jeans.

'Would you like tea?' she said. 'We've got Twinings, Yorkshire, even PG Tips.'

Ruth stared at her. This was becoming more and more dream-like. She heard herself say, 'Yes, please.'

'Twinings? I'm Marie, by the way. It's lovely to meet you.'

She went over to the kitchen area and filled a kettle, then put two teabags into a pot.

'Why don't you take a seat,' said Emilio, gesturing for Ruth to follow him over to the sofas. He sat beside her, not too close to crowd her but near enough that she could smell his aftershave.

Again, she had to stop herself from staring at him. She couldn't remember ever being so close to a man this beautiful.

Eden sat the other side of her.

'I'm sorry,' Ruth said. 'But what is this place? Where are we? How do you know each other?'

'Marie and Emilio are old friends of mine,' said Eden.

'I'm from the West Coast too,' Emilio said. 'And, like you, Marie here is from England.'

'I gathered that. Are you two together?'

Emilio and Marie exchanged a small smile. 'She belongs to someone else,' Emilio said.

Belongs to?

'How are your bruises?' Emilio asked before Ruth could say anything else. 'Any better?'

'A little.'

'That's good.' He shook his head. 'Eden told us you both had rather too much to drink. And the steps were slippery from the rain.'

'I haven't told her what happened yet,' said Eden.

'Oh.' Emilio raised a perfect eyebrow. 'I see.'

'I was going to but . . . we kept getting sidetracked.'

Marie came over with a tray bearing a single china cup on a saucer, as well as the teapot and a bowl of sugar lumps complete with tongs. Long ago, Ruth had fantasised about having a grandmother who would serve tea like this. She had written a blog post about it once, about the family she'd never had. Marie poured the tea into the cup. 'There you go.'

Ruth took a sip, hardly tasting it. But it calmed her down, even though everything felt surreal.

'I fell down the front steps?' she said to Eden, who nodded.

Ruth had to put the teacup down. It was shaking in her hand. 'I don't remember any of that.' Except, if she thought about it, she could picture herself tumbling. Could recall a jolt of panic and pain.

110

Eden laughed softly. 'You were knocking back the tequila pretty fast. What do you remember?'

Ruth concentrated. 'I remember eating dinner. Oh God, dancing in the garden, in the rain. I remember you, me and Adam sitting around talking. Did we hug? The three of us?'

Eden nodded.

'I remember . . . a car?'

'That was my car,' Emilio said.

'I don't understand. And where was Adam?'

'He was passed out,' Eden answered. 'Do you not remember our conversation? When I told you about this place?'

Ruth strained to recall it but nothing came. 'No.'

'You were talking to me about your agent and your career and how unhappy you were. How you didn't think you were being looked after right. You were crying, saying you were completely confused about what to do. Do you remember?'

'I think . . . I think so.' She definitely had a memory of talking about that. But hadn't it been earlier in the evening, with Adam? Perhaps she had repeated herself. It had been on her mind, anyway.

'And that's when I told you I knew people who might be able to help. You got really excited, said you wanted to meet them.' Eden smiled, and Emilio and Marie smiled at her too. So many smiles. Ruth felt like she was bathing in their light. 'You asked me to call them right away, so I did. Emilio drove over, and it was when we went out to see him that you slipped down the steps.'

'And we brought you here,' Emilio said.

'Maybe we should have taken you to the hospital,' Eden said, 'but Marie used to be a nurse and I wasn't sure if you had health insurance. I thought you'd be better off here. Marie checked you over and then I put you to bed and let you sleep. I found the number for the rehearsal studio and phoned them.'

'They weren't very friendly,' Emilio said.

'Eden told me,' Ruth said, with a lurch in her stomach. 'Oh God. Sally . . . I have to talk to her.'

'Why?' said Marie. 'She sounds horrible. Why would you want to work with someone like that? Someone so unforgiving? I'm sorry, but she sounds like a total bitch.'

Ruth was surprised to hear herself laugh. 'Yeah. She is. But she's a genius.'

'She doesn't sound very clever to me, if she's prepared to let you go just because you missed a rehearsal. I think you've had a lucky escape.'

'But . . . my career.'

Eden touched her hand. 'It's going to be fine, Ruth. I promise. We're going to help you.'

Ruth stared at her. She realised she was exhausted, the pain creeping back into her bones, and she felt an overwhelming urge to bury herself beneath the duvet and hide in the oblivion of sleep.

'You seem exhausted,' Eden said. 'Let me help you back to bed. We can talk more later.'

Ruth allowed herself to be led out of the room and back to the bedroom. She fell on to the bed, eyes closing immediately. It was strange, the way the tiredness had come on so quickly.

'I'll come back when you've rested,' Eden said, her voice sounding like it was coming from far away even though she was sitting on the edge of the bed.

'Wait. Does Adam know where I am?' Ruth asked.

'Let's talk about that later,' Eden replied.

Ruth slid towards sleep. As she drifted off – or was it later, during the night? – she heard Eden speak again, although her voice sounded different. Not like hers at all. In fact, it sounded very much like a man's voice.

'You're going to be one of us,' it said.

Chapter 18

Callum came back to the table with our pints. I really didn't want mine. After the other night, when I had been half poisoned by alcohol, it had been a struggle to get through my first drink. But Callum downed his quickly, and I wondered if he was an alcoholic. He had the broken veins around his nose, the watery eyes. Perhaps he had started drinking after his wife died. Or when Sinead disappeared.

'What do you mean, Eden's a recruiter?' I asked. 'A recruiter for who?'

'That's exactly what I asked,' he said. 'And as soon as I asked it, the guy I was talking to on Facebook got cagey. He said he didn't know exactly. Only that he'd heard things. About a secret organisation. A group with no name, or at least no name that anyone knows. He said he's heard them describe themselves as a network. That some people said they were a religion, and others that it was a front for human trafficking, although I haven't found any evidence of that. All he could really tell me was that he'd heard about people disappearing and that when they came back they'd changed. Like, he said he'd heard about this girl, a model who was on smack. Then she vanished for ages and everyone thought she was dead, until she came back and, well, now she's clean and successful. You'd probably recognise her picture if I showed it to you.'

I scoffed. 'She'd probably just been to rehab.'

'That's what I said. But this guy insisted there were loads of examples. He was going to give me a list, said he'd chat to me online the next day and give me more info. Except he never did. His Facebook account disappeared. All the messages he'd sent me vanished too, like the conversation had been deleted at his end.'

I must have looked like I was finding this hard to believe, because Callum said, 'I know. It sounds crazy. This person on Facebook was probably having a laugh at the desperate old guy, yeah? Or maybe you think I'm lying. How can you trust me, a total stranger?'

He had taken the words out of my mouth.

'I can't prove to you that I have a daughter called Sinead who went missing. I might not be who I say I am. But here are the facts. Your girlfriend has vanished, right? You know Eden is a liar and that she has to be involved. And someone just tried to run your ass over.'

I nodded slowly.

'I found out that there was another one of these spirituality conventions happening here in New York two weeks ago. I managed to get hold of a woman who works for the company organising it and paid her – okay, bribed her – for a copy of the delegate list. Eden was on it. So I came here to New York to follow her, hoping she'd lead me to this secret organisation and to Sinead. Instead, she led me to you guys.'

'You saw her at the convention?'

'I did indeed. It took all my self-control not to march up to her and try to shake the information out of her. "Where's my daughter, bitch?" But I knew it would be smarter to follow her.'

There were some French fries on my plate, gone cold now. He picked a few up and stuffed them into his mouth.

'To be honest with you, I didn't know if you were involved too. So since Eden and Ruth went AWOL, I've been following you. I thought you might lead me to them.' He coughed. 'That was until someone tried to run you down in broad daylight. So this is my proposal to you: we team up, help each other find Eden, and get our women back.'

'Our women?'

'You know what I mean. So, what do you say? Are we going to team up?'

He sat back and waited, folding his arms, though he seemed a little nervous, like he was relying on me to say yes: a yes I couldn't give without hesitation.

Because the whole story was incredible. Secret organisations? People disappearing and coming back changed?

But the facts were indisputable. Ruth was missing. Eden was a liar and was involved. And though it horrified me to admit it, someone had tried to kill me.

The police weren't interested. Mona and Jack didn't believe me. No one else seemed to care and I had no other leads to follow.

'I don't really have a choice, do I?'

To my surprise, Callum's eyes filled with tears and he leaned over and grabbed hold of my hand, squeezing it in his large fist. 'We're going to find them,' he said. 'We're going to get them back.'

ω

Callum was renting a short-let apartment on Kent Avenue, close to the Williamsburg Bridge. When I told him I had nowhere to stay, he said I could sleep on his couch.

It was a one-bedroom place, boxy but clean, with A/C that hummed efficiently and windows that all but blocked out the traffic from outside. On the way I had popped into a couple of stores and bought a toothbrush and some spare underwear plus a couple of basic T-shirts. At some point I would have to go back to Jack and Mona's to pick up my stuff, but right now I couldn't face them.

Callum made coffee and we sat at the breakfast bar in the little kitchen.

'Why did we let Eden in?' I asked. 'Why did we trust her?'

'Because you're nice people? Plus she seems harmless, doesn't she? Sweet.'

I thought about what she'd been like at the pool. She certainly hadn't been sweet then. I wondered if that was the only time I had glimpsed the real Eden. And it was hard not to beat myself up about it; how I had allowed myself to be taken in. I suppose it was in my nature to think the best of people. I hadn't suffered enough knocks in my life. Hadn't ever been betrayed or badly let down. I'd had it too easy.

From now on, that was going to change.

'Tell me about Friday night,' Callum said. 'What happened?'

I told him everything I could remember, from the point when Eden had come home with the Japanese food and tequila, up to the group hug. I left out the details of Eden's story because I still couldn't remember them, though I was sure they had to be significant. Why else would she tell us her life story? Unless it was all made up, of course.

'The next thing I knew, I was waking up on the floor.'

Callum scowled. 'Jesus, I should have stayed outside. I would have seen them leaving.'

'It was the middle of the night.'

'Yeah. In the city that doesn't sleep. I shouldn't have either. Let's talk about Ruth. Do you think she would have left of her own accord?'

'I don't know. She was drunk. I guess it wouldn't have been too hard to persuade her. Though I can't believe Eden would have

116

said, "Hey, I'm a member of a secret organisation. Want to come and check it out?"'

'Ha. No.' He twisted his coffee mug around. 'One of the things that's bugging me is why Eden's modus operandi was so different this time. With Sinead, she befriended her, worked on her for months before she whisked her away. With Ruth, it's been days, right? There must be a reason for the urgency.'

I was still trying to wrap my head round the idea that Ruth had been taken by a secret group. But the answer was obvious.

'Eden needed to do it before Mona and Jack came back and exposed her.'

'Of course.'

Something struck me. 'You said people joined and came back changed. Why hasn't Sinead come back?'

'That's the question that haunts me.'

'Maybe there's some kind of test,' I said.

'And not everyone passes it.'

'Jesus.'

We both gazed into the blackness of our coffee cups.

'Let's back up to the night in question,' Callum said. 'Eden knew she had to take Ruth before your friends returned. Friday night was almost her last opportunity. What would she have done if you hadn't gone to sleep?'

This was something that had been niggling at me, in the back of my mind, since it had happened. Eden had plied us with drink, sure, but she couldn't have known I would pass out.

Unless . . .

I stood up. 'I think she might have drugged me. It would explain how horrific I felt the next day, when I finally woke up. I've never felt that bad before, no matter how much I've had to drink. I'm still not one hundred per cent now . . . Or what if—' I broke off. 'Eden must have known that I would tell Jack and Mona about her as soon as they got back, and that I would find out she was an imposter.'

Callum watched me pace the room.

'And she must have realised I would freak out when I found out she wasn't who she said she was. What if she did more than try to knock me out?'

I stopped pacing.

'What if she was trying to kill me? If I was dead, there would be no one to tell Jack and Mona about her. No one would ever know Eden had been there. And there'd be no one to look for Ruth.'

It all made a sick kind of sense. The way I'd felt on Friday night, like I was tripping. The terrible state I'd been in on Saturday. The way that Eden had removed all trace of herself from the house. It was all designed so Jack and Mona would come home to find me dead and Ruth gone. No one would ever know Eden had been there, so . . .

'I'm finding this hard to wrap my head around,' Callum said. 'If you'd been found dead, the police would search for Ruth. She'd be a murder suspect. Eden wouldn't want that to happen, would she?'

'Unless she planned to remove my body.'

He furrowed his brow. 'I don't know. Would she and the others want it to look like you'd both gone missing? And if Eden was planning to have someone come and take your body, why didn't she remove you while you were unconscious? They could have finished the job.'

I shuddered.

'No, I think she only intended to knock you out. No offence, but she probably thought it was safe to leave you alive because she didn't think you'd be capable of tracking Ruth down. Of getting anywhere at all.'

I let what he'd said sink in.

'You're going to have to prove her wrong, son,' said Callum.

Chapter 19

'I need to prove that Eden exists,' I said the next morning, after a restless night on the sofa. 'Do you have any photos of her?'

'No,' Callum responded. He looked a lot less tired than I felt. He'd already been out and had come back with coffee and breakfast. 'I've tried to get one a few times but it's harder than you'd think, secretly photographing someone. I got a couple of blurry shots of the back of her head and that's it.'

'Sinead didn't have any?'

'Not that I could find. I guess Eden doesn't like having her picture taken.'

'Except she took a photo with me,' I said. 'In the bar. We took a few, in fact.'

'Then she deleted them off your phone.' He scratched his beard. 'Did you notice any CCTV cameras there? In the bar?'

I thought back, trying to picture that night. But who notices CCTV cameras?

'I have no idea.'

'Well, you'd better get down there and find out.'

'Aren't you going to come too?'

'Can't. I've set up a meeting with a local journalist. She's an expert in cults.'

'Cults?' It was the first time the word had come up. I realised we had been skirting around it.

'Yep. Apparently this reporter knows everything there is to know about the subject, so I'm going to go have a chat with her. See what I can find out. She's upstate so I'm going to be gone a while.' He paused. 'If you search for cults and secret organisations online, there are dozens of them. Hundreds. But the one we're looking for . . . there's no trace of it.'

'Maybe your contact on Facebook was making it all up.'

He squeezed his empty coffee cup, crushing it. 'It exists. I'm sure of it. And if anyone knows anything about it, it'll be this woman.'

ω

Alison's Starting To Happen, the bar I'd visited with Eden, didn't open until lunchtime, so I spent the morning at Callum's, researching cults on my laptop. The word had a chilling power, conjuring up images of religious fanatics living in communes and compounds. The Jonestown massacre. The sarin attack on the Tokyo subway. Charles Manson and the butchering of Sharon Tate. They preyed on lost people who were searching for something to belong to, looking for meaning.

Yeah, whispered a voice in my head. *Like Ruth.*

I closed the computer. Again, I had to push through my disbelief and try to accept what seemed to be the likely truth. Eden belonged to a cult and had taken Ruth. The question was, why? Why target Ruth? Had she come to Jack and Mona's house with Ruth as her target? That had to be the case; it couldn't be random. But how did she know about Ruth? Again, the answer seemed obvious. Ruth was an actress. She was known in certain, small circles – the theatre world and the kind of people who watched arthouse horror films. Had Eden targeted Ruth because of her role in the movie? That made sense, except Eden had acted like she'd never seen *The Immaculate* before. Her emotional reaction, her surprise at the events in the film, had seemed genuine – although I already knew Eden was a practised liar. A convincing actress in her own right. And that made me wonder if she was in fact an actor, if she was part of theatrical circles too.

Then there was the other big question. How had she known we were at Mona and Jack's house, and that they were away? Eden had seemed to know about the Cunninghams. She knew details about their lives. Or was I imagining that? Had she used generalities, like a medium conning gullible audience members? Or had she parroted back facts we had told her? Perhaps everything she had known about Mona and Jack could be found on their social media accounts.

In fact, Eden could have found out that we were house-sitting for Jack and Mona through *our* social media. Hadn't I tweeted something about how excited I was to be heading to Brooklyn? Did I mention we were staying in Williamsburg? I followed both Jack and Mona on Twitter. If they had tweeted about going to their retreat it wouldn't have been too hard for Eden to put the two things together.

Or maybe it was less complicated. Perhaps Eden had followed us there. Perhaps she had been following us for a while. And maybe she really did know the Cunninghams – or knew someone who knew them.

I opened my laptop again and began to go through my and Ruth's photos. I concentrated on any that had been taken in a public place, scanning the faces in the background, looking for Eden. I went through all the photos from the cruise, including the day we'd docked in New York. I went through the pictures I'd taken around

Brooklyn once we'd started house-sitting, as well as those that Ruth had posted on Facebook and Instagram.

It was remarkable how many blonde strangers there were in the backgrounds of our photos. I kept zooming in, scrutinising them. But none of them were Eden.

I checked the time. I had been down the internet rabbit hole for hours. Alison's would be opening soon.

I grabbed my sunglasses and wallet and headed towards the door, then hesitated. If I was potentially in danger, shouldn't I take a weapon?

I grabbed a small but sharp knife from the kitchen drawer and slipped it into my bag.

ω

Alison's looked very different during daylight hours. The only patrons were a couple of guys huddled in a dark corner with laptops open. I glanced over at the table where Eden and I had sat, and I couldn't help but wonder what she had thought of me. Did she think I was stupid? Easy prey? Maybe, at the back of her mind, she thought she was teaching me a valuable lesson: never trust a stranger.

There was a single barman on shift, who I vaguely recognised from my night here. He had a shaved head and the vampirish complexion of someone who spends their days in a dark place.

'What can I get you?' he asked as I approached.

'Just a Diet Coke, please,' I said.

He handed me my drink, and before he could turn away, I said, 'Do you have CCTV here?'

He stopped dead. 'The cash register's empty.'

'What? I'm not . . . I'm not going to rob you. I was actually hoping you could help me.'

His shoulders relaxed. 'Oh yeah?'

I had already thought through the best way to approach this. After flirting with the idea of pretending to be a cop or private investigator, I had decided to be honest. It was such a crazy story that it went past implausibility and became believable. That was my hope, anyway.

So I told him about Eden and Ruth and me, being as succinct as possible.

The barman narrowed his eyes and glanced at the door then back at me. 'This is a prank, right? I'm going to end up on YouTube, looking like an asshole.'

'It's not a prank. I wish it was.'

He didn't seem convinced. But he seemed intrigued, and I guessed this was a lot more interesting than what usually happened during his day shift. Maybe, like a lot of people around here, he was an aspiring writer or filmmaker who thought he might be able to use this.

'So what exactly do you want me to do?' he asked.

'I was hoping I could take a look at your CCTV footage from last Wednesday evening. If you haven't recorded over it already, that is.'

I immediately regretted saying this, as I'd given him an out. He could easily get rid of me by telling me it had been deleted.

Instead, he said, 'You want to see if you and this girl are on there.'

'Exactly.'

'I don't know . . .'

'Please,' I said. 'I'm desperate. And I can pay you for your time.'

For a moment I thought I'd offended him, and again I wanted to take my words back. But I had misread him.

'How much?' he asked.

I plucked a figure from the air. 'A hundred dollars.'

He didn't seem impressed by that.

'Two hundred if Eden's on there.'

He glanced left and right. 'Two hundred to look. Five hundred if she's on there.' He smiled. 'I've got child support to pay.'

Five hundred dollars would wipe me out. But I nodded. What choice did I have?

'All right. Come back at seven. I'll take a look when the shift changes for the evening.'

I opened my mouth to protest but thought better of it. I didn't want him to change his mind. Before I left, I asked his name.

'You don't need to know that,' he said. 'I'll meet you at seven in the Mexican place across the street.' He grinned. 'You can buy me dinner too.'

Chapter 20

I had hours to kill and no other leads to follow. I walked past Jack and Mona's house, wondering if I should knock, try to persuade them I was telling the truth. But I decided it would be better to wait. Later, if the barman came through, I would have a photo of Eden to show them.

I headed towards McCarren Park with the vague intention of talking to the people at the pool about looking at their CCTV too, in case Eden was on there. But I had second thoughts. I could imagine them reacting badly, demanding to know why I wanted to look at images of lots of women in bathing suits.

I entered the park not far from the spot where the car had tried to mow me down. A small area had been cordoned off with crime scene tape, which added to my unease. Were the people who'd tried to run me down around today? And why did they want to kill me? It wasn't like I'd made any progress.

I was so deep in thought that I didn't immediately notice the man outside the children's playground, where hundreds of kids were running around, having water fights, climbing on the jungle gym and swinging across monkey bars, apparently unaffected by the heat. Just beyond the play area was the public pool. In front of that, a young, well-built man sat on a bench, staring into space.

I didn't recognise him immediately. It was like when you see a familiar actor in a TV show and can't remember where you've seen them before.

It was only when he lifted his face towards me that I realised who he was.

The guy I had christened Mets. The one who had harassed Eden at the pool. He wasn't wearing his baseball cap. But it was definitely him – and he clearly recognised me too.

To my great surprise, he looked scared.

'Can we—' I began.

He jumped up from the bench and ran.

'Hey!' I shouted, as he sprinted away from the playground towards the road. 'Hey!'

I broke into a run, calling after him again. What was going on? He certainly hadn't been afraid of me the last time I'd encountered him. I almost collided with a woman pushing a baby buggy, then a pair of children ran into my path and I skidded to a halt. A young boy gawped up me and I heard his dad yell something, though I wasn't sure if he was shouting at me to watch where I was going or at the kid.

I ran towards the road beside the park, sure I had lost Mets before I'd even started to properly pursue him, but then I caught sight of him across the street, going into an apartment block.

I jogged across the road and approached the building. The door was firmly shut and there was no sign of Mets. It was a large, rather shabby-looking building, far less upmarket than the new apartment blocks down the street. Was this where Mets lived?

I hung around for a while, hoping he would come out so I could ask him what was going on. A large group of kids with skateboards under their arms passed me and went into the building. I thought about following them inside, but the teenage boy at the back of the group eyed me suspiciously – aggressively, even – and I decided against it.

I stood there, unsure what to do, remembering the scene by the pool. Mets and his friend, the one I had christened Muscles, harassing Eden. And I remembered what she had said to him before we'd parted.

Dead men walking.

Had she come back to do what she'd promised?

ω

The Mexican place opposite Alison's was tiny, with just a few benches at the back of the restaurant, where the barman was already waiting. It seemed that most people were getting takeout and, after asking my new friend what he wanted, I joined the line. I was hungry but my stomach was knotted with tension, so I wasn't sure how much I'd be able to eat.

'I don't know your name,' I said, sliding into the seat opposite the barman.

'It's Joe,' he said, with a slight smirk, like it wasn't his real name. I supposed it didn't matter. He grabbed his burrito and immediately began to eat, tucking into it like he was starving, shreds of onion and blobs of salsa plopping on to the tabletop.

'I'm Adam.'

He raised a finger to indicate I should wait till he'd finished eating. So I sat and watched him as he stuffed the food into his mouth. Eventually, he finished and wiped his face with the back of his hand.

'Did you bring the money, Adam?' he asked, so quietly that I had to strain to hear him.

'I did. But how much am I going to need?'

He smiled. 'I was thinking about bumping the price to a thousand, to see how desperate you really are. But this has been fun, and you seem like a nice guy, so five hundred it is.'

'She's on there?'

'Sure is. Well, *you're* on there, and I'm guessing the blonde you're flirting with is the girl you're looking for. You didn't tell me she was so hot.' He laughed. 'No wonder you fell for her femme-fatale charms.'

My God, this guy was a jerk. 'Just show me. Please. Did you print a screenshot?'

'I did better than that. I've got the video here. I downloaded it. Now, the money. Under the table, please.'

I had withdrawn the cash and put it in an envelope that I'd bought from a store up the street. I handed it to him beneath the table and he tucked it into his shirt pocket without bothering to count it.

'*Muchas gracias*,' he said, putting on a ridiculous accent.

He lay his phone on the table and tapped it a few times until an image appeared on the screen: the interior of Alison's, close to the bar. The table where Eden and I had been sitting was at the edge of the frame, but was empty. The picture was full-colour and much better quality than I'd expected.

'This is the start of the evening,' he said. 'Let me skip ahead.'

He slid his finger along the bottom of the screen and then let go so the footage began to play again. My heart flipped. There we were, clearly visible. Eden and me, though you could only see the back of my head until at one point I looked back towards the bar so my face was visible. Eden was leaning forward, saying something, and my shoulders shook like I was laughing. There were quite a few empty glasses between us and we looked like we were having a great time. We *had* been having a great time, and it was easy to see why Joe thought I'd been flirting with her.

'Can you send me this?' I asked.

'No way. If my boss finds out he won't only fire me, he'll sue my ass.'

'But we had a deal!'

I had raised my voice, drawing looks from people in the line, and he put his palms up and said, 'Chill.'

'We had a deal,' I repeated in a hiss.

'Yes, for me to look and show you what I found. I can't give you the video.'

I hesitated. If I grabbed his phone would I be able to get away before he caught me? Before I could decide, he picked it up.

'Here's the best I can offer. I'll take some close-up screenshots of Blondie and send them to you. Okay?'

I tried to protest again but he said, 'That's my best offer.'

I sighed. 'I'm not giving you five hundred dollars for that.'

'No problemo.' He went to rise but I caught his arm.

'Wait. I'll give you two fifty.'

He sat back down. 'You've already given me the money, hombre. I just don't see me giving any of it back.'

I wanted to punch him. Nothing would have given me more pleasure at that moment.

'You're an asshole,' I said.

'So I've been told. What's your number?'

I gave it to him and watched as he manipulated the images on his screen, zooming in on Eden's face at several different angles and taking screenshots. A few minutes later my phone pinged several times and the images arrived.

Here it was. Proof that Eden existed.

Joe, if that was his real name, got up and patted me on the shoulder. He looked down at my uneaten burrito. 'You want that?'

'Take it.'

He snatched it up and left.

ᴡ

I stood outside Jack and Mona's house, gripping my phone like it was a hand grenade that would go off if I dropped it, paranoid that if I let go it would vanish, taking the pictures of Eden with it. I had already messaged Callum to let him know I had the photos and he'd responded with a thumbs-up emoji. I didn't tell him what I was planning, though, as I thought he might try to dissuade me. Tell me to wait. I couldn't, though. I was sick of not being believed. I had to show Jack and Mona the proof. Then, I hoped, they would call Detective Krugman. With photos of Eden, surely he would be able to do something.

The house was bathed in soft light, the sky tinged with pink. It was less humid this evening, the heat not so unbearable; summer was losing some of its fierceness. I rang the bell and waited, the images of Eden ready on my phone screen. There was no reply. I rang the bell again, then peered through the front window at an empty room.

They weren't home.

That took the wind out of my sails. What should I do? I could wait here on the front stoop, but they might be hours. I considered texting the pictures to them, but I wanted to see their faces when they saw the photos. I wasn't only trying to prove I wasn't lying; I was hoping they would recognise Eden, tell me they had encountered her somewhere. Maybe they would even know how to find her.

After mulling over my options, I sent a text to both Jack and Mona.

> *I have photos of Eden and really need to show them to you. I'm outside your place. Are you coming home soon?*

There was no immediate response, and because the messages had sent as texts rather than iPhone messages, I couldn't see if they had been delivered. Maybe Jack and Mona had gone to see a movie, or were at the theatre or somewhere else they wouldn't be checking their phones.

I couldn't just wait here on the stoop. I was too energised and restless. Mets's fearful reaction to me made me believe that Eden had been back to Williamsburg. Maybe someone had seen her. Perhaps she'd been with someone else. It felt like, right now, every scrap of information could be useful.

I went into the frozen yoghurt place across the street. It was a popular hangout for teenagers and people in their early twenties. I showed Eden's picture to the woman behind the counter, who looked at me like I might be a stalker before shaking her head. I needed to work on a cover story.

Next, I went to the Dunkin' Donuts on the corner. A young man with an expression that matched the donuts – glazed – listened to my freshly minted story about my missing friend with little interest, before glancing at the picture and shaking his head.

For the next hour, I went up and down Bedford Avenue and the surrounding streets, telling anyone who'd listen about my friend who'd gone missing, asking them if they'd seen her. All I got were blank looks and shakes of the head, except for the few people who had seen and remembered Eden during that week. Like the guy in the Japanese place who'd served her on Friday night, or the man in the taco truck on the corner. But none of them had seen her since.

Only one conversation was notable. In the liquor store on North Sixth Street, the man behind the counter remembered selling Eden the bottles of tequila last Friday.

'Yeah, I remember her,' he said. 'She irritated me because she was talking to someone on her cell when I was serving her. I hate people who do that.'

'Did you hear what she was talking about?'

He paused, clearly reluctant to give out too much information. I tried my best to look pitiful. 'Her parents are going crazy with worry. But if I can tell them she's just gone off partying with a new boyfriend or something, that would make us all feel a lot better.'

'I get it.' He thought about it. 'I don't remember what she was talking about, to be honest. She said something like, "Tell him not to worry." It sounded like whoever she was talking to was nagging her about something and your friend was pissed. Aggravated.'

A chill ran down my spine. Who had she been talking to? I remembered the day Eden and I had gone to the pool together. Somebody had kept texting her when we were on our way to the park, and Eden had seemed aggravated then too. Was it the same person? I had assumed it was her ex, but I now knew this ex didn't exist.

'There's one more thing,' said the guy in the liquor store before I left. 'At the end of the call, when I was handing over her change, she said something in a foreign language.'

'What language?'

'I'm not a hundred per cent sure. Italian, maybe.'

That was weird. I didn't think Eden was Italian-American. Who would she be speaking to in Italian?

As I stepped on to the street, my phone rang. It was Mona.

'Adam? Where are you?' She sounded a little out of breath, like she was walking fast. 'Are you still in Williamsburg?'

'I'm just around the corner from your house.'

'Okay, cool. I'm five minutes away so I'll meet you out front.'

'Great.' I began to walk in the direction of the house.

I was about to hang up when Mona said, 'Did you already try knocking? Because Jack should be in.'

'Yeah, I did.'

'Huh. Maybe he's in the basement or he's gone out. Anyway, see you in a minute.'

She ended the call.

I reached the house before Mona, and thought about ringing the bell again, but decided I might as well wait. She wouldn't be long. And, sure enough, here she came hurrying along the street. She had her sunglasses up on her head and was dressed smartly.

'Hey,' she said. 'How are you? I had a meeting with a client. I thought I was never going to get out of there.'

Having overheard what she and Jack had said about me, I found it hard to smile. But then she turned to me and laughed, the skin around her eyes crinkling, and I remembered why I'd liked her so much when we met on the cruise. Maybe I shouldn't have been so hard on her and Jack. After all, Ruth and I had let a stranger into their home. They barely knew me and, until now, there had been no proof at all that Eden existed. In their shoes, I might have been just as suspicious and sceptical.

'I take it you haven't heard from Ruth?' she said.

'No.'

She reached out and touched my upper arm, making a concerned sound, and her eyes searched my face as if she were trying to appraise me, to figure me out.

'Let's go in,' she said.

She fished in her bag for her keys and opened the door, going inside ahead of me.

'Jack,' she called. 'Hi. Adam's with me. Just in case you're naked!' She winked at me.

There was no response so she called his name again, this time with a question mark. But the house was utterly silent.

We went into the living room.

'Let me check the basement,' she said. 'He won't be able to hear me if he's down there.' She went out through the back door into the garden, then down the steps that led to the office. She came back almost immediately.

'Nope, he's not down there. I guess he *has* gone out,' she said. She checked the time. It was quarter to nine. 'He can't be asleep already.'

She gestured for me to sit down but I didn't want to. I was too on edge. I'd already experienced two disappearances from this house. Mona looked more worried than she was letting on too. 'I'm just going to check upstairs,' she said.

I waited. My entire body thrummed with tension. I was standing on the exact spot where I last remembered seeing Ruth and Eden, when we had hugged. I felt a deep sense of foreboding.

And maybe it's my memory playing tricks on me, but looking back I remember expecting Mona's scream, so that as it echoed from above me, down the stairs, filling the house, I wasn't surprised.

Chapter 21

A small crowd had gathered outside the house, and the street pulsed with flashing lights from the police cars parked two abreast, blocking the road. I watched as Mona was escorted from the house by Krugman, who whispered in the ear of a uniformed policewoman before gently handing Mona over to her. He was grim-faced as he turned away and met my eye. As Krugman came towards me, the policewoman helped Mona into the back of one of the cop cars and reversed out of the street.

'I'm going to need you to come in and make a statement,' Krugman said.

'Yes. Of course. Did Mona tell you I've got photos of Eden?'

'Hmmm. She did.'

The look he gave me told me that he blamed me for this, at least partly. And he was right to, wasn't he? Jack was dead. I had seen his body myself after Mona's scream sent me racing up the stairs. Jack had been in the second bedroom, the room in which Ruth and I had slept. He was slumped in a sitting position with his back against the far wall, with two holes in his torso: one in his stomach, the other in his chest. I couldn't see his face, just the top of his head where it had fallen forward. He had a bald spot that I'd never noticed before.

Mona had been on her knees beside him, kneeling in a pool of blood, making a dreadful keening sound.

She had turned to me, her eyes a pair of red, watery pits, and shame and regret had washed over me.

Whatever had happened there had to be connected to Ruth's disappearance. By inviting Eden in, I had brought death into this home.

Krugman handed me his card, which carried the address of the station house where he was based. 'I'm going to be busy here for a while but come see me first thing tomorrow. Okay?'

I nodded.

'Good. You didn't see anything, I take it? Mona told me you called round earlier?'

'About half seven, yes. And the house was quiet. I looked through the window and didn't see or hear anything.'

'Hmm. No one hanging around?'

'No. The street was pretty quiet.'

I pictured the holes in Jack's shirt. I had never seen anyone who had been shot before. 'Didn't anyone hear gunshots? And do you want to see the pictures of Eden? I can send them to you.'

He gave me a questioning look.

'Surely this has to be connected? To what I told you about?'

'Maybe. We're going to find out about the gunshots. And yes, you can send the photos to the email address on my card. That would be helpful. We'll need the address where you're staying, too.'

'Okay.'

'How did you get the photos?'

I told him and he nodded.

'See yourself as a detective, do you?' he said.

'I'm just trying to find Ruth. And you guys don't seem willing to help me.'

'Hmm.'

He walked away, head down, back into the building. Jack's body was still inside and I didn't want to see them carry him out. It was bad enough seeing the CSIs go inside in their suits, watching as yellow and black tape was strung up across the front of the house.

I hadn't known Jack long, and for the last twenty-four hours I'd been pissed off with him. But, for a short time, he had been my friend.

Punch-drunk from the events of the day, I stumbled away, back to Callum's place.

ϖ

Walking along the quiet streets that ran parallel to the river, I couldn't shake off the vision of Jack's body. That bald spot on his head. The bullet holes in his torso. Mona kneeling in his blood, wailing.

Had Jack found something out? The house had been silent when I'd got there, and it horrified me to think that Jack had been lying in there while I was waiting outside. Had he been alive, lying there praying someone would find him? Could I have saved him if I'd gone in? I had remembered since that I still had a key to their house, though I'd left it with my belongings at Callum's.

Had his murderer been inside while I was knocking on the door?

I was so deep inside my own head that I hadn't realised I'd taken a wrong turn. I was on a residential, tree-lined street, and there was nobody else around at all. It felt like the middle of the night.

And then I heard footsteps behind me.

Hearing footsteps in New York is hardly an unusual occurrence. But yesterday someone had tried to kill me. And I had just seen a dead man in the house from which my girlfriend had vanished.

What if it was the person who had shot Jack?

I had the knife I'd taken from Callum's kitchen drawer in my backpack. I could stop, confront my pursuer. Get answers. But if it was the killer, they would almost certainly have a gun. What use would a knife be then?

I increased my pace, looking over my shoulder every few seconds. I couldn't see anyone. It was as if I were being stalked by a ghost. Or no, the Invisible Man. I forced myself to stop to see if I was hearing an echo of my own footsteps. All was silent. Breathing heavily, I started walking again, head down, going as fast as I could. I had my phone in my hand, ready to call 911 if anyone came too close.

Will I hear it, will I feel it, if someone shoots me in the head or heart? Is there a moment of knowledge, of realising this is the end, before you die?

But nothing happened. No one came running towards me from across the street. No shots rang out.

I passed the foot of the bridge and found myself at a busy intersection. Life. Movement. People. I had never been so happy to hear the great cacophonous rush of the city. I followed the crowd across, aware that my pulse had slowed, and feeling less afraid as I turned into the quieter street that led to Callum's apartment.

And then a black car with tinted windows pulled up beside me.

I scrambled backwards, looking for somewhere to hide, a wall to hurdle or a garbage can to squat behind. This was it. I would soon be in the morgue beside Jack. I would never know what had happened to Ruth.

The rear window slid down and a wild part of me expected to see the Devil sitting there, ready to offer me a deal for my soul.

It was Callum.

'Get in,' he said.

ಡ

'Where are we going?' I asked. The interior of the car was cavernous but ancient. There was a thick screen between us and the driver, and the smell of decades of stale cigarette smoke clung to the cracked leather. It seemed like the kind of car a mob boss might have been chauffeured around in twenty years ago.

'I want you to meet someone,' he said.

'Who? The reporter you went to see earlier?'

He nodded. 'It'll be useful for you to hear what she has to say. Now, do you want a beer?' He fished out a six-pack of lagers from the footwell. 'It might calm your nerves. No? Suit yourself.'

We drove out of the city. On the way, I told him everything that had happened, from my encounter with Mets up to Jack's murder.

'Holy mother . . . I didn't think things would move this fast.'

'I think someone might have been following me too,' I said. 'Probably the same person who tried to run me over.'

He held up a can of beer. 'Sure you don't want one of these?'

I watched the city recede, the lights of the five boroughs fading as we hit the highway and then found ourselves on curving roads crowded by trees. Callum sipped his beer quietly while my brain replayed the events of the day on a nightmarish loop. I was just about to give in and ask for a beer when he said, 'This is it', and we pulled off the road and drove up a long track into the woods. It was pitch-black, the car's headlights picking out the reaching silhouettes of trees and exposing the dark places between.

We pulled up outside a large cabin and Callum said, 'We're here.'

We got out and I followed him to the front door. I heard a whirr and looked up to find myself staring into a security camera, its red light blinking. Behind us, the car slid away into the night.

The door opened and a dog immediately started barking, loud and close; so loud I thought it might shake the pictures from the walls. A woman shouted, 'Quiet, Julius', and then there she was, beckoning us in. She was wearing a baseball cap, from which a few locks of grey stringy hair had escaped, and, strikingly, yellow-tinted glasses that covered most of the upper half of her face. She was broad and short, a Janis Joplin T-shirt stretched across her chest. She wore a copper bracelet on one wrist.

'Come on, come on.' Her voice was barely audible above the dog, which continued to bark like only the taste of blood would satisfy it. I hurried inside after Callum, and turned to see her peer out at the woods before shutting and locking the door, sliding across one, two, three heavy bolts.

It was dimly lit inside the house. Somewhere nearby, the dog growled, muffled by a closed door. The woman yelled at it again – her shouts had no effect – before turning to face me.

Callum jerked his chin in my direction. 'Wanda, this is Adam. Adam, Wanda.'

I put my hand out to shake hers but she ignored it. Instead, she said, 'Put your arms up', and proceeded to pat me down like an airport security officer.

'He's clean,' Callum said.

'How do you know?' Wanda responded, moving down to my legs and running her hands down one thigh then the other. 'Take off your shoes.'

'Oh, come on,' Callum said. 'He's not wearing a wire. And he definitely doesn't have a weapon in his sneakers.'

'It's fine,' I said. 'It's always polite to take your shoes off when you enter someone's house, isn't it?'

I unlaced my Converse and handed them to Wanda. She shook them and appeared satisfied.

I put them back on while the dog continued to growl and bark nearby. 'That's Julius,' Wanda said. 'Anyone comes near me and . . .' She drew a finger across her throat.

Wordlessly, she led us through the cabin's living room. It smelled of incense sticks and was kitted out with throw rugs and beanbags, piles of books and magazines everywhere: back issues of *Rolling Stone* and music biographies. One of them, I noticed, had been written by a Wanda Brooks. The walls were covered with signed photos of rock stars, mostly from the sixties and seventies. A framed platinum disc hung beside the door. I stopped to marvel at it.

Wanda, who had been about to exit the room, stopped and said, 'Stevie gave me that herself.'

'Wait. You know Stevie Nicks?'

She shrugged. 'Used to.'

'Wanda was a rock journalist,' Callum said. 'Back in the seventies. She knew everyone, didn't you, Wanda?'

'Stevie. Elton. Mick. Jerry. Patti. Bruce. Yeah, I did. But . . .' She leaned forward. Her yellow glasses gave her face a sickly glow. 'It's too dangerous for me to contact them now.'

She left the room before I could ask what that meant, and Callum grinned at me before following her.

I could still hear the dog barking in some part of the cabin as Wanda led us along a corridor that was filled with more framed discs, along with vintage concert posters and magazine covers: *Creem*, *Playboy*, more *Rolling Stone*. We paused in the kitchen and Wanda asked me if I'd like anything to drink.

'Just water, please,' I said.

Wanda winked at Callum. 'These millennials, huh? I've heard they don't drink. Very sensible. Very boring.'

'I wish I didn't drink,' I said. 'I might not be in this trouble.'

She handed me a glass of water and we followed her further down the hallway. There was a door at the end, which Wanda unlocked using a bunch of keys that hung from her belt.

We went inside. The room was full of computers: desktops and laptops, screens glowing in the semi-darkness. There must have been a dozen of them, some brand new, some knackered-looking, including an original Blueberry iMac.

'Wow,' I said.

Wanda eased herself into a huge leather chair, and Callum perched on the edge of a desk beside her. This room wasn't full of rock memorabilia. Instead, the walls were covered with pages from newspapers and printouts from online news pages. I peered at them. All the stories were about cults.

'Take a seat, young man,' Wanda said. 'And tell me everything.'

So I did. When I'd finished, Wanda took her glasses off and I could see excitement shining in her eyes.

'Can you help us?' I asked. 'Help us find Ruth and Eden?'

'I'm going to try.' She looked at me. 'Nineteen eighty-three. I was on tour with this band called Mister Magpie. Holy shit, they were bad. Made A Flock of Seagulls sound like the Beatles. The singer was cute as hell, though.'

Was she about to start regaling us with tales from the road? I opened my mouth to ask her about what was happening in the present day, but Callum gestured at me to be patient.

'That's when I first started hearing about young people going missing. Fans of the band, mostly young women. There was a big group of them who followed Mister Magpie around. Wannabe groupies, a lot of them. Actual groupies, some of them. I thought it would be interesting to talk to them, and found out that a few of the girls had vanished during the tour. There was a lot of whispering about it. I thought they'd probably just gone home – but, well, the rumours were that they'd been enticed to join a cult.' She shook her head. 'And that's what got me interested in the whole thing, though it was just an interest at that point. We never did find out what happened to those missing fans, even though I spent all my spare time trying to dig into it. It still kills me, you know? But I didn't have the resources back then.

'Fast-forward to the end of the nineties. I retired from rock journalism. Too old. Too bored. And then I got my first computer and dial-up internet, and I knew what I wanted to do with the rest of my life. Find the kind of kids I'd failed to help back in the eighties.'

'Remember the early days of the web, Adam?' Callum asked.

I said no. For me it had always been there.

'It was awesome,' said Wanda. 'In 2000, I was on a message board and found a reference to something called Terrium. A self-help organisation, according to them. A cult, according to me.'

'Terrium? What does that mean?' I asked.

'Nothing. It's just a word they made up. Just like they made up a whole philosophy. They lured all these young people to join, usually kids from poor backgrounds, kids who were homeless or drug addicts. Terrium actually had a pretty good drug rehabilitation programme. They'd get people clean. Then they trafficked them into sexual slavery.'

'Oh Jesus.'

'Fastest-growing industry in America,' Wanda said. 'The leaders were actually a married couple. Karen and Brad Keeffe. Evil moth-erfuckers. They made a lot of money. A *lot* of money. I'm proud to say that we brought them down. I knew these cub reporters at the local paper, persuaded them to go in undercover, and they got evidence the Feds couldn't ignore. Rescued a lot of souls. But what struck me was how a lot of them didn't believe they needed saving. They'd been brainwashed to believe they were on a path that would lead to their salvation. It wouldn't surprise me if half of them went on to join other cults.'

'They were seekers,' I said, half to myself.

'What's that?'

'Nothing.'

'Anyway, that experience showed me I could actually make a difference. So I've kept on doing it. Even though it's been like painting a target on my back.' Her voice dropped to a whisper. 'There are a lot of people who'd love to see me dead. Because I'm not only investigating these creeps, I'm telling the world all about them. Warning people.'

Callum gestured to the closest computer. 'Wanda has this incredible database. She's got every cult and secret organisation that's ever existed in the United States on there. And her own YouTube channel too.'

'Really?'

'Yes,' Wanda said. 'Though I have to wear a mask when I'm on-screen. And hide my location, of course.' She leaned forward. 'If they find me, they'll kill me.'

'Tell him what you've found out about the cult we're looking for,' Callum said.

'Yes, of course,' Wanda said. 'I have to tell you, the group we're dealing with is one of the most clandestine of all. They're not a legal entity, unlike many cults. They don't have business accounts and they haven't set themselves up as a recognised religion. Nobody knows where their headquarters is, if they even have one. They don't even appear to have a name, which may be a deliberate ploy. If people can't name them, how can anyone prove they exist? But exist they do.'

'What about former members?' I asked.

'There are no former members,' replied Wanda. 'Once you're in, you're in. For life. That's how many cults are exposed. Members leave or escape. They talk. But there are no whistle-blowers here.'

That sent a chill through me. No one ever left or escaped?

'I have to stress,' Wanda went on, 'that what we know is extremely sketchy, based on rumour and a lot of conjecture. We don't even know how these rumours started, and how much of it is misinformation put out there by this nameless organisation.'

'So how do you know they really exist?'

'Because there are enough tales of encounters with the group to make a pattern. Enough people who changed and became more successful, people who have mysteriously transformed their lives and who appear to have a cloak of protection around them. Enough people who seem to have mysterious friends in high places.'

'Like this model Callum told me about?'

'Jade Thomson? Yes.' The name didn't mean anything to me. 'Except she has recently gone AWOL. According to her agency, she's on a sabbatical. But there are many other examples. Names you'd recognise.'

Callum spoke up. 'I say we grab one of them. Make them talk to us.'

'That would be extremely foolish. Like I said, they have a cloak of protection. We wouldn't get near them. And from what I've heard, they have sworn an oath to never talk, no matter what.'

I put my head in my hands. 'This is mad. It's like the frigging *Matrix* or something.'

'It's nothing that far-fetched, Adam,' said Wanda. 'Everyone knows about Freemasons. We've all heard of the old boys' network. We're *all* part of a network of some kind or another. It's just that, here, we are dealing with one that pretends not to exist.'

'They must have a leader,' I said. 'Someone who founded the whole thing. Do you know who it is? Are there any rumours?'

'Elvis,' she said, deadpan, then exploded with laughter. 'Sorry, man. I can't help fucking with you. No, nobody knows who he or she is. There aren't even any vaguely credible rumours. But whoever they are, I bet you one thing: it's the kind of person you'd pass on the street without noticing.'

There was a silence. The dog had fallen quiet and all I could hear was the hum of Wanda's computers.

'So what can we do?' I asked.

'We're going to find them,' she replied. 'Like I said, we all have networks. I have one too. I have dozens of people helping me all over the country. Citizen journalists. Young people who are as determined to expose the truth as I am. Have faith.'

'I'll try.'

'Do you have any protection?' she asked. 'A gun?'

'Back in Cali,' Callum replied. 'They wouldn't let me bring it on the plane.'

Wanda turned to me. 'What about you? You ever used a gun?'

A gun? I shook my head. 'I'm English.'

She laughed and slapped her thighs. 'Follow me.'

She led us back along the hallway and down some steps into a basement. We reached another door, this one made of solid metal. Wanda produced her bunch of keys again and unlocked it. She pushed it open and flicked on a light.

'What the hell?' I said, as Callum made a delighted noise.

We stepped into the room, which was more of a vault. Or an armoury. There were racks of guns lining three walls. Handguns. Semi-automatics. Rifles and shotguns. In contrast to the rest of the cabin, everything was illuminated by bright fluorescent lights.

'I have to be ready,' Wanda said. 'For when they come.'

I stood by as she and Callum talked about weapons. 'What do you want?' Wanda said. 'I like the Sig Sauer P226, or the Glock 17. Or maybe something small like this? A Taurus Judge? Very easily concealed. Or the Glock 36?'

In the end, Callum went for the Glock 17, plus a box of ammunition.

'How about you?' she asked me.

'I'm good, thanks.' I really didn't want to start carrying a gun around. I had no idea how to use one and no time to learn.

'You sure?'

'I'm sure.'

We went back up the stairs and Wanda said she would call her driver – part of her network of helpers, apparently – and ask him to drive us back to Brooklyn.

'Can I use your bathroom while we wait?' Callum said.

'Uh-huh. Third door on the left.'

He walked down the hallway and opened a door.

'No, third—'

A blur of black fur shot out of the room, straight past Callum, and came bounding towards me, a torrent of barks ringing out. I threw myself back against the wall as Wanda shouted, 'Julius, no!'

The dog skidded to a halt in front of me. It was a Rottweiler. It bared its teeth and growled. I remembered Wanda saying it would kill anyone who went near her and pressed myself further against the wall, wishing I could sink into it.

'It's okay,' I said. 'I'm a friend. Friend.'

Julius took a step closer, lips drawn back, a trail of slobber hanging from his jaw. I turned to Wanda, expecting her to help, but she was smiling.

The dog sniffed me, then dropped to the ground and rolled on to his back.

'He wants you to tickle his belly,' she said, as Callum came back towards us, laughing.

'Did I forget to tell you?' Wanda said with a grin, as I crouched and stroked Julius's tummy. 'He's a pussycat really.'

Chapter 22

It was Wednesday morning. Outside, the city was beginning to wake up, the sun rising on what would be another blisteringly hot day. Ruth, who had woken up at five and hadn't been able to get back to sleep, sat in the bath and examined her bruises. They had faded to yellow and grey. Walking around was less painful and she had stopped limping.

She looked better. But inside, she felt as if she'd swallowed darkness.

Eighteen months ago, when she had begun shooting *The Immaculate*, one of the older actors had taken her aside and given her a torrent of unsolicited advice, all delivered in the plummy, arrogant tones of someone who thought he had life all figured out and couldn't wait to share his wisdom.

'Be careful,' he had said. 'When you are handed the fruits of success, other people will hope you choke on them.'

She'd blinked at him.

'I'm sure you're a good person, Ruthie,' he said. For some reason he had taken to calling her Ruthie. 'And you can't imagine what it feels like to be jealous. But I've been there. I've seen it many times. In this game, we're all like rats in a fire, scrambling for the exit. Fighting, biting, clambering over each other.' He loved his metaphors. 'How do you think the rats who are caught in the fire feel about their former friends who have escaped into the fresh air?'

'Do rats have friends?'

He smiled condescendingly. 'Perhaps not. But actors don't have friends either. Not really. Certainly not other actors, or anyone involved in the arts. We are all competing with each other, like it or not. It's a dog-eat-dog world, Ruthie.'

'Or rat-eat-rat.'

'Quite. Do you have a partner? A boyfriend?'

'I do.'

'And is he an actor?'

'A writer.'

He'd clutched his chest dramatically. 'The very worst. Writers are even more rabidly competitive than actors. I think it's something to do with all the time they spend on their own. Drives them quite mad. Anyway, do be careful, Ruthie. You'd better hope your squeeze attains success at the same time and scale as you.'

She had dismissed his lecture. Or, at least, she had tried to. Because as the film became a critical hit, she couldn't help but hear envy in Adam's voice, even as he praised her. When she'd got the part in the play, she'd imagined she saw fear in Adam's eyes. When she'd talked about her co-star in *Dare* and the chemistry between them, she'd detected jealousy. For a long time, she had been trying to dismiss her suspicions, putting it down to the poison that veteran actor had dripped in her ear. But now she knew.

Adam would be happy she had been fired from the play.

He would be delighted she was failing.

She knew this because, yesterday, Eden had come to her and taken hold of her hands and said she had something Ruth needed to hear. Ruth had sat on the bed with Eden beside her, and listened to a conversation Eden had recorded on her phone that night Eden and Adam had gone to a bar on their own.

'Why did you record it?' Ruth asked.

Eden stared at her hands. 'It's something I do. I record conversations, for my diary. I know I shouldn't, that it's a breach of privacy, but I'm not doing it for malicious reasons and they only ever go into my private diary. I never share them.'

Except for now.

The sound quality was not great – there was a lot of background noise – but both their voices were audible.

> *Eden: It must be weird, though. Dating someone who's on the verge of becoming famous. But also you're going to be famous too, right? A big writer.*
>
> *Adam: I'm not going to be a big writer.*
>
> *Eden: Don't say that.*
>
> *Adam: But it's true. And you're right. A year ago we were equals. We were going to take on the world together. I was going to write the plays and the movies and she was going to star in them. I'm scared. Scared that she's going to leave me behind, that she won't want me anymore. I wish it could be the way it was. Just me and her. Two losers together.*

'I know it's not nice to hear,' Eden had said.

'Then why play it to me?'

'Because I think you need to hear it. I think it's important to know who has your back and who doesn't. You need to know who wants you to fail.'

'I need to talk to him,' Ruth said, trying to pick up Eden's phone.

Eden snatched it away. 'No. That's not a good idea.'

'Why?'

Eden lowered her gaze again. 'There's something else I need to tell you. About Adam. He . . . he hit on me.'

Ruth stared at her. 'When?'

'That night. At the bar. Actually, on the way home. He got really tactile and I guess, well, I guess I was flirting too. But then he tried to kiss me. Don't look at me like that. I didn't let him. Not for more than a second, anyway. And I'm sorry, but he was the same on Friday too, when he was sober, at the pool. He practically begged me to go swimming with him, and the whole time his eyes were all over me. He kept touching me too. I told him it was making me uncomfortable and he eventually stopped but . . .'

'But what?'

'I think he's preparing to move on. He's decided your success is going to kill your relationship and he's trying to protect himself. Make a pre-emptive strike.' She attempted a smile. 'It's a male-ego thing.'

Ruth was stunned into silence.

'I know it must be difficult,' Eden said. 'I know people have abandoned you your whole life.'

'What?'

'Oh, I'm sorry. Adam told me that too. About how you grew up in the foster system. About your mom giving you up when you were a toddler. How all the families who promised to take you in let you down.'

Ruth had to force the words past the lump in her throat. This felt like the biggest betrayal of all. 'Adam told you all that?'

'Among other things. But I can promise you this, Ruth. *We* will never let you down.'

'That's . . . good to hear.'

Eden grabbed Ruth's hand. 'No, I mean it. Seriously. I understand what it's like when the people you trust disappoint you. That's why I'm so happy to have met Emilio and Marie and . . .' The volume of her words decreased and she trailed off. 'It's so important to find friends who won't abandon you. True friends, like the family none of us had.'

Eden had sounded so sincere and emotional that it had momentarily flummoxed Ruth, so she hadn't known how to react. And before she could figure it out, Eden had got off the bed. 'I'll leave you alone now. You probably need some time . . .'

Now, Ruth got out of the bath and dried herself using one of the luxury towels that had been left out for her. Once dry, she put on the expensive, heavy robe and went into the bedroom.

She lay down and told herself, for the tenth time since that conversation, that she wouldn't cry. She would be strong.

Because why should she be surprised? Adam was simply the latest in a long line of people who had let her down. Her birth parents, who had given her up. The social workers who had promised they'd find her a forever home.

Again and again, she had allowed herself to trust.

Again and again she had been let down.

She vowed to herself that that would never happen again. From now on, she was on her own. And she would be stronger solo. Losing the play was a temporary setback. All of those people who had abandoned and betrayed her – she was going to show them.

ω

Ruth woke up, unsure how many hours had passed, surprised that she had fallen asleep.

She sat up and stretched, her train of thought from earlier that morning coming back to her. Her vow to change.

It was time to get out of here. To start her comeback. The new, harder, take-no-shit-and-trust-no-one Ruth.

She went over to the wardrobe. Yesterday, Eden had brought the clothes she'd been wearing the night she'd got drunk, along with bags filled with new clothes. 'I went shopping for you,' Eden had said, laying out an array of beautiful tops and trousers, skirts and dresses, shoes and even underwear. 'I knew you'd want something new to wear when you left here and I got a little carried away.'

Ruth looked through the clothes now, trying to decide which outfit would most suit her re-entry into the world.

Jeans and a vest top. A simple outfit, except the jeans were made by Gucci and the top was Armani. How could Eden afford all this stuff? Who were these people?

As if Ruth thinking about her had summoned her, there was a knock at the door and Eden came in.

'How are you?' she asked.

'I'm okay. I'm feeling good, actually.' She mentally puffed herself up. 'I've decided it's time I got out of here. I need to go back to Jack and Mona's, get my stuff, call my agent. I'm probably going to head straight to LA. Hey, maybe you could come with me.' It all came out in a rush.

'Maybe,' Eden replied. 'But before you go, there's someone I'd like you to meet.'

Eden moved aside to reveal a man standing behind her. He had a neatly trimmed beard and wore an expensive-looking suit plus old-fashioned horn-rimmed glasses. When he smiled, even though he was in his forties, his forehead didn't crease. There was something plastic about him. A shine. He was good-looking, though.

He stepped past Eden into the room and, without asking, pulled Ruth into an embrace. His body was hard, muscular. And he smelled amazing, wearing a cologne she'd never encountered before.

He held on to her and she found that she was speechless. A little unsteady on her feet, as if his cologne was intoxicating. Behind him, Eden stood in the doorway, eyes cast to the floor.

'I've been so looking forward to meeting you, Ruth,' he said.

Chapter 23

I turned up at the station house at eight the next morning, Wednesday, bursting to tell Krugman everything that had happened. I'd already emailed him the photos of Eden and I imagined he would be keen to talk to me.

I had spent a restless night on Callum's couch, half convinced an intruder with a gun would come bursting through the door at any minute. I was chilled by what Wanda had said about how no one ever left the nameless cult. Surely that meant that if they tried to recruit someone and that person resisted, or refused, they would be disposed of so they couldn't reveal the cult's existence.

What if they were planning to dispose of Ruth?

I'd left the house shortly after seven thirty, before Callum woke up, leaving a note telling him I'd see him later.

I waited for thirty minutes in the reception area of the station house. The officer behind the desk kept looking at me. After a while, she came over.

'Detective Krugman's been held up. Do you want to come back in thirty minutes? Go get yourself a decent cup of coffee?' She aimed a grimace at the vending-machine coffee I was holding.

'I'm good,' I said. 'I'll wait.'

Forty-five minutes passed and I was about to approach the woman behind the desk when Krugman came out of a side door and strolled over to me. His face was dark with stubble, his shirt was creased and there were sweat patches under his arms. I guessed he'd been up all night.

I stood up, ready to follow him to, I assumed, an interview room, ready to tell him about what Wanda had told us, even though I could picture his disbelief. But he said, 'You can go.'

'Sorry?'

'We caught the bastard who did it. He's confessed already.'

'He? I don't—'

Krugman cut me off. 'It was a burglary. He breaks in, thinking the house is empty, Jack disturbs him and the guy panics. Two hours later the dumb asshole gets arrested trying to rob somewhere else.' He shook his head with disgust. 'You know, I've been doing this job a long time but this is the first time I've had to deal with the death of one of my friends. Such a goddamn waste.'

'Wait, you're saying it had nothing to do with Eden?'

'That's exactly what I'm saying.'

I couldn't believe it. A disappearance and a murder within a few days of each other, at the same address?

'Are you absolutely sure?'

'The guy confessed to me himself.'

'But . . .' I didn't know what to say.

'I've just been on the phone to Mona, telling her the news,' he said. 'I'm not sure if it sunk in.'

'Where is she?' I asked.

'She's staying at a hotel until the house is, y'know, cleaned up.'

A cop walked past and nodded grimly at Krugman.

'Anyway, I've got to go. I stink.'

'Wait,' I said as he turned away. 'What about Ruth? She's still missing. What are you going to do about that?'

'It's not my department. I told you, if you want to report her missing you need to fill out a form. I can get one of my colleagues to help you.'

'She's not just missing,' I said hurriedly. 'She's been taken. And I know you were sceptical about the whole thing, because I heard you and Jack and Mona talking in the garden.'

He raised both eyebrows. 'Oh yeah?'

'And maybe I don't blame you. But I have proof now that I wasn't making Eden up. I sent you the photos.'

'Some girl in a bar? Sorry, but that ain't exactly proof.'

'What? So you still don't believe me?'

He went to walk away but I followed him, speaking as fast as I could. 'Eden's a recruiter for a cult.'

He gawped at me. 'A what?'

'A cult. No one knows their name but they recruit people and . . . make them more successful. I've been talking to someone whose daughter was taken by them, and she never came back, because they kill people who won't join. And they also kill anyone who threatens to expose them. Someone tried to run me down outside McCarren Park.'

To his credit, Krugman didn't act like I was a raving lunatic. He stood there calmly, letting me talk.

'The guy who's helping me, his name's Callum Maguire, his daughter's called Sinead Maguire, and I've also talked to a journalist, an expert in cults, and she confirmed this group exists.'

'What journalist?'

'Her name's Wanda Brooks.'

'Uh-huh. And you know what this cult is called?'

'No. Nobody does.'

'Or where they're based?'

'No.'

He folded his arms. Was he smirking? 'Do you know anything about them at all, other than that they make people successful?'

'Not . . . really.'

He laughed. 'Adam, you're a nice guy. That's obvious. But you're wasting my fucking time.'

'But—'

'Shut up. Maybe the police in England can waste their time investigating fairy stories, but this is New York City. I just caught a killer, a man who shot one of my friends. I need to process the asshole and then I've got to go home and take a—'

'It's not a fairy story.'

'Don't interrupt me. I believe you when you say Eden exists. I don't think you'd lie to me about that. But a recruiter for a cult? Sweet Jesus. All that happened was that your girlfriend got blind drunk, overslept, got fired, and now she's holed up somewhere with her new friend. As for someone trying to run you down . . . You drive on the wrong side of the road over in England, don't you? You were probably looking the wrong way when you stepped out.'

'But there have been two crimes at one address in one week,' I said. 'Surely that can't be a coincidence.'

'No. There's been one crime. The murder of my friend. And the asshole who did it is already behind bars.'

He turned and walked away.

'You're wrong,' I called.

He ignored me, slamming the door behind him.

Chapter 24

McCarren Park was already busy, with bathers lining up for the pool, children in the playground and joggers running around the perimeter. I sat on a bench and watched the entrance to the building I'd seen Mets go into. It had only been yesterday, but so much had happened in the last twenty-four hours that it felt like much more. At the same time, today was the fifth since I'd last seen Ruth, and the world – my world, at least – seemed like a very different place.

Sitting on the bench, I thought over what I knew so far. There wasn't much.

I needed to know if Mets had seen Eden since that day at the pool. If she had said anything that would help me find her.

After thirty minutes he hadn't appeared, and – fed up of waiting – I crossed the street and pressed a random buzzer on the building. No one answered so I pressed another. This time, a sleepy-sounding man answered.

'UPS. I got a parcel for apartment twenty-three,' I said, attempting an American accent.

To my surprise, he buzzed me in.

As I went in, an elderly lady came down the stairs, struggling with a large bag. I rushed up to help her.

'Thank you,' she said as I put the bag down by the exit. She studied me with sharp eyes. 'I don't think I've seen you before. Just moved in?'

I smiled. Rather than inventing an elaborate lie about him being a friend, I decided to take a gamble. 'I'm actually looking for someone. I think he might be in danger, and I need to warn him.'

'In danger?'

'Yes. It's pretty urgent, actually. If I don't find him . . .' I left the rest to her imagination. 'The thing is, I don't know his name. But he's young, around twenty, and built, and he usually wears a blue baseball cap with the Mets logo.'

'Huh, there are a lot of those around.'

'I know. But I think you'd recognise this guy. He's good-looking, blue eyes, spends a lot of time at the pool across the street.'

'Sorry, can't help you.'

She left the building. *Now what?* I could randomly knock on doors, but that would probably lead to someone calling the police. I might be better off going back to the park and hanging around.

Or, I thought as I spied the fire-alarm button on the wall of the lobby, I could do something radical.

I smashed the glass and hit the button. Immediately a bell rang through the air, deafening me. People began to appear from the floors above, some dressed, some in robes, a mixture of ages. Most of them came down slowly, looking at each other and sniffing the air, wondering if it was a false alarm.

There was a crowd of around ten people in the lobby now, none of them making much of a move to leave the building, probably due to the absence of smoke. Somebody went off to find the super while others wondered where the hell he was.

'I saw someone hit the alarm,' I said above the din. People gathered around me. 'He was in his early twenties, wearing a blue Mets cap. A big guy.'

An old man turned to his neighbour. 'That sounds like it could be Jesse. Carol's grandson.'

'Carol?' said the neighbour. 'She's in thirty. Hey, where's Carol? Anyone seen Carol?'

I felt a little guilty for falsely accusing Mets of setting off the alarm – would he get into trouble for it? – but reminded myself what a douchebag he had been at the pool. Then someone came down the stairs with a lady of around seventy. At the same time, the super appeared and turned off the alarm, to sighs of relief all round.

'What's this about my grandson?' Carol barked.

'This guy said he saw him hit the fire alarm,' said the old man who had first identified Mets.

Carol narrowed her eyes at me. 'How do you know it was my Jesse?'

'Do you have a photo of him?' I asked.

She did. She produced a top-of-the-range iPhone and showed me a picture of her and her grandson together, smiling at the camera. It was him.

'He's a good boy,' she said. 'He gave me this phone. Let me call him now. Get this straightened out.'

The other residents of the building drifted back to their apartments while Carol searched for Jesse in her contacts. I looked over her shoulder. There was his address.

I left her waiting for him to answer and made a quick exit.

ຕ

Jesse lived in a tall, drab building on a quiet street in Greenpoint, about fifteen minutes away.

I pressed the intercom and, after a few seconds, a voice said, 'Yeah?'

'Jesse? My name's Adam. I need to talk to you.'

'You're the Brit. From the pool.' My accent was that strong? 'It was you, at my nana's place?' He strained to project aggression, but there was fear in his voice he failed to mask, I was sure of it. 'Where's your bitch at? She with you?'

His choice of words made me flinch. 'I'm not really her boyfriend. We just made that up to stop you hassling her.'

'Yeah, well, we stopped.'

'I need to ask you some questions,' I said quickly, before he could click off. 'The woman I was with at the pool, Eden, I think she's done something to hurt my actual girlfriend. Will you please let me in? Or come out and talk to me? I promise I don't mean you any harm. Eden's not my friend. Not anymore.'

I could almost hear his brain ticking over, trying to figure out if this was a trick.

'Come up,' he said, and he pressed the buzzer to let me in.

He was waiting in the doorway of his apartment. As I came towards him, he peered over my shoulder to check there was no one with me, then beckoned me in and shut and bolted the door behind me. He wasn't wearing his baseball cap today. But as he turned towards me I saw he was holding a small handgun.

I sucked in a breath. Two days ago, someone had tried to run me down. Yesterday, I had seen my first dead body. Nobody had ever pointed a gun at me before, and my first thought was that I should have accepted Wanda's offer. But, perhaps because of everything that had happened to me during the past few days, I wasn't as scared as I would've thought I'd be. Perhaps it was because I'd heard fear in his voice. Had seen it when he ran away from me. And maybe that was foolish of me. Scared people are more prone to making rash decisions.

'Put your arms in the air,' he said.

I obliged, and he came over and patted me down with his free hand. Apparently satisfied, he told me to sit down. Again, I did as he asked.

He noticed me glance around the neat apartment and said, 'My mom's at work.' There were fresh flowers in vases, shelves full of romance novels, and framed photos of a grinning, gap-toothed little boy on the wall. Jesse went over to the window and peered down at the street. He was as jittery as anyone I'd ever seen.

'Why don't you put the gun down, Jesse?' I said in the calmest voice I could muster.

'Uh-uh.'

'We can't talk while you've got that thing pointed at me.'

Still, he hesitated.

'Come on, Jesse. I don't have a weapon. You're bigger than me. What am I going to do? Please, put the gun down.'

With agonising slowness, he obliged. He sat in an armchair and rested the pistol beside him, so he could easily grab it if he needed to.

'Why did you run away when you saw me?' I asked.

He narrowed his eyes at me. 'I didn't run away.'

'Okay.' Macho pride. One of the greatest obstacles to honest communication. 'But you do seem scared of something. It's Eden, isn't it? What happened? Did she come back? With reinforcements?'

He didn't respond. I wasn't sure if it was because he didn't trust me or because he didn't want to admit he was afraid.

'All right, listen,' I said. 'I'll go first.'

So I told him everything I knew, going back to Eden turning up at the house. The only thing I omitted was Jack's death, as I thought that would make him even more scared. He listened with ever-widening eyes. He really was like a little boy. When I'd finished, I waited, convinced he would accuse me of bullshitting him.

Instead, he said, 'A cult? Like the Manson family or some shit? I watched this show on Netflix. That dude was sick.'

I wasn't sure if he was using 'sick' in the positive sense.

'But it totally makes sense,' he said. 'Shit.'

'What do you mean?'

'The guys who did it. They were freaky, you know what I mean? Like they were . . . *too* normal. Does that make sense?'

I could only stare at him.

'Soon as we saw them coming towards us, I said to Brandon—'

'Wait, who's Brandon?'

He stared at me like I was stupid. 'The guy who was with me at the pool.'

Muscles.

'I know you think he was a jerk, but he was my best friend since I was, like, six.'

Why was he talking about him in the past tense?

'Tell me what happened,' I said.

His gaze fixed on a point across the room. 'So, it was, like, seven thirty, something like that? Not quite dark. We'd been hanging at the pool and we were going to go home, get dinner, before hooking up with these girls we met.'

'You were heading out of the park?'

'What I said. Only, these two guys started coming towards us. These preppy-looking dudes, young but wearing suits. I thought they were Jehovah's Witnesses or some shit.'

'Hang on, what day was this?'

'Sunday.' That was the day Jack and Mona got back.

Jesse went on. 'Anyways, they come up to us, like they're gonna try to talk to us about Paradise or whatever, and Brandon and me look at each other, like, this is gonna be fun, and then one of them, the taller one, holds up a picture – a picture of that bitch you were with.'

I wished he'd stop saying that. 'Eden.'

'Yeah. Her. And the guy says, "You recognise this girl?" I right away think, *Shit, has she sent her older brothers or something to look for us?* And then my boy Brandon says something like, "Yeah, we fucked that bitch right here in the park and she fucking loved it", laughing, you know? And the guy – the guy who wasn't holding the picture – he shoots his arm out like this, and Brandon . . . Brandon just, like, crumples to the ground. It took me a second to realise this dude had stabbed him. Right here. In the heart.'

He looked up to Heaven. 'The cops said he woulda died instantly. He wouldn't have felt no pain. And then the guy turned to me, the knife dripping with Brandon's blood, and he said, and this is the freakiest part, "Protect one, protect all". And I think if he didn't, you know, stop to say that, if he'd gone for me right away, I'd be dead too. But the couple of seconds he took to stop to say that, it gave me a chance. I kicked him in the balls.'

I couldn't help but laugh.

'Not the kind of move I'd usually pull. But he'd just killed my boy. I panicked. I kicked him right where it hurt and ran like fuck before the two of them could react.'

'And did they chase you?'

'Yeah. For a while. But I'm fast and I know that park like it's my own backyard. I ran all the way back here and did something I never thought I'd do. Called the cops. Turned out someone had already found Brandon's body and called them. Then I spent the next twenty-four hours answering their motherfucking questions.'

'What do you mean, they looked like Jehovah's Witnesses?'

'Like I said, they were wearing suits. Nice suits, I think. Like, real expensive-looking. They were white and old – in their thirties, at least. Later, when I was talking to the police, I realised they didn't look like Jehovahs. They looked like they worked on Wall Street.

Like those rich assholes who've all moved to Williamsburg recently, you know, in those fancy apartments by the river.'

'And they said what? "Protect one, protect all"?'

'Yeah.' He leaned forward. 'That sounds like some kind of cult shit, doesn't it?'

It certainly chimed with what I knew so far.

'Have you seen them since?'

'Nope.' He held up the gun. 'But if those motherfuckers turn up again I'm gonna send them to meet their ancestors.'

He didn't sound very convincing.

'Do you know which detective is in charge of the investigation into Brandon's murder?'

'Yeah. Big guy. Treated me pretty nice, for a cop. What was his name? Oh yeah. Krugman, that was it. Detective Krugman.'

Chapter 25

I stood outside Jesse's apartment building, paralysed by indecision. I tried to call Callum but it went straight to voicemail. I left a message, asking him to call me, then began to walk back towards Williamsburg, staying on busy streets where I figured I would be safe. When I had to cross the road, I hurried, making sure there were other people crossing at the same time. I didn't go anywhere near the park.

Halfway there, two guys wearing suits and Ray-Bans came towards me along the street. My pulse accelerated and I stepped back into a shop doorway. I pulled the backpack off my shoulder and stuck my hand inside, scrambling to find the knife I'd taken from Callum's apartment. I found it and got ready to defend myself. I swallowed, breathing hard, braced to fight.

The two men walked past, laughing at a shared joke.

I blew out a long, relieved breath and stood in the doorway for a minute, waiting for the adrenaline to leave my system. I felt like I was turning into a new version of myself. One who lived in a world where violence was expected. Where anyone who passed by could be part of this secret, threatening alternate reality. The old me wanted to run back to Callum's and hide. But the new me was determined to keep going, to keep looking.

And as I carried on towards the house where Ruth and I had stayed – drawn back there once again – I realised how foolish I had been to feel envious or paranoid about Ruth's impending success and my relative failure. Fame, money, recognition – none of it was important. All that mattered was that I found Ruth and made sure she was safe.

I stood outside the Cunninghams' house and thought, *It can't be a coincidence.* Jack's death had to be related to Eden and the cult and the men who had stabbed Brandon.

But how? How could it . . .

An idea came to me.

I had previously assumed that Eden and the cult had decided to recruit Ruth because they had seen her work and found out, through social media, that she was in New York. But that explanation had never quite sat right with me. It involved too much luck.

A better explanation could be this: Jack or Mona had told someone that an up-and-coming actress was coming to house-sit for them. That someone had looked Ruth up and decided, for whatever reason, that she would make a perfect recruit. So they sent in Eden to check her out.

It was the most likely explanation I could think of right now.

I needed to speak to Mona.

I know you probably don't want to see anyone at the moment, I texted. *But could we meet?*

I only had to wait a minute for a response.

ω

I hung around the reception of the Lotte New York Palace, under-dressed and out of place in my shorts and T-shirt. The concierge gave me a look that Sally Klay would have been proud of. In fact, this place reminded me of the cruise ship, full of wealthy older people, and I wondered why Mona had chosen to stay here. Perhaps temporarily living somewhere so grand and otherworldly helped provide a kind of cushion; a way of barricading herself from the ugly side of urban life. Or maybe it was simply that she was rich, and this was the kind of place where she felt comfortable. She had, after all, chosen to go on a cruise.

I didn't have to wait long. Mona appeared, walking over from the lifts like someone who was in physical pain but trying not to show it, like the Little Mermaid when she chooses to stay in human form. She held herself erect, her eyes hidden behind sunglasses, dressed all in black.

I stood as she approached and gave her a hug.

'How are you?' I asked.

'I don't know how to answer that.' Her voice was flat; the irony and fizz that made her so much fun to be around was missing. 'Numb, I guess. Everything seems dulled. Like, this is maybe a weird comparison, but when you switch from watching a TV show in HD to whatever the other one is called.'

'Standard definition.'

'Yes, that's it.'

'I'm so sorry,' I said again. 'But . . . at least they've caught the guy who did it.' She merely nodded so I went on. 'Krugman told me it was a burglar.'

'A kid, he told me. Some nineteen-year-old kid trying to get money to buy drugs.' I wished I could see her eyes. Then I might not have felt like I was talking to a robot.

'Do you know his name?' I asked. 'The guy who did it?'

'Dennis told me. But what does it matter?'

'I don't know. I was just wondering . . .'

I had been wondering if the burglar was a member of the cult, or someone they had hired to kill Jack, perhaps because they feared he would remember who he had spoken to about Ruth coming to stay – the person who had led Eden and the cult to our door.

Or maybe I was wrong about that. Maybe Mona or Jack had spoken to Eden directly.

'Can I show you Eden's picture? Just so you can tell me if you recognise her.'

I got my phone out before she could protest. I already had the photo of Eden open. I held it up so Mona could see it.

For a moment, I thought she was going to refuse to look at it. But then she took her sunglasses off – her eyes were bloodshot and puffy – and leaned forward. She studied the picture for several seconds.

'I don't know her.'

'Are you sure?'

'I'm certain. She looks like a thousand other pretty West Coast girls. I've never seen her before in my life.'

'But she knew you,' I said. 'She knew details about your lives. What about Jack? Might he have spoken to her?'

'How am I supposed to know that?' she snapped at me, then looked contrite. 'I'm sorry, Adam, but my husband has just died. I really don't want to think about any of this.'

'I know, I know. I'm the one who should be apologising. But Ruth is still missing and I have to know where she is.'

Mona didn't recognise Eden, and I would never be able to ask Jack. So I went back to my other theory: that one of them had inadvertently spoken to another member of the cult.

'Did you or Jack tell people about me and Ruth coming to stay?'

'Why are you asking that?'

I could imagine her reaction if I told her I thought Jack might have been murdered by a cult. She wasn't a dumb kid like Jesse. 'Just humour me, please. Did you tell anyone?'

She thought about it. 'I don't know. I told people we had house-sitters coming. A couple of Brits we met on a cruise. But I didn't tell anyone your names because who would be interested? It's not like we had Emma Watson and Daniel Radcliffe coming to stay.'

'What about Jack?' I asked. 'Might he have told people?'

'I don't know, Adam.' She appeared to be about to start crying and I felt terrible, but I had to find out if Mona knew anything that might help me.

I pressed on. 'They knew we were going to be there. If you didn't tell anyone, it must have been Jack.'

'And then what?' Now she sounded irritated. 'You think Eden came looking for Ruth? That she, what, watched that weird movie Ruth was in and became obsessed with her?'

'Yes,' I replied, again not wanting to mention the cult.

'And what? This crazed fan, Eden, has made off with Ruth? Got her locked up in a basement somewhere? Like in that movie, *Misery*?'

'That wasn't a basement.'

She stared at me.

'But Ruth *is* in danger. I'm certain of it. Earlier today I spoke to this guy who told me his friend was murdered because of something he said to Eden.'

'What are you talking about?'

I was going to have to tell her about the cult. I started to attempt to explain but Mona cut me off.

'This is insane. You're insane. This Eden person didn't come looking for Ruth. Ruth's gone off for God knows what selfish reason. And you're bothering me when I'm trying to grieve for my husband.'

Her voice cracked and she put her sunglasses back on. But she couldn't disguise that she was crying.

I opened my mouth to say more but forced myself to stop. I was convinced I was right. Eden had known either Jack or Mona. She had known their names and other details about their lives. And Jack must have been the source of that knowledge, either because he had talked to Eden or she had found out through a third party. Furthermore, I was sure Jack's death had to be connected to Ruth's disappearance.

I still didn't have the answers, particularly to the question of how the burglar was connected to all this, but Mona didn't know anything. There was no point pressing her.

'I'm sorry. I didn't want to upset you. I really didn't.'

She raised her voice. 'Well, you didn't succeed.'

A member of hotel staff was coming over. Mona stood up and I stood too.

'Don't come to Jack's funeral, Adam. You're not welcome.'

The member of staff arrived by Mona's side. 'Is everything all right, madam?'

She pulled herself upright.

'This gentleman is leaving,' she said, pointing a shaking finger at me. A tear trickled down her face, catching the light from the chandelier. She made no attempt to wipe it away.

Chapter 26

According to a map I found online, Columbia University's Department of Psychology was on the east side of the main Manhattan campus. I went through the gates and up some steps, and wished I could appreciate being here, a place where so many brilliant minds had been nurtured. Sally Klay had studied English literature here. As I approached the library it wasn't hard to picture the young Sally, sitting beneath a tree, book in one hand, cigarette in the other, dreaming of the day when the city beyond this campus would be hers.

I had made Mona cry. I wasn't proud of that. But I was still convinced I was right. And where was the most likely place Jack would have talked about Ruth and me coming to stay, as well as the place where he might have met Eden? His workplace. Here.

I found Schermerhorn Hall and paused outside, looking up at the inscription above the door. *For the advancement of natural science. Speak to the Earth and it shall teach thee.*

I went inside. There was hardly anyone around on campus, and this building had that empty, out-of-season feel. But on the way here I had checked and discovered that the summer programme for undergraduate research was still running. A young woman passed me in the hallway, not glancing up from her phone, her footsteps echoing behind her. I followed the signs to the psychology department and saw it: a door bearing Jack's name. They hadn't yet taken the sign down.

The door next to Jack's bore the name 'Prof. Niven Kyle'. It was slightly ajar. I knocked and a gruff voice called, 'Come in.'

I stepped into the office. It was exactly as I had expected. A computer. Piles of books everywhere. Degree certificates on the wall. A photo of a smiling woman with her arms around a teenage girl on the desk. Professor Kyle was in his fifties with grey hair and an open-necked shirt, sleeves rolled up to the elbows. He peered at me curiously. 'Yes?'

'Were you a colleague of Jack Cunningham's?'

He gave me a suspicious look. 'I was.'

'I'm Adam. I was house-sitting for Jack and Mona until they got home from New Mexico.'

'Oh yes? He mentioned something about that.'

So Jack had told people they had house-sitters coming in. But I knew I had to be careful. For all I knew, Professor Kyle could be one of them. He might be the person who had sent Eden in to recruit Ruth. He didn't seem alarmed by my presence, though.

'Were you still staying there when it happened?'

'No.'

'Thank goodness for that.' He sighed. 'Terrible business. I'm relatively new to this department so I didn't know Jack particularly well, but everyone around here is very upset.'

'It's been awful for all of us,' I said. I had begun to concoct a story. And I decided I needed to take a risk. Professor Kyle really didn't seem like he could be a member of a death cult. 'This might sound selfish but I can't help but think it could have been me or my girlfriend if we'd still been there, or if the burglar had come along a week earlier.'

He perked up. A man with some knowledge to share. 'It's a perfectly natural reaction. It's called counterfactual reflection. Szpunar and Schacter did a very interesting study into it.' He caught himself. 'But I'm sure you don't want to hear about that.'

I smiled politely. 'I've also been wondering if this burglar knew Jack and Mona were going away and didn't think they'd be back yet.'

'Haven't they already caught the guy who did it? I imagine that's one of the questions they asked him.'

'I know. But the police won't talk to me and I can't help but wonder. Did Jack tell everyone he and Mona were going away?'

'He was pretty open about it. But wait, are you suggesting that someone tipped off this burglar? Someone here?'

'Oh no, I wasn't—'

'Because he told everyone he had people coming to house-sit. So even if he mentioned it to all his students, which is possible because he was very excited about his trip, everyone knew the house was going to be occupied.' A memory must have popped into his head. 'Your girlfriend – she's the actress?' He furrowed his brow. 'Or are we supposed to say "actor" for both men and women these days? We get so many memos about this sort of thing but I find it hard to keep up.'

'"Actress" is fine,' I said. But my theory was looking more correct by the minute. Jack *had* told everyone about Ruth.

'Did you hear people talking about her? Ruth, I mean?'

'Um, not really. I think a few people in the film school had seen her movie. Jack seemed very excited that a soon-to-be movie star was going to be staying in his house. He said he met you on a cruise, is that right? And your girlfriend is about to appear on Broadway?'

Now this was getting out of control. I had hoped Jack would have only told a few people, but it seemed it had been common knowledge. Hundreds – thousands? – of people, any one of whom might be a member of the cult, or who might have talked to Eden about it. How on earth was I going to find the source? Unless, of course, the person he'd told had been Eden herself.

'This might sound strange,' I said, 'but can I show you a photo?'

'A photo?'

It would be easier to tell him part of the truth. 'I don't know if this is connected to the burglary, but while Ruth and I were at the house, this woman turned up and said she was friends with them. Mona says she has no idea who this woman is. I think she might be someone who found out Ruth was going to be staying there . . .'

'A stalker?' His eyes widened.

'Her name's Eden,' I said, taking my phone out and showing him the picture.

'Sorry, I don't recognise her.'

I sighed.

'Did she give you the impression she was a student here?'

'No, but maybe she visited the campus? Took part in research or something?'

Kyle stroked his chin. 'Wait here.'

He left the office and came back a few minutes later with a woman who was around a decade older than him. She had crescent-shaped lines in her cheeks that made me think she smiled a lot.

'This is Brenda. Our administrator. She knows everything that goes on around here.'

I showed Brenda the photo of Eden. She peered closely at it, taking the phone from my hand and putting her glasses on. She tilted her head to one side then the other. My hopes surged.

'Sorry. Don't recognise her,' she said. 'She looks a little like this Swedish girl who's studying here, but it's not her.'

I sighed. It was a dead end.

Brenda led me towards the exit and held the door open for me. To my surprise, she followed me outside and shut the door behind her, glancing around to make sure no one was listening.

'The reason I paused so long when you showed me that photo was because . . .'

She appeared to have second thoughts.

'Please tell me,' I said.

'It's just . . . I hate to speak ill of the dead. Especially the so-recently deceased. But when you told me you were looking for a young woman who might have known Jack, I braced myself. Because Professor Cunningham had something of a reputation. He liked young blonde women. Women who are easily impressed. That girl in your photo. She was exactly his type.'

Chapter 27

I took the subway back to Williamsburg, trying to recall Jack's reaction when I'd told him about Eden.

Who the hell is Eden? he had said.

Had he been lying? Had he been cheating on Mona with her? Was she the latest in a long line of conquests, most of them presumably undergrads or research subjects? That would explain two things. Firstly, how Eden found us. He probably would have boasted to her, like he apparently had to everyone else, about this hot actress who was coming to stay. Secondly, it explained why he had denied knowing who she was. He couldn't risk Mona finding out.

I thought about going back to the hotel to see Mona, to tell her what I'd found out, or to Dennis Krugman. But I needed proof, didn't I? Mona wouldn't talk to me anyway, and I really didn't think she'd appreciate being told now, while her grief was so raw, that her dead husband might have been sleeping with another woman. I'd already made her cry once today. And Krugman? Well, I was prepared to share what Brenda had told me with the police if it led to me finding Ruth. But so far, it had proven impossible to get him to take anything I said seriously. I doubted he would make the trip to Columbia to talk to Brenda, especially as Jack was his friend. And there was absolutely no proof that Jack had ever met Eden, let alone had a fling with her. Krugman would laugh me out of the station house.

But if I could prove he had known Eden, the police would have to take me seriously. They would be able to get a warrant, get Eden's address.

Or maybe I could still get it myself, from Jack's home office, which was in the basement apartment. He had said he didn't use it much because of all the storage boxes that cluttered the place up, but maybe he kept notes there. It would be the perfect place to keep the contact details of his conquests, because Mona hardly ever went down there. There might even be photos.

I double-checked that I still had keys to the house. I didn't have the key to the basement, but I knew where it was kept. It was hanging on a hook in the kitchen.

I got off the train in Williamsburg and headed straight to the house. It was still light, and as I turned off Bedford there were lots of people coming and going. Commuters arriving home from work. Dog-walkers and shoppers. I approached the house, trying to look casual, and nobody gave me a second glance. The crime scene tape had been removed, which was a blessing as it meant the house wasn't drawing attention from passers-by. And if any of the neighbours saw me, they would probably recognise me, and think I was running an errand for Mona.

I let myself in and shut the door behind me.

The house was eerily silent and stiflingly hot, too, without the air conditioning on. I didn't look at the stairs, not wanting to be reminded of the sight of Jack's body. Would there still be blood-stains on the floor or would someone have come to clean them up?

I went straight through to the kitchen and there it was: the key to the basement.

I could almost hear my own heartbeat as I opened the back door and went down the steps. I turned the key in the lock and stepped inside.

I was hit instantly by a musty, stale smell – the result, I guessed, of the apartment being left empty over the summer, though I assumed Jack had been down here since they had returned home, and Mona had popped down here shortly before finding her husband's body.

It was a small apartment, the same size as the ground floor of the house, with one main room, a galley kitchen and a small bathroom. I stood at the centre of the room and looked around. There were cardboard boxes stacked up against the wall, some old framed pictures leaning against them.

The desk was positioned over by the front window, with a view out on to a little patio area. I cursed. There was no computer on the desk. Jack had a MacBook and I guessed he brought it down here when he wanted to work. The laptop was probably still up in the house. It would be password-protected.

But maybe, in one of the desk drawers, I would find something. A scrap of paper bearing his password. Maybe something miraculous: a letter from Eden or a notebook containing her name and address. Secret love letters or notes. Proof that Jack knew her. Anything I could take to Krugman.

I started to pull open the desk drawers, inspecting anything that looked interesting. There were old bills, subway tickets, drafts of papers Jack had been working on. I searched inside books, checked that there was nothing taped to the underside of the drawers. I looked all around for hidey-holes.

But there was nothing useful. Nothing to suggest that Jack had had a secret life at all.

I put everything back in the drawers. I needed to go upstairs to look for Jack's laptop, try to guess the password. I also knew it wasn't too hard to unlock a MacBook. There were guides online.

I took a last look around – and heard a creak above my head. I froze.

The creaking sound came again, followed by a series of duller sounds, heading towards the back of the house. Footsteps.

Somebody was up there.

The footsteps continued, passing over my head. Then they stopped. From what I could tell, they were by the back door.

A car went past outside, and someone yelled something on the street, drowning out the sounds in the building.

I strained to hear. Was it Mona? How exactly was I going to explain what I was doing down here? I couldn't tell her I'd left something behind and had come back to get it, because we had been told not to come into the apartment. I was going to have to tell her everything I'd found out.

Except the footsteps sounded too heavy to be Mona. Too heavy to be Eden too. She had always walked around like a cat, silent and stealthy.

It's the person who killed Jack, said a voice in my head. *The real killer. Or the men who killed Brandon.*

I ran to the front door, but it was locked from the inside and I only had the key to the back door.

The footsteps came down the steps towards the apartment.

I looked around for somewhere to hide. Could I squeeze in behind the boxes? I tried to pull some of them away from the wall but they were heavy and I didn't have time. I remembered the knife in my backpack and threw the bag to the floor, kneeling and fumbling to open it.

The back door opened.

Detective Dennis Krugman stepped through.

'Oh, thank God,' I said.

He shook his head slowly. He seemed disappointed in me, like I was a teenager who had been caught smoking again.

'You should have gone home, Adam,' he said, raising his gun.

180

Chapter 28

The man, who Ruth assumed to be the person in charge here, released her from his embrace and stepped back. The scent of his cologne lingered in the air between them and he beamed, showing a set of perfect teeth, almost certainly veneers. There was something familiar about him, but maybe it was just that he reminded her of Jack. He had that same look: the youthful, handsome academic. Or a tech billionaire.

He spoke to Eden. 'You can go,' he said, closing the door behind her. Then he turned his attention back to Ruth. 'I hope I'm not disturbing you.'

'No, not really . . .' The resolve she'd felt just ten minutes ago was fading. She struggled to bring the feeling back. 'I was just saying to Eden, it's time for me to go. I'm really grateful to everyone here for looking after me but I have so much to sort out.'

'I understand. Where are you planning to go? Back home?'

'No. California.'

'Ah, Hollywood. Of course.' He went over to the window. 'Man, I can never get enough of this view. It's quite something, isn't it?'

'Er, yes. But I'd quite like to be back at street level again.'

He laughed like this was one of the best jokes he'd ever heard. 'Down there among the dirt and the noise and all the traffic fumes? I love this city but I've got to tell you, I like it best up here. I can see everyone. Everything. *The cloud-capp'd towers, the gorgeous palaces, the solemn temples, the great globe itself.*'

'*The Tempest*, Act Four, Scene One.'

He showed his shiny teeth again. They appeared to glow. 'My favourite of all the Bard's great works. I wish I could have seen your Miranda.'

Ruth was taken aback. 'You know about that?'

'Of course. I've been following your career with enormous interest.' She noticed that his accent was from outside New York. A trace of the South, though she wasn't an expert. 'I was so looking forward to seeing you on Broadway. Sally Klay.' He tutted. 'I tried to speak to her myself, to beg her to reconsider, but I couldn't get past her assistant. She'll come to regret it, though.'

'I doubt it,' said Ruth, with a stab of pain. Again, she fought to bring back the resolve she'd had before this man arrived. To put all that behind her. To move on to bigger things.

'Oh, she will.' Beneath the friendly tone, she detected a shard of ice. 'If that's what you want. It's all about the future, isn't it? And it's clear to me that you could be a star. One of the biggest.'

That must have been what he meant when he said Sally would regret it.

'You say you've been following my career. Have you seen *The Immaculate*?'

'Of course! I devoured it. You're incredible in it.'

'Not many people have seen it.'

'Huh. Ridiculous. Everyone should witness your talents, Ruth.'

She couldn't help but experience the tingle of pleasure that came whenever she received fulsome praise. But she said, 'You're embarrassing me.'

'Talented and modest.' He smiled. 'I could hardly believe it when Eden told me you were here. I've been away on business and was terrified you'd be gone when I got back. I mean, what an opportunity . . . It feels like fate. Destiny!'

She had no idea what he was talking about.

Before she could ask he said, 'It must have been disorienting to wake up in a strange place and to find out that the people you trusted have let you down.'

As he spoke, his eyes locked on to hers. It was disconcerting. She never felt comfortable with excessive eye contact, another thing she blamed on her childhood; the way the social workers would stare at the ground when making promises. But with this man – and she realised he hadn't yet told her his name – she found it hard to look away. It wasn't a sexual attraction. He was too old for her, for a start. His brilliantly white teeth were off-putting. And she had never been attracted to overly confident men. There was something about him, though. His intensity. The interest he was showing in her. The way he looked at her, it was almost as if he was trying to hypnotise her, and she had to break eye contact.

'Has anyone explained anything to you?' he asked. 'About who we are?'

'No, not really. Eden just said you were all friends. But she's been maddeningly vague.' She found she was beginning to mimic the way he spoke.

He stroked his chin. He was definitely familiar. Was it really only that he reminded her of Jack?

'That's what we are. Friends. And we're hoping you'll be our friend too, Ruth.'

He sounded so sincere that she couldn't help but laugh.

'That sounds . . . nice. It's always good to have more friends. But like I said, I've got so much to do. I have to talk to my agent, and collect my stuff from Jack and Mona's, and . . .'

'That's fine,' he said. 'If you're sure you feel well enough.'

'I do.'

'But could we talk for a little while longer? I'm such a fan. It would be a shame to let you go so soon. Are you hungry? I could get someone to bring us something?'

Actually, she was hungry. But she really had to get going.

Except when she opened her mouth to say no she heard 'Okay' emerge.

'Wonderful,' he said. He went to the door and spoke to someone. Had they been lurking outside the door?

'I have some business to attend to,' he said. 'But will you wait here so I can tell you all about us?'

'I'm not sure . . . I really need to get going.'

'Please, Ruth. I won't be long, I promise. And it will be worth it.'

She wanted to leave. But she also really wanted to hear what he had to say.

'Okay,' she said. 'I'll wait. But after that, I'm going. I need to get on with my life.'

'Of course,' he said, with another smile. 'I can't wait to tell you what we can do for you.'

Chapter 29

Krugman came towards me, the gun still pointed in my direction. Two guns pointed at me in one day – but this time, I really believed the person brandishing it would use it. Again, I wished I'd taken the weapon Wanda had offered, though what use would it be if I didn't know how to use it?

'Put your hands behind your back,' he said.

'Wait . . .'

'*Put your fucking hands behind your back.*'

I did as he asked, and he marched over and snapped a pair of cuffs over my wrists. He reached into my pocket and took out my phone, switching it off.

'You're coming with me.' He began to pull me towards the door.

'Wait. What have I done?'

'Breaking and entering.'

'But I've got a key.'

He ignored me and continued to drag me towards the door. I tried to resist but he prodded the gun into my flank and said, 'You want me to add resisting arrest?'

I walked. He marched me up the stairs and through the house to the front door, then out on to the front stoop.

There was no one around. While I had been downstairs, another of New York's summer storms had started, and rain lashed down, emptying the street. A rumble of thunder accompanied me as Krugman made me walk down the steps. His unmarked car, a mud-brown Toyota, waited by the kerb. He opened the back door and pushed me inside. He chucked my backpack, which he'd worn on his way out of the house, on to the front passenger seat.

He got in and started driving. I tugged at the cuffs, but it was no use.

'Where are we going?' I asked after a little while. 'The station house is in the other direction.'

'Shut up.'

We drove through the city, Krugman swearing at the clogged-up traffic. From the occasional glimpse of street signs, we appeared to be driving south-west. Krugman had a bottle of Diet Coke, which he sipped from occasionally. My mouth was dry, heart pounding. I tried to think of a way out of this. But every time I tried to speak, to ask him where we were going, he snapped at me to shut up.

After a long, slow crawl through Brooklyn, we crossed a long bridge. A sign told me we were now on Staten Island. This was bad. Really fucking bad. Because there could only be one explanation for what was happening. He was part of it. He was one of them.

Krugman kept driving. When I tried to speak again he put the radio on – a station playing classic rock – and turned it up to drown me out. Creedence Clearwater Revival sang about a bad moon rising. At one point, Krugman's phone rang but he pressed a button to send it to voicemail.

The traffic was sparser here, and before too long we crossed another bridge, heading out of New York City. It was dark now and still raining, the windscreen wipers sweeping back and forth. I watched them, trying to focus on the hypnotic motion in an attempt to stay calm. On the radio, Elton John was singing and I thought of home, wishing more than anything that I was back there now, sitting in the beer garden of a pub with a pint. I tried to visualise myself there but it didn't work. I wasn't home. I was handcuffed in the back of a car, speeding down US Route 9, and I felt it in the pit of my stomach. I was going to die.

It took some effort to get the words out. 'You're going to kill me.'

He didn't reply. Instead, he turned off the highway on to a quieter road. A couple of cars went by in the opposite direction, and then we were driving through woodland, along a curving road. There was no one else around. We passed a 'Deer Crossing' sign and Krugman slowed down. He appeared to know exactly where he was going, turning on to a track that led deeper into the woods, his headlights illuminating the trees that crowded around us like voyeurs at a public hanging, trying to get a last look at the con-demned man.

Once we were a fair distance into the woods, so no one would spot the car from the road, he slowed to a halt.

'Wait here,' he said, and opened the door.

Krugman got out of the car and went to the boot, disappearing from sight for a moment. When he came back into view he was car-rying a torch – a flashlight, as he would call it – which he'd already switched on. He held a shovel too.

A shovel. To bury my body.

He opened the back door.

'Get out,' he said.

'No way.'

He stuck the gun in my face.

'You know something, Adam? You should have gone home. Or just waited.'

'For Ruth to come back? Changed?'

He narrowed his eyes. 'That what Callum Maguire told you? That asshole is next. I'm gonna enjoy dispatching that mother-fucker, after what Eden's told me.'

What did that mean?

'What about Wanda Brooks? Don't deny it – you told me you'd talked to her. You know where we can find her?'

'No. We met her in public.'

He put the gun against my forehead. 'You sure?'

'I swear. She wouldn't let us go to her place. She's totally paranoid.'

'Hmm.' He seemed to believe me.

'Who else you been talking to, huh?' he asked. 'I know you went to see Mona. And I also know you went to Columbia. What did they tell you?'

'Nothing. They wouldn't tell me anything.' I didn't want Krugman going there and murdering Professor Kyle and Brenda. 'I showed them Eden's photo but they said they couldn't say anything because of confidentiality. Listen, I—'

'Shut up! Talking, talking, always talking. Jesus Christ. You're worse than Jack. Now get the fuck out of that car.'

He grabbed my arm and yanked me out, twisting me round so he was behind my back. He held on to my upper arm.

Behind me was the road that cut through the woods; ahead I could see nothing but trees. I felt like they were watching me, a solemn crowd, silent and still. Witnesses to an execution.

A path, muddy from the recent rainfall, led into the woods.

'Let's go,' said Krugman, letting go of my arm and pushing me ahead of him.

I forced myself to walk, one foot in front of the other, my way illuminated by the beam from Krugman's torch. As we entered the woods, the trees closing around us, welcoming us in, I heard a car drive by on the road. Krugman paused and glanced over his shoulder. I thought about calling out but there was no point – they would never have heard me – and by the time I'd dismissed the idea, the road was quiet again. The car gone. I considered running, wondering if I could lose myself in the trees. That might be my only chance. But I would be in the pitch-darkness, hands cuffed, pursued by a man with a flashlight and a gun. I knew I wouldn't get anywhere.

'Why did you kill Jack?' I asked. 'Were you worried he was going to own up to knowing Eden?'

I thought he might deny it, but he said, 'You know, Jack begged for his life. Like a little kid begging not to be beaten by his dad. Is that what you're going to do?'

'Would it do any good?'

He laughed.

'Ruth will want to know what's happened to me,' I said. 'She'll know who was responsible. She'll go to the police. The real police.'

He shoved me forward so I stumbled and almost fell. 'I am the real police.'

We carried on walking, deeper into the woods. It was almost dry here, the canopy of trees providing protection from the rain, but the air still burned with the scent of the summer storm. Something landed on my face – a bug, some kind of fly – and I tried to shake it away, realising my cheeks were wet. I had been crying without knowing it. Crying for Ruth. Perhaps, though I was loath to admit it, for myself.

A little way into the woods, close to a ditch that ran alongside the path, Krugman said, 'Stop.'

A breath shuddered through me and I clenched my teeth. *Keep your dignity. Don't beg.*

'Face the ditch,' he said. 'And stay still.'

I had my back to him. I closed my eyes, grateful he hadn't instructed me to get on my knees.

189

'You religious?' he said. 'Got anything you want to say?'

I was finding it hard to hold back the tears now. I was thinking about my family, back in England. My mum and dad. How they would never know what had happened to me. How this would hang over them for the rest of their lives, a terrible mystery.

'Please,' I said. 'Don't hide my body. My mum . . .' I was too choked to say any more.

'Sorry,' he said. 'Can't do—'

And somewhere nearby, a twig snapped.

'What the fuck?' said Krugman.

I turned. He turned too, sweeping the beam of the torch through the trees.

'Who's there?' he yelled.

I saw it at the same time as him. A figure, stepping out from the foliage, like a piece of night breaking off, shadow emerging from shadow.

Krugman aimed, but the shadow moved fast, evading the beam of light. Another twig snapped and the figure jolted to a halt.

Two guns went off at the same time.

Chapter 30

Krugman lay still, just a few feet away from me. I hurried over to see if he was still breathing – he was – at the same time that Callum stepped out from between the trees. It was so dark with the torch lying on the ground that I could barely see his face. But then he said, 'Sorry to have cut it so fine.'

'Are you shot too?' I asked.

'Me? I'm fine.' He strode over and joined me, crouching beside Krugman. 'Still alive. Good.'

Blood bloomed across the front of Krugman's shirt where the bullet had struck him in the belly. Instinctively, he had laid his fingers across the wound.

'We need to get him to a hospital,' I said. 'Where's your phone?' Krugman had taken mine after he pretended to arrest me.

Callum addressed Krugman directly. 'You want us to do that? Call an ambulance?'

Krugman stared up him. His eyes were glassy. He coughed and droplets of blood appeared on his lips.

'I could patch you up, call 911. *Officer down.* They'd probably send a helicopter, am I right? You'd be fine. But first, tell us where they are.'

'Where's Ruth?' I added.

Krugman didn't speak.

'Come on, man,' said Callum. 'Time's ticking away. Do you really want to die? Is this really how it ends for you? Shot in the woods by an old guy like me? You got kids? A wife? You ever want those things? Just tell us, where can we find them?'

Krugman coughed again. More drops of blood.

I tugged Callum's arm. 'He hasn't got long. Give me your phone.'

'Not till he tells us where they are.'

'Callum . . .'

'You hear that, Detective Krugman? This young man wants to save you, even though you were going to kill him and bury him out here where no one would ever find him. All he wants is to find his girlfriend, talk to her. So where is she?'

Krugman went to speak. A croak came out, along with more blood. I put my ear close to his mouth.

'Protect one, protect all,' he said.

Callum swore, then pulled Krugman's hand away from the bullet hole. It was a horrific sight, a red mess, and I could hardly bear to watch. Callum ripped apart Krugman's shirt, buttons popping and falling on to the damp earth on which he lay.

I thought he was going to try to staunch the flow of blood. Instead, he picked up a small but sharp twig from the ground and jabbed it into the open wound.

Krugman screamed.

'What the hell are you doing?' I yelled.

Callum withdrew the twig. Its point glistened black in the shine of the torch. 'I'm a desperate man, Krugman. Now tell us where to find them.'

But the pain had made Krugman pass out.

'Mother of Jesus,' Callum said, slapping Krugman on the cheek.

'Are you a sadist?'

'No, Adam,' he hissed through clenched teeth. 'But we need to find out where they are. If he dies without telling us, we'll be back at square one. Worse than that. After this, we're going to have every one of those bastards looking for us.'

Krugman made a groaning sound.

'Let me try to reason with him,' I said.

Callum's eyes twinkled and he whispered, 'The good cop, bad cop routine, eh? Dealing with the evil cop. I like it.'

'Just let me talk to him,' I hissed.

He put his palms up. 'Okay, okay. Be my guest.' He reached into Krugman's pocket and plucked out his phone, positioned it against the detective's thumb to unlock it, then stood and took a few steps into the darkness.

'Krugman,' I said, speaking gently. '*Dennis*. He's not going to let me call an ambulance unless you tell us what we need to know. He's going to hurt you again.'

Krugman moved his lips and, once again, I leaned closer to hear.

'She's his now,' he said.

'His? Who is he?'

He lifted a hand and pointed a trembling finger at me.

'Dead men walking,' he whispered, echoing what Eden had said to Jesse and Brandon at the pool.

Then he made one more sound, 'Hmm', before falling silent.

'Oh shit,' I said.

Callum came over, reached down and closed Krugman's eyelids. 'I'd say a few words but I don't think anything's going to help him get into the Kingdom of Heaven.'

I stood up. There was blood on my jeans and on my hands. I staggered a few feet away and threw up behind a bush.

'Nice one,' said Callum. 'We're going to have to clean that up. DNA. Though if we tell the cult where he is they'll probably do it for us. They're not going to want Krugman's straight colleagues trying to figure out what happened here.'

'What do you mean, call them?'

He held up Krugman's phone. 'Last call received, sent to voicemail. About an hour ago. There's no name attached and the number is withheld.'

'That was when we were driving here. Have you listened to the message? Was it them?'

'Let's have a listen. How do you get it on loudspeaker?' While he fiddled with the phone he said, 'Jesus, my hand is shaking.' I could see now that he was sweating heavily. Greasy droplets clung to his beard.

'Have you . . . have you ever done that before?'

'Killed someone? Christ, no.' He looked into my eyes. 'I wasn't lying. I'm desperate. And these people, son. They're scum. They're evil.' His voice cracked. 'I just want my little girl back. If they've hurt her, if they've . . . I'll kill every last one of them.'

Finally, Callum managed to get the message to play. The voice was clear in the dark, silent woods. It was a man.

'*I'm guessing you're busy. Call me when you're done.*' The message ended.

'That's it?' I said. 'At least we've got the phone.'

'We can go through his messages. And maybe we can figure out where he's been with it. Is that possible?'

'I'm not sure. But you should disconnect it from 4G, so it can't be wiped remotely.'

'I'm terrible with these things. How do you do that?'

'Give it here.'

He handed it to me. As I took it, the phone beeped. Krugman had received a text.

'Oh my God,' I said, reading the message.

194

Where are you? What's happening? I need to see you. I miss you xxx

'What is it? Who's it from?' Callum asked, trying to take the phone back. I held it out of his reach, and another text arrived from the same person.

Is he dead yet?

I stared at the screen in shock.

The messages were from Mona.

I held the phone up so Callum could see. 'Holy shit,' he said. 'She's one of them?'

The phone beeped again.

For fuck's sake, if you won't reply I'm calling Gabriel.

'Gabriel?' I said.

Callum took the phone from me and, after thinking for a moment, began tapping at the screen. Tapping out a reply.

Sorry, had my hands full. All is good. It's done. But it got a bit messy. Tell Gabriel I need to lie low for a couple of days xxx

Mona's response came almost instantaneously.

Poor baby. But at least Adam's out of the picture now. Hope you're not hurt but if you are I'll kiss it better when I see you xxx

Callum hesitated for a second and wrote, *Can't wait xxx*

He handed it back to me. 'There, I've bought us a couple of days. But I think you should still switch the 4G off.'

I did it on autopilot, unable to focus on what I was doing.

Mona. It wouldn't sink in.

Callum looked over at Krugman's body, then nodded at the shovel that lay on the ground beside him. 'You're younger than me and I just saved your life. You can dig the hole. There's probably a pair of gloves in his back pocket. You might want to use them.'

'What are you going to do?' I asked, discovering that there was indeed a pair of gloves there. Krugman had come prepared.

Callum had his own phone in his hand now. 'I'm going to try to figure out who Gabriel is. And where we can find him.'

Chapter 31

'I haven't told you my name,' he said when he returned. It was hard to keep track of time here but Ruth thought it had been more than a few hours. She had been on the verge of giving up waiting. 'I'm Gabriel.'

He took a seat at the table and gestured for her to join him.

'Gabriel. Like the angel? Sorry, you probably get that all the time.'

'Every now and then. But we're all angels here – of a kind, anyway. Guardian angels. Except, well, we watch over each other.'

There was a knock and Emilio came in, carrying a tray of sand-wiches and coffee. Once again, Ruth was struck by how insanely beautiful he was, as if he'd been designed on a computer. It was difficult not to stare at him. The way he moved, the fluidity of the simplest gesture, like setting the tray down on the table, captivated her too. If anyone around here was an angel, it was Emilio.

Ruth's eyes lingered on Emilio as he left. Gabriel noticed.

'You like him, don't you?'

'I . . .'

'And he told me he likes you too.' He poured artificial sweet-ener into his coffee. 'You're single now. You can do whatever you like.'

Her face must have shown surprise because Gabriel said, 'Don't tell me you're planning to go back to that loser? Adam, is it?'

'I need to talk to him.'

'Even though he put the moves on Eden?'

'I don't know. I haven't heard his side of the story.'

Gabriel opened his mouth, then clearly thought better of what he was going to say; she could see the swerve. 'I feel sympathy for him, actually. It's not easy to cope when the people we love outshine us. Jealousy, envy, fear of abandonment. It's all so human. And there's this terrible tension, of having to pretend you want someone to succeed while secretly wishing they fail.'

She cast her mind back to the actor and his talk of rats scrambling to escape a fire, and she realised she had no idea what she was going to do about Adam. She loved him – but was she still in love with him? They didn't have sex very often these days, which she blamed on being tired and distracted. Her heart had long since ceased skipping a beat when he walked into a room. But she cared about him. And, like Gabriel, she understood why he felt insecure; why he might want to hold her back. She had felt the same when other kids in the system had found families to adopt them. Earlier in her career, she had felt envious of her peers when they landed hot roles while she was rejected. As Gabriel said, it was human. Natural. And she didn't really blame Adam for making a pass at Eden either. She found, in fact, that she cared far less than she thought she would. And that was a bad sign, wasn't it? When your boyfriend tries to cheat on you and you don't really care?

She realised Gabriel was talking. She tuned in to hear him say, 'That's one of the reasons I created this.'

'This? I still don't know what this is.'

He got up and went over to the window, pressing a button on the control pad to open the blind. Ruth was surprised to see that night had fallen. 'Come,' he said.

She wouldn't usually respond to a one-word command, but she found herself getting up and joining him, gazing out at the city once again: all the lights of New York, the shining capital of her dreams.

'Watch this,' Gabriel said.

Gabriel pressed another button on the pad and, to her surprise, the window popped open, swinging slowly inwards. At the same time, on the exterior of the building, a balcony slid horizontally out from the wall.

'Cool, huh?' he said, sounding like a little kid who'd discovered a nifty secret feature on one of his toys. 'I had this put in when this place was built. I like to be able to get out into the air, to properly see and smell and hear the city.'

'Hang on. When this place was built? You own this building? The whole thing?'

'Oh yes.' He stepped out on to the balcony and held out a hand. 'Join me?'

They must have been at least fifty storeys up. Just the sight of the open air before her put a knot in her stomach.

'Come on,' he said, and, determined not to seem afraid, she took his hand and stepped out. There was just a metal bar to protect them. For a second she had an intrusive thought: the urge to throw herself off. She pictured herself falling, spinning to her death like a rag doll dropped from a roof.

'You okay?' Gabriel asked. He wore a huge grin and was still holding on to her hand.

'I'm fine.'

He squeezed her hand but then finally let go. For a few seconds they stood in silence. A million lights beneath a sliver of moon. It was still warm, even up here. Ruth thought she could feel the heat rising from the ground: the heat of industry and commerce and art and life. It felt good to feel the air on her face again after a few days locked inside. She closed her eyes and took a deep breath, and when she opened them again, Gabriel was gazing at her intensely.

'Tell me something, Ruth,' he said. 'This is a city of eight million people. London has a similar population. So many human beings. So many potential friends and allies. How many true friends – by which I mean people you can absolutely trust – do you have in each of those cities? A dozen in each?'

'I wish.'

'How many, then?'

'I don't need anyone else,' she said. 'I only need myself.'

'Oh, Ruth. Do you really believe that? It's so sad. Human beings need each other, don't you agree? But I understand how hard it is to make real friends. Modern life makes it so difficult. The competitiveness. Our peripatetic lifestyles. The fact that whenever you try to have a conversation with someone they're distracted by their phone, wondering if they could be involved in some better interaction online. People these days think that a "like" on an Instagram post constitutes friendship.'

'Huh. That's true.'

He warmed to his theme. 'Like people who look over your shoulder when they're talking to you at a party, hoping to talk to someone more useful. Doesn't that drive you crazy? And don't get me started on relationships.'

She watched a plane drift slowly across the sky and thought about Adam. Did he care that she wasn't around? What was he doing right now?

'We're stronger together,' Gabriel said, gazing down at the city below. 'But only with people we can absolutely trust and rely on. Do you have that with Adam?'

Tears pricked her eyes. 'I did once.'

She swiped at her cheeks, embarrassed.

'I know what it's like to be let down, Ruth,' Gabriel said. He was leaning against the barrier now, staring at a blinking light on the horizon. A faint breeze stirred his hair.

'All the people here, including me, were let down by our families. Some of us had fathers who beat us or abused us. Some of us had mothers who were more interested in the bottle or the needle than giving us what we needed. Many of us looked for help among our teachers, or a priest, or some other authority figure. All of us were disappointed. We know what it's like for someone to tell us they love us one minute and betray us the next. We're all like you, Ruth.'

He turned to meet her eye. That intense gaze again. The one she found hard to break.

'That's why I decided to change things. I went out and looked for people like me, people with nobody to rely on, and we made a pact. That whatever happened, we would look out for each other. Over that time, it's grown. Friends find friends. Each new friend joins us in our pact, and the friendship group grows. It's a beautiful thing. If someone in Arizona needs assistance, a friend in Oregon can help them. If a friend in California is in trouble, someone they've never met – but who has taken the same oath as them – can get them out of it. We help each other find work. We help with legal problems. We share knowledge and advice. I would call it a family except, well, families always let you down. This is better than a family.'

'And you're the leader?'

'We have no leader. I'm just the person who started it, and I still give others guidance.'

'Like a priest?'

'Hardly. More like, I don't know, an elder. This isn't a religion. We worship no god. We have no crazy belief system. We have no name, no leader. We don't meet up in the desert and burn effigies.

This isn't a cult.' He said the word like it tasted bad. 'We have certain rules that we all follow – we vow to help and protect each other – but that's it.'

He looked at her with such intensity it was uncomfortable, almost sexual. No, not *almost* sexual. It reminded her of the way Adam used to look at her when they were in bed together, when he was inside her. She found herself growing hot.

'And sometimes,' Gabriel said, 'we find someone who could use a hand.'

She waited, short of breath.

'Like you, Ruth.'

She realised she had been waiting for this.

'I've seen your work,' he said. 'I can see how talented you are. How special. You've got something, a quality, that is rare. I don't just mean that you're a great actress, though you are, or that the camera loves you, though it does. It's something more than that. Something that only comes along once in a generation. I imagine it's how people felt when they first saw Meryl Streep, or Audrey Hepburn.'

She was used to people sucking up to her, lavishing her with fake praise and flattery. But this didn't sound like that. Gabriel seemed so sincere, almost painfully so. The emotion in his voice, the way his eyes shone – it was almost too much to take. She finally managed to look away. She had to.

'That's . . .' She didn't know what to say. To be compared to Meryl and Audrey! These were words she had dreamed of hearing. But, at the same time, she found it hard to take it seriously, despite Gabriel's earnest expression. She was torn between a base desire to believe him and allow herself to bask in the warmth of his praise, and another instinctive reaction: to reject what he was saying, to listen to the voice of self-doubt, the one that told her she would fail, the one that said she was nothing special. An unwanted brat. A girl who no one could really love.

'I need to go inside,' she said, suddenly dizzy.

'Of course.'

They stepped back into the room and Gabriel pushed the buttons again. The balcony slid back with hardly a sound into the floor beneath their feet, and the windows swung slowly out and snicked closed. It was utterly insane, and beautiful.

They sat back at the table. She sipped at her coffee but it had gone cold.

'I'll get you another,' Gabriel said.

'No. Please. It's fine.'

'If you're sure. Perhaps I should let you rest now. Think about what I said. I'm sure you'll have lots of questions.'

She nodded.

'But I'd like you to stay here a little longer, so we can have a chance to talk again once what I've told you has sunk in. And you should talk to Eden and Marie and the others.'

She found herself nodding.

He rose to leave.

'Wait,' she said. 'I'm sorry, but I'm confused. You say you can help me. That you want me to join you. But I don't understand what that means. What it entails. And I really don't understand why I have to stay here.'

'You don't. Of course you don't. But I wasn't sure if you had anywhere else to go.'

'I thought I'd go back to Mona and Jack's.'

'Ah.' He frowned. 'Eden didn't tell you?'

'Tell me what?'

'About what happened to Jack . . . I'd rather let Eden tell you.'

He opened the door – and Emilio almost fell into the room.

'Is everything okay?' Gabriel asked.

Emilio gathered himself. 'Sorry, I was about to knock. I need to talk to you.'

'Of course.' Gabriel turned back to Ruth. 'Apologies. I'll send Eden in. But we can continue this tomorrow.'

To her surprise, he dashed back into the room and took hold of her hands, gripping them enthusiastically. 'You're so smart, Ruth. So special. Never let anyone tell you different. You deserve the world.'

He let go of her hands and moved towards the door, where Emilio was waiting, but then turned to her a last time.

'And I can give it to you.'

PART THREE

Chapter 32

I got off the PATH at Newark Penn Station and took an Uber to the address Wanda had given us. It wasn't her cabin this time, but a diner outside Newark.

'Can't risk you leading them anywhere near my place,' she had said on the phone. Callum had told me Wanda constantly switched burner phones. 'Not now you've raised the stakes so much.'

The Uber dropped me outside the diner and I went in, spotting Wanda in a corner booth. She seemed nervous but excited. She had her baseball cap on and, instead of the yellow-tinged glasses, a pair of aviator shades.

'Are you one hundred per cent certain no one followed you?' she said, checking over my shoulder.

'As sure as I can be. I'm pretty sure they think I'm dead anyway.' I told her about the message Callum had exchanged with Mona the night before, pretending to be Krugman. I also summarised what had happened in the woods. My muscles still ached from digging the grave in which we had buried the detective. By the time we'd finished I had been covered in dirt and sweat and the dead man's blood. Luckily, the ground had been damp and quite soft, but I wondered if that would make it more likely that an animal would dig the body up. Last night I'd had a nightmare in which I'd been in the woods with Ruth, delighted to be with her again, telling her I thought I was never going to find her, and then Krugman had appeared, covered with mud, lurching towards us through the darkness.

I didn't expect to sleep well for a long time. I had buried a man's body. A cop's body. And before that, I had been convinced I was going to die.

I knew there was darkness in my future. That one day I was going to have to deal with all this shit. But right now, I would simply have to hold it all together. For Ruth. By focusing on trying to find her, I could just about keep my mind off what had happened. What I'd done.

Last night, I had watched Wanda's YouTube channel, checking out around a dozen of her videos. In the clips, she wore the kind of mask one might wear to a masquerade, a creepy-looking black-and-silver affair that covered everything except her mouth and chin. She talked about conspiracy theories and how to recognise if someone you knew was on the verge of joining a cult. She detailed a recent epic investigation that had led to the conviction of the leader of a so-called multi-level marketing company, for false imprisonment and fraud. I was astounded by the number of views and comments she got. Her followers loved her. There was an irony to it that didn't need pointing out.

'Where's Callum now?' Wanda asked, beckoning over the waitress.

'He's in the lobby of the Palace Hotel, waiting for Mona to appear so he can follow her. She's never met him or seen him, and he assures me he's good at tailing people. He followed Eden all over New York without her noticing, so . . .'

'He's very determined,' said Wanda.

'He's desperate,' I said, echoing what Callum had told Krugman.

Wanda nodded. 'I've met a lot of men like him. A lot of men who can't quite believe that the little girl who used to call them Daddy and wanted to be around them all the time could allow herself to be taken away. To be brainwashed. It's a hard thing for a parent to deal with.'

The waitress appeared and took our orders. I wasn't particularly hungry so just ordered coffee and toast.

'Do you think all cults are inherently bad?' I asked when we were alone again. 'I mean, we all hear about the ones who brainwash their followers and take their money and exploit them. The ones who convince their members to kill themselves or murder people. But do you think there are any that actually do good?'

The question sounded odd even to me, but Wanda took it in her stride.

'It's an interesting question. There are certain groups that are often described as cults, but they call themselves new religious movements. NRMs. Like the Brahma Kumaris and Sahaja Yoga. And people who join them describe themselves as "active seekers". I've read articles that talk about how these groups can be empowering, especially for women. Certainly compared to the cults most people hear about, anyway.'

After the waitress had brought our coffees over, Wanda went on. 'The problem with all of them, including the better ones, is the way the guru, or leader, controls everything. A lot of these people see themselves as godlike. You have to be pretty damn egotistical to set up a religious movement – and then they go crazy on the power. I've seen it again and again. They all say, or pretend, they're trying to help other people. But nearly always, they just want to help themselves. And you know what most of these cult leaders want to help themselves to, apart from the contents of the bank accounts of their followers?'

I had a pretty good idea, but simply said, 'What?'

'Their followers' bodies. Or should I say, their *female* followers' bodies. It's amazing how many cult leaders decree that they need multiple wives. That it's a great honour to sleep with the leader. Look at David Koresh and all the babies he fathered. All the under-age girls he raped.'

I put down the coffee cup that was halfway to my lips. My hand was shaking and I suddenly felt too nauseous to drink.

'And what about Gabriel? Do you think he's like that?'

'Do I?' She produced a small notepad from her pocket. 'I'll tell you this: David Koresh and all those cult leaders who create or take command of a group so they can get laid, they're not the exception. They're the rule.'

'And have you got anything that might help us figure out who he is?'

'Maybe. We know the identities of three members of the cult. Mona Cunningham, still alive. Detective Dennis Krugman, deceased. Eden, alive as far as we know, surname unknown. Then there's the mysterious Gabriel.' She opened the notepad and consulted something she'd written. 'We're discounting Jack, right? We don't think he was one of them?'

'I don't know. He's been with Mona since they were at college. I don't know if she could have been a member of a cult without him knowing about it.'

Wanda shrugged. 'People keep secrets from their spouses all the time. I'm guessing he didn't know his wife was banging the friendly neighbourhood cop.'

'I thought Jack was cheating on her too. With Eden.' But now I knew Mona was the link to Eden. 'Looks like I was wrong about that. But I don't understand why Krugman killed Jack. After I got the photo of Eden I texted both Mona and Jack and told them I was outside their place. I think the moment Mona got that text she must have called Krugman and told him to deal with Jack before I showed him the photo. But I don't know why.'

Wanda thought about it. 'She must have known Jack would recognise Eden. Mona and Eden are both members of the cult. Perhaps Jack had seen them together somewhere. I bet they met up to discuss the plan to recruit Ruth, and Jack saw them together. His wife was cheating on him. The poor bastard might have been suspicious, following her around.' She shrugged. 'It's a logical explanation, anyway. The other thing I'm wondering about is how Krugman got into the house while you were outside.'

'Through the back door?'

'I guess. But he got there damn quickly.' A sigh. 'Maybe we'll never know.'

Wanda glanced towards the door, as she had done a dozen times already. Fleetwood Mac was playing in the background and I thought Wanda might make a comment about it, but she was too distracted.

'Here's another thing that's bugging me,' she said. 'Why go to all this trouble to recruit Ruth? What's so special about her? And yeah, I know she's your girlfriend, that you think she's special. But what sets her apart from a thousand other young women?'

'She *is* special, that's what. Everyone says it. She's got that magic ingredient – whatever it is that makes some people stand out. Like your friend Stevie Nicks. It's talent, charisma, beauty. Strength. Ruth has it too.'

Wanda nodded like she got it. 'Let's get back to the question of who Gabriel is. There's nothing in any of my databases related to people called Gabriel. So then I thought maybe he's named himself after the angel. Maybe the whole cult is based around angels. It's a thing. And yeah, there are plenty of groups that worship angels and Gabriel above all of them. I spent quite some time going down that route but I think it's a blind alley. From what we know of this cult, they're not Christian. They don't seem to be religious at all. So that made me think we're looking for someone whose name actually is Gabriel.'

'Is it a popular name in the US?'

She laughed. 'Guess what? I looked that shit up. It's very popular now. It peaked in 2008, when just under thirteen thousand babies in the US were given that name. But it wasn't that popular in the seventies or eighties, which is probably when our Gabriel was born.'

'Thank God he's not called John.'

'Ha, yeah. Or Adam. Anyway, the next step was to see if I could find anyone called Gabriel who has or had a known relationship with either Mona Cunningham or Dennis Krugman. Old classmates. Former co-workers. College buddies. I checked Mona first. Total dead end. She went to a private all-girls school and she's never had a job apart from a series of businesses she's run herself, and there was no way I could get hold of a list of her clients. There was no one in her college class called Gabriel either. I even checked her Facebook page and all her social media to see if they were dumb enough to be connected online, but no luck.'

Yet again, she looked over at the door. A Britney Spears song was playing now. I guessed Wanda didn't know her.

'I didn't get anywhere with Mona so next I looked at Krugman. There was actually a Gabriel in his class at elementary school, but he died six years ago. Again, he's not connected to anyone called Gabriel on social media. And, unfortunately, I can't access police HR files to see if he's ever worked with someone with that name.'

'Krugman must have come into contact with a lot of different people,' I said. 'Other cops. Lawyers. Criminals.'

'Oh yeah. I thought I wasn't going to get anywhere with Krugman. Was about to give up. And then my research assistant found this.' She had taken off her shades and her eyes shone. This was what she had been waiting to tell me. Building up to it. It was like watching one of her YouTube videos: the creation of drama before the reveal.

I snatched the sheet of paper from her hand. It was a printout of a newspaper story from 2014.

NEW YORK CITY PUBLIC SERVICE AWARD WINNERS ANNOUNCED

Beneath the headline was a photo of a group of men and women, proudly holding large medals. Second from the left was Krugman.

'He won the Law and Order Award for some big case he was involved with,' Wanda said. 'But see this guy next to him?'

She pointed to a white man in his late thirties beside Krugman. Like Krugman he was wearing a tux and was smiling for the camera. But the smile, though it revealed an immaculate set of teeth, didn't reach this guy's eyes.

'That's Gabriel Dearman,' Wanda said. 'He received a special Service to the Community Award for building a youth centre in Brooklyn.'

'Who is he?' I asked, unable to take my eyes off him. There was something vaguely familiar about him. Maybe it was just that he looked like a thousand other guys.

'He's one of New York's lesser-known billionaires. There are stories about him in the business press, but he's publicity-shy. Seems he made his money through a lot of smart investments in tech companies.' She named a half-dozen corporations who had come to prominence in the last decade. 'Owns one of the tallest buildings in Brooklyn – his own Trump Tower, if you like. Except he's not ostentatious like Trump. It's not called Dearman Heights or anything like that.'

She showed me the location on her phone.

'Do you think he could be our guy?'

'I think there's a very good chance of it. Because guess what else I found out?'

'Don't keep me in suspense,' I said.

'He went to college with Jack. Columbia, Psychology, Class of '99.'

'Holy shit.'

'Holy indeed. And Mona was at Columbia at the same time, wasn't she?'

'Yes. She was dating Jack.'

'So the likelihood is that she knew Gabriel too.'

I stared at the photo of Gabriel Dearman. This was him. It *had* to be.

'I'm going to do some more digging, see what else I can find out about him,' Wanda said. 'Like I said, he's very private. Tell Callum not to go banging on Dearman's front door, okay?'

'Why?'

Wanda leaned forward. 'Firstly, you don't go around yelling accusations at guys like this. He can afford the best lawyers and the best security. Spook him and he could be in the Cayman Islands within hours. We have to be extra-careful, okay? That's vital. If Dearman gets any inkling we're on to him, he'll be gone. And who knows what wreckage he'll leave behind? We already know how the cult feels about witnesses. What they do to them. You don't want them to cut your girlfriend's throat and leave her in the woods, do you?'

How was I supposed to respond to that?

'Keep your head down,' Wanda said. 'Wait for me to call.'

Chapter 33

On the way back to Brooklyn, I called Callum.

'Any news?' I asked him.

He made a disgusted noise. 'Big shopping day.'

'Shopping?'

'What I said. Mona came breezing through the hotel lobby, then headed straight for Fifth Avenue. Went in and out of around five fancy stores, then into Saks. Gotta tell you, it's not easy tailing a woman around a department store with all the assistants coming up and asking you if they can help. Had to pretend I was buying something for my wife. Anyway, she finally walked out of there with a black dress in a bag.'

'For the funeral.'

'I guess. And then she headed straight back to the Palace. The only interesting thing was that she kept checking her phone – like, compulsively. Even more than your average sixteen-year-old. She's antsy, worried about Krugman.'

I swallowed. Surely the cult had known Krugman's plan for me? Those woods could be a regular burial ground for them. How long before they sent someone to search for him? The police had to be looking for him too, surely.

'Anyway,' Callum said. 'I'm going to hang here for a little longer. I figure the more anxious she gets, the more likely she is to go looking for her lover. What did you find out from Wanda?'

I filled him in.

'Gabriel Dearman, huh?'

'Does that mean anything to you?' I asked.

'Nope.' He went quiet for a second, thinking. 'Maybe I should use Krugman's phone to text Mona, ask her to meet back at HQ or something. See where she goes.'

'Don't. It's too risky. What if they're tracking Krugman's phone? The moment you turn it on you'll give your location away.'

'Yeah. You're right. Plus I left the phone at the apartment anyway.'

I ended the call, hoping he wouldn't do anything stupid.

ϖ

Back at Callum's apartment, I had a shower, trying again to scrub myself clean after the events of the previous night, convinced there were still specks of Krugman's blood on my skin. When I got out, Wanda called me, using one of her burners.

'One of my researchers managed to track down an old neighbour of Gabriel's, from when they were kids,' she said. 'This guy lives in Alaska now so he should be safe. Probably. This guy's tough, anyway. The type who knows how to react if a bear comes running at you. His mom used to be friends with Gabriel's mom too, so he's received a trickle of news about him over the years. The type moms love dishing out: *So-and-so's son is doing great. Why can't you be more like him?* A chuckle.

'What did you find out?' I asked.

'So, Gabriel was born in '76 in Raleigh, North Carolina. Grew up in the 'burbs. Parents divorced when he was nine, and dad did a vanishing act. According to my source – or more accurately, his mom – Dearman Senior was something of an asshole. A con man. Always coming up with some get-rich-quick scheme or other, none of which worked. But he identified pretty early on that computers were going to be the future, so he bought Gabriel a Commodore 64 when he was six or seven, and a book teaching him how to code.'

'It's a familiar story,' I said.

'Yep. All these tech geeks started out like this, didn't they? Apparently, Gabriel wasn't just into computers. He was a book-worm. Learned to read when he was three, was gobbling up Shakespeare when he was eight and actually understanding it. My source said Gabriel was into drama too. Always trying to get the teachers at their elementary school to put on Shakespeare plays. He told everyone he was going to be a famous playwright when he grew up, though in the interview I found with him online he said he'd always wanted to be a movie director. So I guess that ambition changed at some point. He also said in this interview that he's a huge movie buff still, that he has a massive cinema at home and that he buys all the new movies when they come out. Like, all of them. He's building his own massive library.'

'So he would have seen *The Immaculate*,' I said.

'That Ruth's movie? Yep. I think we can safely assume that.'

I remembered telling Ruth, when I saw the film, that it was going to attract the attention of casting directors and producers. I'd had no idea that it would also attract the attention of someone like Gabriel Dearman. But if this was indeed the case, I could understand it. Ruth's performance was so powerful, so hypnotic, that I could see how it would have captivated his attention. A rich man, with secret power, used to getting what he wanted, frustrated by the things money couldn't buy.

Deciding he wanted Ruth to be part of what he'd created.

'What else did your source say?' I asked.

Wanda cleared her throat. 'By the time they got to junior high, Gabriel was designing computer games. Good games. He used to copy them on to cassette and sell them at school. My source remembers one called *Tempest* in which you were the ruler of this island and had to control all these characters, make them do what you wanted.'

'Just like in the play.'

'Yep.'

'The play Ruth was in when Mona met her.'

Which had come first, I wondered? Had Mona encountered Ruth on the cruise and told Gabriel about her – this hot young actress who was appearing in a play he was obsessed with? Or had he seen the movie first, then discovered Ruth was going to be appearing in his favourite play? He would have seen it as a sign, surely. And then sent Mona to make contact with her.

It could have been either scenario.

Wanda went on. 'Apparently, Gabriel's computer-game enterprise ended when some bigger, tougher kids tried to muscle in, insisted that he had to pay them for protection and a sixty per cent cut of what he was making. He refused, and these kids beat the crap out of him. He ended up in the hospital, needed eye surgery. These kids all blamed each other and the cops could never prove which one of them had done it, plus they had rich parents who could afford good lawyers so they got away with it.' She paused. 'All those kids are dead now. They died over a five-year period. A series of accidents.'

I let this sink in. 'What happened next?'

'This is where it grows more murky. Gabriel moved to a new school so my source lost direct contact with him. But his mom told him later that Gabriel had gone to Columbia to study psychology, which was a big surprise to everyone. They thought he'd do computer science or maybe even drama.'

'He wanted to learn how people tick,' I said. 'So he could manipulate them. Control them. Just like Prospero.'

In *The Tempest*, Prospero rules the island he has been exiled to along with his daughter, Miranda. He causes the shipwreck and uses sorcery, and a spirit called Ariel, to monitor and direct the actions of the other characters.

'You think he's modelled himself on this fictional character?' Wanda asked. 'You're a playwright too, aren't you? It sounds like the kind of interpretation you'd come up with.'

'True.'

'All I know is that, for a few years after that, Gabriel disappeared. My source doesn't know what happened to him and I haven't come across anything online yet. But the article I found told me that he began to build up his portfolio of stocks and shares in dot-coms and other tech companies in the early 2000s. He was an early investor in this start-up that Google bought for a billion. Then he invested in property too. He's seriously rich. Seriously, seriously rich.'

I wondered if he'd also bankrolled Mona's businesses. Maybe even helped her buy the house in Williamsburg. Or perhaps it was the other way around. Mona's family were rich, weren't they? Maybe she'd loaned him money for his first investments. That made sense.

I remembered the first time I'd met her, in the lounge bar on the cruise ship. I had been sitting in the corner, writing, and she and Jack had sat at the next table, soon drawing me into a conversation. Mona must have realised I was Ruth's boyfriend and had targeted me for information. Soon, she would befriend us both – or pretend to. It had happened just a few months ago, but it seemed like a lifetime.

'From everything I've found out, I'm convinced he's our guy,' Wanda said. 'He lives in his tower in Brooklyn, in the penthouse.'

I brought up Google Maps on my computer and found the address she had given me earlier. It was just a few miles north of Williamsburg. I switched to Street View, so I could see the tower. Fifty storeys of glistening glass and steel, though Street View only showed its base.

'She's there,' I said. 'Ruth. She has to be. So what's the plan? Do we call the police?'

'And say what? We think one of New York's richest men is operating a cult out of his luxury building?'

'But . . . if he's holding Ruth against her will. And what about Callum's daughter, Sinead?'

'We have no proof Gabriel is holding anyone against their will. We have no proof of criminal activities at all.'

'What about Brandon? Jesse's friend? The one who was knifed in the park. They murdered him.'

'Again, we have no proof that's linked to Gabriel or his people.'

'And Jack? Krugman shot him. Then got some poor sucker to confess to it.'

'Adam, do you really want to go to the police right now and talk about Krugman? Are you out of your mind?'

She was right.

'So what are we going to do?' I asked.

'I can start working on a story. Talk to more people. There must be cleaners, maintenance staff in that building we could talk to. We can go through Gabriel's financial dealings, look for irregularities . . .'

'No! That's too slow!' I stared at the map. 'There must be something—'

I heard a car screech to a halt outside. A door slammed and then the car pulled away quickly, speeding off until I could no longer hear it.

I wouldn't normally have thought anything of it – this was Brooklyn; it was noisy all the time – but in my heightened state of paranoia, I went over to the front window, still holding my phone, and looked down at the street.

There was a man standing outside the building. I could only see the top of his head, but as I watched he looked left then right before approaching the front door.

The buzzer rang.

At the same time, Wanda was saying something in my ear. I tuned in to hear her say, 'I'll call you back later.'

'No, wait—'

But it was too late. She had hung up, and she had called me from a blocked number so I couldn't ring back.

The buzzer sounded again. I returned to the window. After a few moments the man stepped away from the door – and looked up at me.

Our eyes met.

He was in his thirties, with dark hair. Chiselled. He looked like a film star. He stared at me, not moving, not breaking eye contact.

I raised my phone, zoomed in and took a photo of him.

He didn't like that. He stepped out of my line of sight, back towards the apartment. I expected him to start pressing the buzzer again, but all was silent.

I went over to the front door of the apartment and peered out through the spyhole. Nothing.

I should call the police. But Wanda's words echoed in my mind. How could I tell them what was going on without telling them about Krugman's death?

The silence seemed to stretch on forever. Perhaps the man was gone. I went back over to the window and, fumbling with my phone, tried to call Callum. It went straight to voicemail. I left a message, then sent him a text, telling him there was someone here.

And then I heard it.

Scratching at the apartment door.

He was inside the building, trying to pick the lock.

Chapter 34

Ruth had been pacing for an hour, wondering if anyone was going to come and see her – Gabriel had promised he'd be back to continue their conversation from yesterday – when Eden came into the room.

Ruth started talking immediately. 'Gabriel told me about Jack. Why didn't *you* tell me?'

Eden hung her head. 'Oh, Ruth. I'm sorry. I was planning to . . .'

'Do you know when the funeral's going to happen? I want to go. And I need to get in touch with Mona, to offer my condolences. Have you seen her? How is she?'

'I spoke to her. She's as you'd expect. The coroner has just released the body so I think the funeral is going to be in a few days' time. We can go together. Assuming . . .'

'Assuming what?'

'Did Gabriel talk to you about us?'

'He did.'

'And how are you feeling about everything?'

Ruth laughed. 'To be honest, I don't understand it all. He was saying he can help me, that he wants me to join you, but I don't get what that means. He said he can give me the world.' She shook her head. It was such a grand statement – so vague and broad – that it was virtually meaningless.

'Gabriel is a fan,' Eden said.

'Yeah, he said. To be honest, I find it quite embarrassing.' When he had been talking to her, looking into her eyes, it had all felt real. Important. But now . . . 'I just want to get out of here. I really want to talk to Mona. You've all been very kind, but it's time to move on.'

Did she imagine it, or was that a flicker of annoyance on Eden's face? But it vanished as soon as it had appeared.

'Gabriel doesn't want you to go. Not yet.'

'I know. He wants me to hang around, talk to him some more. But honestly, Eden, I'm tired of talking. I'm going stir-crazy. I need to get out of here. I have to get on with my life. Also, I really need my phone back.'

'I told you, it broke when you fell.'

'Yes, but surely the SIM didn't break? Give me that and I can put it in a new phone.'

Eden didn't respond to that. Instead, she sat on the bed. 'Ruth, I'm going to be blunt with you. If you walk out of here now, you might go on to be successful. You've got talent, looks. You're a good actress. But you also have a black mark against your name. You're the woman who walked out of her first big Broadway role before it had even begun.'

'I didn't walk out!'

'Doesn't matter. That's what the world thinks. You also told me that your agent isn't very good. Maybe none of that matters. Maybe Hollywood won't care, and in a couple of years' time I'll be watching you collect your first Oscar. But the road ahead is going to be hard. How many actresses go to Hollywood with an indie hit behind them thinking they're going to make it? I lived there, Ruth. I saw it. The streets are littered with broken dreams. Only

223

the toughest, the best, the ones with the most self-belief and the most luck break through.'

'I know that.'

'Do you? Do you really? You're talented. You've got charisma. And maybe you have the self-belief, though you hide it well. But luck – that's something you can't control. And that's where we come in.'

'But what does that mean? What exactly do you do?'

Eden got up from the bed. 'It's simple. We're a network. We have money. Vast amounts of money. We have connections. We have power. We can make things happen for you. And we can teach you as well. Teach you to be stronger. Teach you to believe in yourself.'

'I do . . .'

'Really? I'm talking absolute confidence. We can turn you into a person who glides through life. Who gets everything she ever wanted. We can make you happy. And you'll belong. You'll have friends better than any family.'

It sounded so good. Eden was telling Ruth everything she had ever longed to hear, offering all the things she'd been looking for throughout her life. But surely it was too good. Too easy. Ruth had fought for everything she had gained in her life so far. Fought to survive the care system she'd grown up in. Refused to believe all the people who told her acting was too hard, that she would never make it. Nothing had ever been handed to her on a plate – yet here was someone offering to do just that.

Her instincts told her to mistrust. That nothing in her life could ever be this easy.

But what if this was the fork in the road? The moment where her life could go one way or the other? Success or failure. Ambitions fulfilled or crushed.

Eden was offering her what sounded like a magic pill. Would it be insane to turn it down? To try it at least?

She didn't know what to do.

'I was a wreck when I met Gabriel,' Eden continued. 'A shaking, weak, self-loathing creature. A drug addict.'

'You never told me that.'

'I know. Because that's the old me. The me I try to forget. And unlike you, I did have a family, but wished I didn't. My dad . . . My dad is an asshole. One of the worst human beings to ever walk this planet. I had been taught that I deserved nothing but misery and poverty and abuse.' Her eyes filled with tears. 'And then I met Gabriel and he showed me the way things should be. *Could* be. He taught me to be strong, to believe in myself. He gave me protection against both the wolves and the sheep. He saved me, Ruth. And he can save you too.'

Eden took hold of Ruth's wrists, holding on tight. Her eyes shone not just with tears but with a religious fervour. An ecstasy.

'Join us,' Eden said. 'And he *will* give you the world.'

The temptation was almost unbearable; it was like she was being torn in two. Once again, she felt the way she had when Gabriel had been talking to her, caressing her ego, soothing her fears away. She was thrown into an imagined future, one in which she was adored and respected; a world of luxury and security. She pictured herself cradled and loved.

'Do it,' Eden said, 'and he'll give you everything. All of himself.'

The way Eden said it, with a hint of lasciviousness, made Ruth snap out of the dreamy state she had been falling into. 'What does that mean?'

Eden didn't respond straight away.

Ruth pressed. 'What do you mean, *all of himself*?'

'Just your loyalty. Like I said, it's a network. We all help each other. When you're in a position to help another member, you'll do so.' But she sounded uncertain, like she was backtracking.

'He won't want to sleep with me?'

Eden hesitated again.

'He will, won't he?' Ruth said. A memory had come back to her. That first night after she woke up, meeting Marie. What had Emilio said? That she belonged to another? 'Do you belong to him, Eden? Do you have to sleep with him too? Do all the women here?'

She thought Eden would deny it, but instead she said, 'Sometimes. But only because we want to. He doesn't make us.'

'Oh my God. But it's expected, isn't it?'

Eden tried to take hold of Ruth's hand. 'You'll enjoy it. He's a skilful lover. He's a teacher in the bedroom too.'

Ruth snatched her hand away. 'I'm actually going to be sick. He was going on and on about loving my work, saying how great I am. But really, he just wants my body.' Nausea bubbled up in her. 'He's nothing more than a glorified stalker.'

It was as if they'd been hypnotising her and suddenly she was back in the real world. What had she been thinking? How could she have allowed herself to be tempted?

She knew how. They'd been working on her. Trying to brainwash her.

Well, it wasn't going to work.

'I want to leave now. Where are my clothes? I want my SIM card too.'

Eden looked slightly panicked. She glanced up at the wall, towards what Ruth had assumed was a smoke alarm.

'Is that a camera?' Ruth asked. 'It is, isn't it?' She gazed up at it. 'Are you watching me now, Gabriel? Have you been spying on me the whole time, like some disgusting peeping Tom?'

'Ruth, you're making a big—'

She pushed Eden away and pointed a finger at what must be a camera. She raised her voice. 'Let me tell you something, Gabriel. I will never sleep with you. I will never even touch you. You're a fucking creep. You're not going to induct me into this . . . this sex cult.' She sucked in a deep breath. 'You're nothing more than Charles Manson with a fancy apartment. And if you think I'm going to let your diseased dick anywhere near me, you're insane. Now let me the fuck out of here.'

She waited. Eden shook her head, like someone who had just watched a co-worker call their boss an asshole.

The door opened.

Gabriel came in. Ruth heard Eden gasp beside her, and Ruth herself took a step back, because he looked furious. Capable of violence.

'You're an ungrateful bitch, Ruth,' he said with a tremor in his voice. 'Do you know how much trouble we went to, to get you here? How much trouble you're still causing? You're staying here. You're going to fulfil your destiny.'

'My destiny? What the hell are you talking about?'

But he didn't answer. Instead he grabbed hold of her by the arm and bared his teeth in her face. He was shaking with anger. She tried to pull away but Gabriel held on to her like a vice. He dragged her across the room and pushed her on to the bed.

'Get the others,' he said to Eden.

Chapter 35

I ran towards the door, intending to slide the deadlock across.

It was too late. The door swung open to reveal the dark-haired man standing there. His hand moved inside the blazer he was wearing.

I spun and scrambled into the living room, shutting the door and grabbing a chair, which I tilted and jammed beneath the handle. I looked around desperately. The knife I had taken from the kitchen was still in my backpack. But where the hell *was* my backpack? I had no time to find it. The man was rattling the door. The chair would only hold him back for seconds and, this time, Callum wasn't here to save me.

Then I saw it. The fire escape that zig-zagged up the outside of the building. Access was through the window. As the man kicked at the door, I grabbed the window frame, praying it would open easily.

It did.

I stepped out on to the fire escape at the exact same moment the chair fell away and the door crashed open. The man came through and raised his gun. It was still the afternoon. If he shot me, it would surely attract attention from people on the street. But I wasn't thinking about that. I was too scared to think much of anything at all.

There were steps going up and down, but I had an image in my head from movies I'd seen, of people escaping across New York rooftops, so I went up. I didn't look back, just continued to climb as fast as I could. The iron steps were slippery from a rain shower that morning, and I almost lost my footing, desperately grabbing the railing.

I reached the next platform and glanced down to see my pursuer coming out through the window.

There was one more platform above me, on the top floor of the building, then a final staircase that led up to the roof. As I reached the last platform, he said my name, just loud enough for me to hear. I froze for a second, looking straight into my pursuer's eyes as he raised the gun again. He had a clear shot.

'There's nowhere to go,' he said, coming up the steps towards me. At the same time, I looked up at the roof. It stood alone, the distance between this building and the next too far to jump. I had made a mistake going upwards. I was trapped.

He came closer, up the steps towards me, raising the gun one last time.

He didn't shoot.

'Put your hands where I can see them,' he said.

I raised my arms, palms towards him.

'Come back down,' he said. 'Slowly.'

I went back down the steps, hands still held up, treading carefully so I didn't slip. He kept the gun trained on me. When we reached the platform beside the open window, he gestured for me to go through first, then followed, pointing the gun at me all the time.

'Where's Maguire?' he said.

I hesitated. If I lied and told him Callum was close, he might decide he needed to kill me on the spot, then lie in wait for Callum.

'Manhattan,' I said.

'Doing what?'

'I don't know.'

He stepped closer, jabbing the gun in my direction. 'Don't bullshit me.'

I felt like I had no choice but to tell the truth. 'He was watching Mona at the hotel. But I don't know where he is now.'

I couldn't tell if he believed me.

'How did you know we were helping each other?' I said.

He rolled his eyes. 'I saw him push you out of the way of my car.'

So much was going through my head that I didn't stop to question how he knew who Callum was and what he looked like. If asked, I probably would have guessed that Sinead must have told him. Shown the cult members a photo of her dad.

'And how did you find us?' I asked.

He smirked. 'You're amateurs, Adam. You brought Krugman's phone back here, didn't you?'

I realised what he meant. 'Oh shit. There's a tracker inside it?'

'Yep. And not the usual Find My iPhone shit. A proper tracker.'

I guessed that was something they did with all their phones. Was that why Eden had been so happy to give Ruth her spare phone? So she could keep track of her? Had the cult been responsible for the phone theft in the park too?

Of course they had. How many steps behind them would I always be?

'So which one of you shot Krugman?' he asked. 'Maguire, I'm guessing.'

I didn't contradict him.

He made a clucking sound with his mouth. 'We're going to make arrangements so Krugman gets a proper funeral. We look after our own.'

'Like Mona looked after her husband?'

'Jack wasn't one of us. But you know about that? Did Krugman tell you?'

'I figured it out. I know about Krugman and Mona too.'

He raised an eyebrow. 'Smart. You know a lot. Now pick that chair up and sit on it.'

I did as he asked. He moved behind me and cuffed my hands. Then he grabbed another chair and sat down too, the gun still on me. He took out his phone and tapped out a text with his other hand. Reporting back to Gabriel, I guessed.

'What's your name?' I asked.

He didn't reply.

'Come on,' I said. 'You know mine.'

He mulled it over. Eventually, probably believing there was no harm telling a man who would be dead soon, he said, 'Emilio.'

'Where's Ruth?' I asked.

He smiled. 'Are we playing quid pro quo? You know I'm the one holding a gun, Adam?'

Despite the situation, there was something weirdly likeable about Emilio. He was charming. He looked like the good-looking boy next door, the one everyone wants to be friends with.

'I just don't want to go to my grave not knowing that she's okay,' I said.

'Huh.' He looked thoughtful. 'She's fine. Not that you really care.'

'What do you mean?'

'You were envious of her success. You wanted her to fail.' He looked genuinely disgusted.

'I never . . .' I stopped. Why was I trying to defend myself to this guy? After what he and the rest of the cult had done? 'You think that's worse than abducting her?'

Emilio laughed. 'She hasn't been abducted, Adam. We're looking after her. Protecting her.'

231

'Protect one, protect all?'

He raised his eyebrows. 'Where did you hear that?'

As he said this, my phone beeped in my pocket. Emilio reached in and plucked it out.

'What's the code?'

I told him and he unlocked it. I couldn't see the screen but I guessed he was reading the message that had just arrived. I assumed it was from Callum. Emilio put my phone into his blazer pocket. 'Such a mess. This bitch had better be worth it.'

'You're talking about Ruth.'

'Yeah. She's cute. Got that whole Princess Diana thing going on. Looks like butter wouldn't melt. That's exactly how Gabriel likes them. Though it didn't work out so hot for the last actress he became obsessed with.' He laughed, then got up. He produced a gag from his pocket and tied it around my mouth.

ϖ

We sat like that for thirty or forty minutes, him not speaking, me unable to speak. Whenever I looked around, or even glanced up, he would snap at me, telling me to keep my eyes on my lap. I no longer thought of him as the boy next door. His good looks masked something rotten. While we waited, he treated me to a litany of all the things Gabriel was probably doing to Ruth right now, like he was reading off a list of PornHub keywords. I did my best to tune out, to let the filth wash over me. I think he saw it as a minor punishment for all the trouble I'd put him through. Or maybe he was just doing it to stave off boredom.

And then came the unmistakeable sound of someone turning a key in the door.

'Don't move,' Emilio whispered, getting up quickly. 'Make any kind of noise and I'll fucking hurt you. Your girlfriend too.'

He went into the hallway just as I heard the door open.

'Surprise,' I heard Emilio say.

A moment later, they appeared in the living room – Callum first, then Emilio behind him, the gun pressed into his spine. Callum had his hands up but his eyes darted around. I wondered if he had his gun on him, but then noticed Emilio was holding it in his other hand.

'Sit down,' Emilio said, nodding towards the chair he'd been sitting in.

Callum obliged. He shot me a searching look and I wanted to tell him about the tracking device in Krugman's phone, but of course I couldn't.

'I've heard so much about you,' Emilio said to Callum.

'I'm sure,' Callum replied, darting another look in my direction.

'Yeah. I've heard all about what an asshole you are.' He raised his gun and pointed it at Callum's forehead. 'This is from Eden,' he said.

Callum was calm. He stared at Emilio as if daring him to do it.

'Eden? How is she?' Callum asked. 'How is my daughter?'

Chapter 36

The van's rear doors opened and two pairs of arms – Emilio and the man he had called for assistance – threw me inside. I landed on my front, scraping my cheek on the metal floor. My wrists were still cuffed behind my back and I lay still for a moment, gathering my breath before rolling on to my side and struggling into a sitting position.

'Are you all right, son?' said Callum, who was over in the corner of the van, behind where the driver would be.

I was still reeling from what he had said. *How is my daughter?* 'Why didn't you tell me that you're Eden's dad?'

The van lurched into motion, sending me rocking backwards, only just able to keep my balance. Nearby, a car engine started up, presumably Emilio. And then we were moving.

After lowering the gun, Emilio had laughed in Callum's face. 'Don't worry, *Dad*. I'm not going to shoot you. I wanted to see if you'd piss your pants. Eden wants to kill you herself.'

'She knows I'm looking for her?' Callum had asked.

'Of course she does.' Emilio had taken a couple of steps away, then had second thoughts. He'd gone back and spat in Callum's face. 'That's from me, for Krugman. But also for what you did to Eden. You deserve everything that's coming your way.'

He had gone into the other room and made a call, then come back and switched on the TV, settling on ESPN, where two men were talking about baseball. Despite everything, I noticed that the show caught Callum's interest.

'We're staying here till sunset,' Emilio had said.

Now, in the van, I repeated my question to Callum, adding, 'Why did you lie to me?'

'Because I didn't think you'd help me if you knew Eden was my daughter. I knew that you blamed Eden, or would soon blame her, for making off with your girlfriend. I needed you to think we were in exactly the same situation.'

I tried to wrap my head around this. I remembered the story Callum had told me the day he'd stopped me from being run over. The story about raising his daughter on his own after his wife died. He'd said that his daughter, Sinead, had met Eden and run off with her to join the cult. 'Did you make up the part about your wife dying?'

'No. That's all true. But it was Eden who went off the rails after her mom died.'

'Not the fictional Sinead.'

'That's right. And I don't know who recruited Eden. It might have been this Gabriel asshole himself. Or the jerk driving this van.'

'And what about the rest of it? The anonymous guy on Facebook who told you about the cult. Is he real?'

In the gloom, I could only see Callum's outline, but I saw him hang his head a little. 'No. I invented that part.'

'So what happened?'

'Does it really matter?'

'Yes, it fucking does.'

The van swung around a bend and I leaned against the side to stop myself from toppling over.

'We really are from Bakersfield. That's true. And we moved to Los Angeles after Mary died. She was my wife. It wasn't easy, bringing up a teenage girl on my own. We fought a lot. Eden acted out, got mixed up with the wrong people, got into drugs and drinking and skipping school. Maybe I was too strict.'

I was sure he wasn't telling me the whole truth about his parenting style, but decided not to push it.

'She left home when she was eighteen. Moved in with some guy, a dude in a band. I didn't see her much after that. Every now and again she'd come round asking to borrow money, which I'd always give to her. Once, I came home and found her going through her mom's old things, crying. That was a good night. We talked about her childhood, watched an old home movie. I cooked dinner and she stayed the night. I thought . . . maybe she was going to come back to me. That it was all going to be okay. But when I woke up the next morning she was gone, along with all the money in the house and her mom's old jewellery.' I heard him swallow. 'That was the last time I saw her.'

'Until when?'

'A few months ago, I got a call from an old friend. He'd seen Eden at a spirituality convention near Palm Springs. I wasn't making that bit up. He said she was with a famous model.'

'Jade Thomson?'

'Yeah. Jade was launching her own range of crystals or some bullshit and my friend said he thought Eden was her assistant. After that, I tried to get in touch with Jade but it was impossible. At the same time, I tried to find out as much about her as I could. What I told you about Jade vanishing and coming back changed, like she had this new charisma, this inner glow that made the camera love her even more, that was true. And Eden was hanging out with her, or working with her.'

The van was idling now, apparently stuck in traffic.

'That's when I heard the rumours about Jade being part of a cult. There were these guys on 4Chan, these hackers. You know 4Chan?' I'd heard of it but never used it. I knew it was essentially a message board where users posted anonymously. 'One of these hackers said a friend of his got into Jade's phone and found a load of nude pics. These creeps try to do it to all the female celebs. This guy then sent a blackmail demand to Jade.'

'Let me guess. He ended up dead.'

'Yep. There was all this speculation on 4Chan about what happened, but one poster swore that Jade was a member of a cult. Other users were telling him that was crap but it rang true, because of some weird stuff Eden had said the last time I saw her.'

The van started moving again.

'After that, I went to all the conventions I could find where Jade's crystal business was listed as an exhibitor. Jade was never there herself and neither was Eden. Until three weeks ago, at the convention in Brooklyn. Jade was making a personal appearance, launching a new range, and I went along.'

'Eden was there?'

'She was. I knew if I approached her on the spot, she'd freak out. And I wanted to find out if I was right about her being in a cult. So I followed her. You know the rest. So—'

'Stop talking.'

I didn't know if Callum was telling the truth now. It was clear from what Emilio had said that Eden hated her dad. He definitely wasn't telling me the whole story.

I remembered how he'd been that night in the woods, with Krugman. Killing him had hardly seemed to bother Callum at all. And the way he'd stuck that twig into Krugman's wound; the sadistic pleasure he'd appeared to take from it . . . I thought I had a good idea of why Eden had really left home. Why she had run away to join a cult, especially one that gave its members protection.

It wasn't hard to see the appeal of that; how easy it would be for Gabriel to persuade vulnerable young people to join.

'Where do you think they're taking us?' Callum said after a little while. 'To their HQ, or back to the woods to dispose of us?'

'I don't know,' I replied. 'But I'm guessing you'll get to be reunited with Eden, wherever we're going. Eden with a gun in her hand.'

'Yeah,' he said quietly.

Chapter 37

'I'm so disappointed in you. *So* disappointed.'

It was dark outside, and Ruth could see herself reflected in a mirror on the wall of the bedroom they had taken her to. This room was larger than the one in which she'd been staying, and was dominated by a king-sized bed. The mirror hung level with the bed to her left, and she knew, though she fought the knowledge, that it had been positioned there for one reason.

She was on her back, her arms stretched out behind her, wrists fastened to the bedposts. Before tying her to the bed, Marie and the other woman – an Amazonian with muscles like a shot-putter – had made her change into a pair of white cotton pyjamas. They had strip-searched her first – just in case, they said, she had hidden anything about herself, anything that could be used as a weapon. Then they had forced her to shower and scrub herself clean, the water so hot it had turned her flesh a vivid pink.

This was, she knew, the penthouse. Gabriel's apartment. On the way through the main living space, which had floor-to-ceiling windows that looked out across Brooklyn and towards Manhattan, she had taken in the huge TV. Ruth's own image had been frozen on it. The scene in *The Immaculate* in which her character is told she is destined to save humanity. On the sixty-inch screen, a fake tear glistened on her cheek.

Now, Gabriel paced the strip of floorboard beside the bed.

'So fucking disappointed, Ruth.'

He leaned over her, thumping the mattress beside her. His calm, superior demeanour was gone and his eyes were wild, his skin blotchy with fury. It was as if the picture he kept locked in the attic had come to life, and here it was, confronting her. Breathing all over her.

'I thought you were the one,' he said, his voice loud in her ear, like he couldn't control the volume. 'You know how long I've been looking?'

She didn't respond.

'There were so many! All of them with something. All of them beautiful and young and fit. All of them sweet and funny and gentle. All of them with some talent. Some kind of X factor. But none of them were right, Ruth. Some of them were too keen on the idea of having power. Some of them wanted too much. One or two of them wouldn't stop weeping. Do you know what that's like? To have that fucking noise in your head? That boo-hoo-hoo?' He mimed a crying woman. 'They all seemed right until we got them here.'

Ruth managed to speak. 'And where are they now?'

'Gone,' he said. 'Long gone.'

The way he said it made her go cold.

He sat on the edge of the mattress and lay a hand on her upper thigh. She tried not to flinch. She didn't want to make him angry. She didn't want to be long gone. He idly stroked her leg through her pyjama bottoms, fingers bending then unfurling, and she tried not to imagine where his hand would go next.

'You seemed so perfect,' Gabriel said. 'When Mona called me from the cruise to tell me about you, told me you were playing

Miranda, I had to track down a copy of your movie. And when I saw it – boom!' He lifted his hand from her thigh and slapped himself on the chest. 'I knew I'd found her, after all this time, after all those mistakes. The girl who was worthy to sit beside me. To join me at the top of the world.'

He lay his hand on her thigh again. 'Maybe even the mother of my children. The next generation.'

She shuddered, and she knew he felt it because of the look on his face. Not anger. No, it was the look of a greedy little boy who'd been told he couldn't have the toy he wanted for Christmas.

'Do you remember the first time we met?' he said.

She blinked at him. When was it? Yesterday? The day before? Time had almost ceased to exist since she'd been brought to this place. The days ran into one another. Why was he talking about it like it was a long time ago?

'You don't recognise me, do you?' he said. 'It was in the park. You'd just lost your phone. That phone that contained all those special pictures of you.'

He licked his lips.

She recoiled. 'It was you. You set it up.'

But he wasn't listening. 'You won't believe how many times I've gazed at those photos, Ruth. I couldn't believe how perfect you were.'

So the remote deletion of her pictures hadn't worked. His eyes raked over her body now like he was seeing her naked again. She felt violated. Sickened.

'I went to so much trouble to get you here,' he said. He watched himself in the mirror as he spoke. 'Because I knew you were worth it. And I thought you would be easy to persuade. A woman with your background. In and out of foster care. Desperate to belong to something. Hungry for success. Aware of how cruel the world can be. Not many friends. A boyfriend who you suspected was jealous of you. All the ingredients were there, and I thought I'd just have to show you how easy things could be for you.' He touched her stomach with his fingertips. She felt his hand tremble. 'I wasn't lying, Ruth. You could have had everything. Perhaps I should have taken it slower. Let you get to know me better. Eden wasn't supposed to tell you everything.' He sighed. 'And now it's too late.'

'Maybe . . . maybe it's not too late, Gabriel,' she said, trying to meet his eye. *Act, Ruth*, she told herself. *It's the one thing you're meant to be good at, so act like your life depends on it.*

Because her life *did* depend on it.

'It sounds so wonderful. To be protected. To not be at the mercy of all the predators and sharks out there. And success and fame and glory – it's all I've ever wanted. To show all those people they were wrong. All the people who rejected me. Like my birth mother. She's still alive. Still out there somewhere. I want her to see me on the big screen and realise what a terrible mistake she made.' She caught his gaze in the mirror. 'I shouldn't have said those things. I wasn't . . . I wasn't thinking straight. But if you give me another chance, I'll let you manage me. Let you protect me.' She forced herself to say it. 'Let you love me.'

He stared at her. His breathing had grown heavy, pupils slightly dilated. His hand was flat on her belly now, beneath her pyjama top. He kept it perfectly still.

'And I'll love you too,' she said. 'I'll give you all the love you never had.'

She could see he wanted to believe her. He was *desperate* to believe her.

But he withdrew his hand and leaned close to her, his nose inches from hers. She could smell his breath. Could smell the darkness inside him.

'How stupid do you think I am?' he said. 'I saw the disgust on your face. Believe me, I've seen that look on women's faces before.'

She could believe that, all right.

He stood.

'Please don't kill me,' she said.

'I'm not going to kill you, Ruth. You know why? I don't need you to want this to happen. I don't need you to be a fully active member of our network, going out into the world, becoming a star. All I need is for you to be here beside me. In my tower. In my bed.'

She stared at him.

'Eventually, you'll learn to like it. And if you don't . . .' He shrugged.

His hands moved to his belt buckle.

'No. Please. You can't—'

There was a knock at the bedroom door. Irritation flashed in Gabriel's eyes. 'Who is it?'

Eden came into the bedroom. She didn't even look at Ruth.

'Emilio's back.'

'Are they both with him?'

Eden nodded.

'Good.' He rubbed his hands together, then grinned at Ruth. 'I guess this can wait till later. Till after.'

'I'll stay here and watch her,' Eden said, finally glancing down at Ruth.

'Are you sure you don't want to come with me? To see your father? After all the things he did to you, I thought you'd want to be there.'

'I do. I just . . . ' Eden said. 'It's a big thing. I need to psych myself up for it. You talk to him first, and I'll keep an eye on Ruth.'

Gabriel nodded and left the room, leaving the two women alone. Eden sat down on the bed.

'Oh, Ruth,' she said.

Chapter 38

The van doors opened and Emilio instructed us to get out. The driver stood beside the vehicle along with another man and a woman. I had to shuffle out in an undignified way, until Emilio grabbed me and pulled me forward. Callum followed and I looked around. We were in an underground car park. Emilio and the others marched us over to a lift. The door pinged open, and Emilio and the man and woman I'd never seen before pushed us inside.

I didn't see anyone press a button, but in the next moment we were gliding skywards.

At least it wasn't the woods.

I glanced at Callum. It was obvious he was trying not to seem nervous.

'Finally going to meet your man Gabriel, are we?' he asked.

'You're Eden's father,' said the woman. She was six foot and built like a nightclub bouncer. I'd heard the other man call her Brittany as we'd got into the lift.

'I am indeed,' said Callum.

Brittany spat in his face.

'Seems you're not very popular around here,' I said.

Brittany turned to me. The lift was taking a long time to get to the top. 'You're the actress's boyfriend. Eden should have poisoned you the night she left that house.'

'I guess she was afraid the real cops would get involved,' I said.

Brittany snorted and addressed Emilio. 'Since when are we afraid of the police?'

But I knew their fear of a proper criminal investigation must have been what prevented Eden from killing me that night. And maybe they thought Ruth would be harder to convert if I was dead.

The lift stopped moving and the doors opened.

We were led out into a corridor where there were more people, all young and good-looking, and they took us into an apartment and patted us down. The blinds were drawn and the room was dim, with just a sofa, a table with two chairs, and a pair of doors that led, I assumed, to a bedroom and a bathroom. There was a little kitchen to the side. Then they all vanished except Emilio and Brittany, plus someone I took to be a security guy. He was holding a gun.

'Strip,' said Brittany.

Callum said, 'What?'

'I'm really not interested in looking at your dicks,' she said. 'Just do it.'

I took my clothes off. Beside me, Callum did the same. The A/C in the apartment was cranked high and I shivered, hands cupped over my genitals.

'Now put those on,' Emilio said. Two sets of clothes were laid out on the sofa. A plain grey sweater and matching trousers. Clean underwear and a pair of canvas sneakers. We both did as they asked, dressing side by side in silence.

There was a light rap at the door. The security guy opened it and another man came in. It was him. The man from the photo.

'You're Gabriel,' I said.

'Adam,' he replied, coming over and appraising me. He did the same to Callum. 'And you're Callum Maguire.'

'Not going to spit in my face, are you?' Callum asked.

Gabriel just smiled. 'I've heard a lot about you. All the things you did to Eden when she was a child. I've held her in my arms while she told me all about it. I've kissed away her tears.'

'All lies, I'm sure,' said Callum. 'That girl had a good upbringing. Firm, to be sure, but fair.'

Gabriel took a step closer to him. There was a look of genuine disgust on his face. 'Is that what you thought when you were beating her? When you made her hold out her arm so you could stub your filthy cigarettes out on it?'

Instinctively, I moved away from Callum. Emilio grabbed hold of my elbow to stop me going further.

'I never did that,' Callum said.

'I've seen her scars.' Gabriel moved a fraction closer. 'She told me about how you crept into her bed at night too. When she was seven.'

'Oh Jesus,' I said.

Gabriel turned to me. 'And you've been helping him.'

'I had no idea. I didn't even know he was Eden's dad until today. All I want is to find Ruth. To make sure she's okay. If she's happy here, wants to be here—'

Gabriel gave his head an annoyed shake and put a finger to his lips. 'Hush.' It was Callum he was focused on now. He slowly circled him. 'I know what you did to her mother too. Your wife. Mary, wasn't it? All the beatings. The abuse. The control. I heard about how you made her take off her top and poured hot oil on to her skin because she burned your dinner. How you made her clean your shit stains out of the toilet with her bare hands. How one Christmas you hurt her so badly you almost went to jail, but your wife wouldn't testify against you because she was too scared.'

Callum's expression hardened. 'Don't come over all morally superior, Gabriel. You're the leader of a *cult*. I bet you do exactly the same to anyone who fucks with you.'

Gabriel stopped moving. 'I never – never! – hurt members of my family. People who join me need never worry about their well-being again.'

'Tell that to Detective Krugman,' Callum said. 'Now, I want to see my daughter. Like Adam says, I just want to know she's happy. To look her in the eye and believe she wants to stay here. And then I'll go back to California and leave you alone.'

'Bullshit,' said Emilio.

We all turned to look at him.

'He doesn't care if she's happy. He's scum. He killed his wife . . .'

Callum frowned. 'She killed herself.'

'Because you drove her to it. Eden told me—'

'Enough!' The roar came from Gabriel. His face was purple, a vein throbbing on his brow. 'I'm sick of listening to—'

Callum took a swing at Gabriel, who tried to step back but was too slow. Callum's fist connected with his cheekbone.

Within a second, Emilio and Brittany had Callum on the floor. Gabriel stood there, stunned, nursing his cheekbone.

'Give me the gun,' he said, taking a handgun from his security guy, who had been standing guarding the door throughout.

Emilio had Callum on his front, pinned to the ground with his arms behind his back. 'Doesn't Eden want to do it herself?' Emilio asked.

Gabriel lowered the gun. 'Let him up.'

Emilio and Brittany got to their feet, leaving Callum on the ground. Slowly, he pushed himself into a sitting position. Gabriel pointed the gun at Callum's face.

'Get up,' he said.

Slowly, Callum did as he was told.

'Emilio, get Eden. I want this done now.'

ω

Gabriel and Emilio led me out, leaving Callum behind with Brittany. Then Gabriel's security guy came with us into another room. As we entered, Gabriel turned to Emilio and said, 'Get everything ready.'

Emilio nodded and walked away before Gabriel shut and locked the door. Now it was just me, him and the security guy.

'Ready for what?' I asked.

He didn't reply, and as he looked at me, it came back to me. I had thought he looked familiar when I first saw the photo of him. Now I knew where I had seen him before.

'You were in the park. When Ruth's phone was stolen.' He was the man who had given chase, the one who had spoken to us and told Ruth to report it to the police. He'd been clean-shaven then and had been wearing sunglasses. But it was definitely him.

'Well done. You clearly have a better memory for faces than Ruth.'

'Why were you there? Because you wanted to get a proper look at her? In the flesh?'

I guessed he had stolen Ruth's phone so Eden could give her a new one with a tracker inside, in case he needed to keep tabs on her. And as a bonus he had got access to all Ruth's private photos.

'You're disgusting,' I spat. 'When did you first become obsessed with her? Was it before or after the cruise? Did Mona tell you about her existence?'

He didn't respond. Instead he walked over to the window while I continued to rant at him.

'What have you done to her?' I demanded. 'Have you brain-washed her? Forced her to join your cult?'

He pressed a couple of buttons on a panel on the wall and, to my astonishment, the glass slid away and a balcony emerged, jutting out into the open air. I was silenced, staring out at the night, the illuminated city, as wind gusted into the room.

Gabriel grabbed me by the front of my shirt. I tried to resist but he was stronger than he looked, and the security guy stepped forward, gun in hand.

Gabriel pushed me on to the balcony and against the thin rail, gripping my throat, breathing in my face. I could feel the fifty-storey drop behind me, hear the distant drone of a helicopter. I tried to grasp hold of the rail as Gabriel shoved me up against it, and made the mistake of turning my head for a second to look down, only to imagine myself falling, down, down, to smash on the pavement below.

'How many other people know about us?' Gabriel demanded, spittle landing on my face. 'Who have you talked to?'

'None.'

'Liar! I know about Wanda Brooks. Who else? Ruth's under-study? What did you say to her?'

'Nothing.' The word came out strangled and he loosened his grip on my throat a little.

'How many people do I need to kill?' he spat.

I didn't speak. I really didn't believe he would push me. This wasn't the middle of nowhere. A body hitting the ground would draw the police, TV news crews, crowds of onlookers. Maybe Gabriel saw this realisation enter my eyes, as he suddenly dragged me back into the room and threw me to the floor.

'Want me to kill him?' the security guy said.

Gabriel paced around me. I could see and feel the anger coming off him. Maybe I shouldn't push him further, I thought, but I couldn't help myself.

'Callum and I figured out how to find you,' I said from my position on the floor. 'Other people will too. You're nowhere near as smart as you think you are, Gabriel. You're not special. You're a narcissist. A megalomaniac. A small man with a god complex. And one day the law is going to catch up with you and take all this away. I'd like to see how special you think you are when you're rotting in a cell.'

'I want you to understand something,' he said, jabbing a finger at me as he walked around me. The angrier he got, the faster he paced. Behind him, I saw the eyes of the security guy widen, like he was shocked by Gabriel's behaviour.

'Even if one day someone betrays us, if I have an accident, if this building burns to the ground with me inside, it won't matter. When *I* die, I will live on in the hearts and the heads of the people who follow me. I'll live forever, in them. I am immortal.' His voice had reached a hysterical pitch. 'We're everywhere, Adam. *Everywhere.*'

His eyes were almost popping out of his head with rage. I could tell there was a lot more he wanted to say. But he caught himself, took a deep breath. The vein still throbbed on his forehead, but apart from that he appeared calm.

He turned to the security guy. 'I'm going to send Brittany in. Get Wanda Brooks's address out of him. Do whatever you have to do.'

ϖ

I don't like to think about the thirty minutes that followed.

Brittany came into the room, and she and the security guy – whose name, I soon learned, was Nick – dragged me into a bathroom and filled the tub with cold water. Then they pushed my face beneath the surface, holding me under until my lungs burned and I was convinced this was it. It's hard to describe the feeling of panic, of desperation – the need for it not to happen again.

They demanded Wanda's address. Everything I knew about her. They yelled at me, they screamed threats. They pushed my face into the water. They spoke kindly, soothingly, said this would all stop if I just told them everything. Then they yelled at me again. Held my face beneath the water for so long I was sure I would die.

I tried to hold out. I really did. But in the end, when I couldn't take it anymore, I gave up everything I knew. I had to persuade them that I didn't know her actual address; was only able to describe the route to her cabin and what it looked like. I told them about the diner where we'd met.

Then they dumped me on the bed, shivering and ashamed, and left me alone in the room.

I lay there, wet and cold, wondering how long it would be before they found Wanda's cabin. Wondering if Callum was already dead; and where Ruth was and what was happening to her. Gabriel had mentioned getting ready for something. Did that involve Ruth?

And how long would it be before they killed me?

Chapter 39

Eden picked out a short white dress for Ruth.

'Put this on,' she said.

They were still in the penthouse. People kept coming and going; Eden's phone beeped every few minutes. They kept talking about preparations, but no one would tell her what they were preparing for. Eden had a bottle of champagne and she offered Ruth some, tried to persuade her to drink it. Ruth refused, even though her nerves were shot and she craved something to take the edge off her feelings. When Eden ordered her to do her make-up, she found her hand was shaking too much to apply it, so Eden sat her down and did it for her. Then another woman came in and styled her hair, teasing it into curls.

'Beautiful,' Eden said when the woman left, and she stood behind Ruth and told her to look in the mirror. 'Don't you think you look beautiful?'

'I feel sick.'

Eden spun the chair around and grabbed Ruth's chin, crouching before her.

'You need to stay calm,' she said.

'I need to get out of here.' She grabbed Eden's wrists. 'Please, Eden. Help me. You can't let this happen.'

Eden broke away. 'Shut up. Stop being so pathetic.'

Ruth couldn't help it. She started to cry.

'Oh, for fuck's sake, you're ruining your make-up. Now I'm going to have to start all over again.'

Emilio came into the room.

'We're ready,' he said.

Eden snapped at him. 'Give us five minutes.'

'But Gabriel—'

'I said, give us five minutes.'

Emilio looked Ruth up and down. 'What's the matter with her?'

'She's scared. Wouldn't you be?'

He rolled his eyes. 'It's a great honour. To be with the most powerful man in America? If I was a woman—'

'Oh, fuck off, Emilio,' said Eden. She was wiping away the mascara that had run down Ruth's cheeks. 'Go tell Gabriel his bride needs a little while. He's waited this long. He can wait another five minutes.'

Emilio hesitated. 'Did you deal with your father?'

She nodded. 'It didn't take long.'

He gave her a searching look. 'How did it feel?'

'Not as good as I expected.'

'I'm sorry. What about the body? We need to dispose of it.'

'It's taken care of. I took him down to the basement. I'll get someone to bury him tomorrow. Or burn him. Whatever.'

'Okay. Cool.'

'Your dad was here?' Ruth said after Emilio had gone, not quite able to believe what she had just heard. 'What happened? Did you *kill* him?'

'I don't want to talk about it.'

'But Eden . . .'

253

'You should be more worried about yourself,' Eden said. 'Now, please, sit still. I don't want them dragging you out of here before you're ready.'

Eden finished applying the fresh make-up. Then she crouched before Ruth again.

'Listen to me. I know this is scary. But you're going to have to be brave.' She stood up and took hold of Ruth's hands. 'It won't be as bad as you think.'

But Ruth could tell she was lying.

'Eden . . .'

'Don't. No more questions. Let's get this done.'

Chapter 40

I pressed my ear to the door and heard the sounds of industry. Footsteps going up and down the corridor. The lift pinging. Snatches of conversation as people walked past, the odd word standing out.

Gabriel.

Tonight.

Ceremony.

Ceremony? What did that mean?

And then they came.

Brittany was dressed for a party in a sleeveless black trouser suit that exposed her huge biceps. Nick, the security guy who had helped her torture me, wore a tuxedo with a rifle slung over his back like it was part of the outfit.

'Come,' said Brittany. She grabbed my arm and escorted me down the corridor to the lift, Nick following behind. She pressed the button and the three of us ascended one floor. From the buttons in the lift, I knew we were one floor from the top, where the penthouse presumably was.

'Is Callum dead?' I asked.

'Callum? Who's that?' she responded with a smirk.

The lift opened to reveal an empty corridor with a door at either end.

'Go on and check they're ready,' Brittany said to Nick.

'What's going on?' I asked after he'd left. 'I heard something about a ceremony. What does that mean?'

'You'll see.'

Nick came back. 'They're ready.'

Brittany led me down the corridor and opened the door.

She pushed me inside and hands grabbed at me. There were people all around me, as if I'd entered a crowded nightclub, minus the pounding music. There were a hundred people here, give or take, and I wondered if this was all of them, the whole cult, or just a portion. I looked around to see if there were any other faces I recognised and caught a glimpse of the model, Jade Thomson, whose picture I'd looked up after Callum and Wanda told me about her. Emilio was there too, plus the driver of the van who had brought me here. There was no sign of Eden, though. Or Ruth.

I was pushed through the throng and into a space where the crowd had parted. They encircled me. The men were in dinner jackets, the women in cocktail dresses, dripping with jewellery. I stood there and tried not to show how scared I was.

One side of the circle – the side furthest from the door – parted to reveal the full extent of the room. It was a huge space, with a glass wall stretching its entire length, the glowing lights of New York beyond; the same view I'd had from the smaller room in which I'd been kept. Around the perimeter, dozens of white candles flickered. On one wall hung a massive portrait of Gabriel, looking every inch the cult leader.

And here he was, in the flesh.

He stepped into the gap that had opened when the crowd had moved aside, framed by the glass wall and the city, his flattering portrait to his right. Like the others, he was wearing expensive eveningwear, including a black velvet jacket that appeared to shimmer in the low light. Mona stood beside him, wearing a red dress. I tried to catch her eye but she ignored me, like I wasn't worthy of her attention.

'This,' Gabriel said in a booming voice, a hand pointed in my direction, 'is the one who has caused us so much trouble. The one who killed Dennis.'

'But I didn't—'

My voice was drowned out by a great hissing noise, as if a giant serpent had slithered into the room. I looked around me at the faces, all those beautiful faces made ugly by hatred. Somebody spat at my feet and a man tried to get to me, to land a punch, but another held him back. A hundred nameless strangers glared at me. But they all hated me.

'He's lying to all of you,' I shouted.

'Quiet!' a dark-haired woman snapped, and the people around her echoed her. A man bared his teeth at me and drew a finger across his throat.

Gabriel spoke again, hushing the throng. 'Tonight – together – we will show this man what we are all about. And we will show him what happens when you attempt to hurt us.'

So that's why Gabriel hadn't killed me yet. I was part of this display of power.

A whisper of excitement ran through the crowd.

'Protect one, protect all,' somebody shouted, and the chant went up.

Protect one, protect all.

Gabriel let them chant for a minute, basking in the din, and then raised a hand. Instantly, the mob fell silent.

'Take him,' he said, and Brittany and Emilio stepped forward, grabbed hold of me and dragged me past Gabriel to the far end of the room, near the glass wall. I checked over my shoulder and saw Nick standing behind me, his rifle still slung over his back.

'Now you're going to see,' Brittany whispered in my ear before aiming a subtle jab into my kidneys.

She gripped my arm just above the elbow and Emilio did the same on the other side. 'You're going to enjoy this,' he said. He wore the grin of a raver whose ecstasy tablet was starting to kick in.

The crowd was hushed now. All I could hear was breathing.

'Now, let's forget this unpleasantness,' said Gabriel. 'Tonight we have two new members to welcome. Two beautiful young souls. Are you ready?'

A cheer went up, a chorus of yeses.

The door opened and two people came in. One of them was a red-haired woman, clad like all the others in a designer dress. She held the hand of a blond man in his mid-twenties, with a dimple on his chin and cheekbones to kill for. He was wearing a long white robe with a hood.

Gabriel approached the young man and embraced him for a few seconds before turning back to the crowd. 'This, as many of you already know, is Danny.'

There was a chorus of 'Welcome, Danny!'

Danny looked around with a sheepish smile as the crowd clapped and cheered and called out 'Welcome' and 'One of us'. It went on and on until Gabriel called for quiet.

'Danny has been brought into our family by Marie. So please, all of you, thank Marie.'

The redhead who was holding Danny's hand grinned as everyone cheered and shouted their thanks.

'Please, Marie,' said Gabriel, 'help prepare Danny. Everyone else, stand back.'

Marie whispered something in Danny's ear. From my place on the other side of the room I couldn't be certain, but it looked as if his Adam's apple bobbed and a fearful look crossed his face. But with Marie's encouragement, he walked into the centre of the circle. Somebody pushed forward a bench, like one you might find in a gym. Marie stroked Danny's forehead and kissed him on the cheek. Then she unfastened the robe and it fell into a puddle around his feet.

The crowd fell silent as Danny, clad in just his underwear, lay on his back on the bench.

'Thank you, Marie,' Gabriel said, and she melted into the crowd, leaving Gabriel alone beside the prone young man. His skin was smooth and hairless, like a professional swimmer's, and the briefs he wore left little to the imagination.

'It is time for Danny to wear our mark,' Gabriel said. 'The mark of belonging. Of loyalty. The mark that everyone in this room wears.'

'A mark?' I said. 'What—'

'Shut up,' hissed Brittany, jabbing me in the kidneys again.

Gabriel said something to Danny, and he nodded but it looked like he was trying not to appear scared.

Gabriel raised his arms. 'Danny, do you promise to abide by the rules as they have been explained to you?'

'I do.' There was a tremor in his voice.

'Please say it again,' Gabriel said gently.

'I do. I *do*.'

A ripple of laughter ran through the crowd; a release of tension.

'I like your enthusiasm,' said Gabriel, and they all laughed again. I could see Gabriel soaking it all in, the attention and approval of his crowd causing him to puff up. 'And do you promise to protect your fellow members as they will protect you?'

Jesus, I thought. *It's like a wedding.*

'I promise.' Danny's voice sounded weak – a mix of excitement and fear. He glanced at Marie. Was sex going to be part of this?

259

Was she going to take him to a bedroom after this to consummate his marriage to this so-called network? Or would she mount him right there in front of everyone, with the crowd cheering them on? Nothing would have surprised me now.

'Do you swear to keep our existence a secret and to help eliminate any threat against us?'

'I swear.'

Gabriel knelt beside the young man. 'Then you are ready to join us. From now until your dying day. *Juctim tamquam unum.* Together as one.'

'Together as one,' echoed the crowd.

Was that what the liquor store owner had been talking about when he'd described Eden as speaking Italian? I could see it: members of the cult signing off their phone calls with their Latin slogan.

'Now it is time to wear the mark.'

Gabriel put a surgeon's mask across his face and produced something from his pocket. It looked like a large pen.

'Hold him still,' he said, and a pair of men strode forward, each taking hold of one of Danny's legs. Then another pair of men appeared by his shoulders. One of them produced what looked like a flat strip of leather, and slipped it between Danny's teeth.

Gabriel pressed a button on the pen-shaped object he was holding.

'You like barbecue?' Brittany whispered in my ear.

Gabriel held the object over Danny's lower body and waited for a moment. I could see a red glow from the tip of the pen. Then he pulled down the waistband of Danny's briefs, and touched the pen to the soft, smooth flesh of Danny's pubic area.

Danny's whole body convulsed like he'd been given an electric shock, his groin and belly rising from the bench a few inches before slamming back down. A terrible sound came from his throat, a scream of pain strangled by the strip of leather between his teeth.

'Hold him down!' Gabriel shouted, his voice muffled by the mask. Around him, I saw his followers put their hands over their noses and mouths to protect against the smell of burned flesh. But I guessed they had all seen – and smelled – this before. They had all been through it.

Gabriel lowered the cauterising pen again, touching the shaved area of Danny's groin. Again, the young man convulsed, but Gabriel's helpers held him flat. I didn't want to look but couldn't help myself. I had to see. It was like watching someone undergo dental treatment without anaesthetic, and I didn't understand why they hadn't given him something to dull the pain. Or perhaps pain was part of the experience. He would remember this experience forever. If he ever had doubts, he would recall what he had put himself through to join. If he found himself coming close to sympathising with a person he had been asked to harm or kill, he would remember his own pain. Perhaps he would see anyone who hadn't been through this as weak, soft.

But right now, Danny only had one thing on his mind: the burning agony of a red-hot filament being drawn across his flesh.

The crowd had closed around Gabriel so my view was blocked, but I could hear Danny's grunts. The smell had reached me now, and it was even worse than the noises. Brittany was right. It was like meat cooking – no, it *was* that, precisely; raw flesh sizzling and burning. The stench of seared human skin filled the room and I saw a young man near Gabriel gag. Another had gone green. I tried not to breathe through my nose, but then I thought I could taste it at the back of my throat.

I knew if I survived – and I really didn't believe that was possible – I would never forget this. Would never get that taste out of my mouth, that smell from my nostrils.

At long last, ten minutes after it had begun, Gabriel stepped back and shouted, 'One of us!'

261

The crowd roared.

Danny was helped into a sitting, then standing, position. His face was pink and streaked with sweat and tears. But he was smiling. Gabriel placed his palms on Danny's cheeks and kissed his forehead. The crowd continued to cheer. Two of the helpers led Danny out of the room, followed by Marie.

'What was it?' I said to Brittany. 'What did he brand him with?'

'It's a cauterising pen. Hurts like fuck.' She grinned at me. Her eyes glowed with the mad fervour of a true believer. 'You want to see?'

I nodded.

'Show him, Emilio.'

With a smile, Emilio unbuttoned his trousers and pushed them down at the front to show me. Despite what I had just witnessed, I was shocked by the mess of scar tissue there, the pink lines and curves that covered an area about four inches in diameter.

'What is it?' I asked again. It looked like an incomplete circle with two mountain peaks inside.

'It's our symbol,' she said. 'The symbol of togetherness.'

And then I saw what it was. It wasn't a circle and mountains. It was two letters: G and M.

Gabriel and Mona.

They were branding members with their initials.

Before I could say anything, the crowd burst into applause again. The crowd had reshaped itself into a circle around Gabriel. He held up his hands again to silence them.

'Bring her in,' he said.

Chapter 41

Eden came into the room. She was dressed up like all the other people here, though her dress was black and simple. As she came in, she nodded at Gabriel and Mona, who were standing side by side, and then her gaze cut through the crowd and found me. I glared at her but she didn't react, just held my eye for a moment before stepping aside.

Ruth entered.

She was wearing a short white dress, and I gasped when I saw her. Over the years, I had seen her at her weakest moments: waking from one of her many nightmares about being a child who had been sent to live with a monstrous foster family, one that had terrorised and mocked her; comforting her when she came home from an audition that had gone badly. But I had never seen her like this.

She was hunched over, arms wrapped around herself as if she was freezing. Her skin was so pale she appeared bloodless. Her hair had been done, and she was made up like a bride on her wedding day – an analogy I tried to push away – but she was clearly scared. Weakened and cowed by whatever had happened to her here.

Eden leaned over and brushed a strand of hair from Ruth's face. But she still stared at the floor.

'Ruth!' I called, but she couldn't hear me above the rising hub-bub, the ripple of excitement that ran through the room.

I pulled against Brittany and Emilio's grip, desperate to get to her, but they held me firm. The crowd stepped back, clearing a space, just as they had when Danny had been branded.

'Bring her forward,' Gabriel said.

Eden pulled Ruth into the centre of the space so she stood before Gabriel. Mona stayed on the inner edge of the circle. Gabriel gestured for Emilio to come over, and said something in his ear. Emilio produced a handgun from inside his jacket – from my time in Wanda's armoury, I recognised it as a Glock 36 – and stood behind Ruth and Eden. Brittany continued to hold on to me, with Nick behind us.

Gabriel raised his hands and, again, the murmuring crowd fell silent.

'Tonight, we have gathered to welcome two new members.' A long pause. 'But as you all know, we only allow people to join us who deserve it.' He pointed a finger at Ruth. 'This woman does not deserve to be one of us.'

A gasp rippled through the crowd.

What was he talking about?

Gabriel went on, his voice growing louder. 'She has brought nothing but chaos ever since she came here. Dennis is dead. Mona lost her husband. He was not one of us, but it caused great pain to our co-founder.'

A murmur of sympathy; hands reaching out to console Mona. Did these people really believe she cared, when she had been screw-ing Krugman? I noticed, though, that Eden seemed shocked. Like this wasn't in the script.

'I have a confession,' Gabriel said, resting his hand on his chest and adopting a solemn tone. I had to hand it to him: if he ever wanted to go into politics, he'd probably end up as president. It was like watching Obama or Trump at one of their rallies, the crowd eating out of his hand.

'I thought Ruth here was special. I thought she was – and I feel foolish saying this – the one who was destined to be by my side. The woman I've searched for all these years. Look at her. Look at her beauty, the light that shines out of her, even when she stands before us, wretched and guilty. I allowed her beauty to dazzle me. To fool me.'

He reached out to touch Ruth and she squirmed away, looking at him in disgust.

He grinned darkly at her and went on. 'Then I discovered I had invited a serpent into our garden. And I couldn't accept it. I thought I could force her to join us, even though that goes against everything we stand for. Every one of you here volunteered to become one of us. All of you came to us willingly.'

A murmur of assent. Someone said, 'Hell, yeah.'

'And I was going to put us all in danger by making Ruth join. I was foolish. I was weak. I was reminded that, after all, I am just a man. A man, bewitched by beauty.'

He turned in a circle, reaching out to the onlookers. 'I am sorry for what I was going to do. I hope . . . I hope you can forgive me.'

It was quite a performance. And I half expected someone, anyone, to start laughing. But they were taken in by it. All of them. Only Eden looked perturbed by what was going on, as if she was pissed off that Gabriel had changed the script without telling her. Ruth looked around at the crowd like they were collectively insane.

And they were. A madness had fallen over this group, a madness that reinforced itself as they fed off each other. It was a kind of mass hysteria. Gabriel had said he had been bewitched by Ruth, but these people were the bewitched ones.

It was terrifying, and I could see that terror in Ruth's eyes.

'We forgive you,' someone said. Another person repeated it. And then they were all saying it. *We forgive you. We forgive you.* And then, 'There's nothing to forgive.'

A new chant went up: *Nothing to forgive. Nothing to forgive.*

It took them two or three minutes to quieten down. Gabriel basked in it, mock-humble, like a preacher accepting donations from his flock. Then he put his hands up and they hushed.

'Thank you,' he said. 'Thank you all. I am touched.' He swallowed. My God, he was a fraud. Again, he reminded me of a politician, or a preacher. 'But now we have business to attend to.' He pointed at Ruth. 'Not only did this woman reject us, but she brought a stranger to our door. A stranger who has threatened our very existence by spreading lies about us. A man who enlisted the help of a journalist in an attempt to expose us.'

Dozens of pairs of eyes turned towards me and the hiss went up again, the invisible serpent returning to the room.

'Don't worry, don't worry,' Gabriel said. 'The journalist will be dealt with. We now know where she lives. But what do we do to people who betray and threaten us?'

'We remove them,' somebody said.

'We kill them,' said another.

'Bring him forward,' Gabriel said.

Brittany dragged me into the middle of the circle and held me firm before Gabriel. I was close enough to punch him. I would have tried it, if Brittany hadn't been holding on to me. Though if I was going to die anyway . . .

Ruth was just a metre away. She stared at me. And I noticed that she didn't look so scared anymore. At some point during Gabriel's long speech, her demeanour had changed. Like she'd switched from playing one role to another. And I realised I'd seen this before. I'd witnessed her vomiting from nerves a minute before

266

a play began. Then, when the curtain went up, she strode on to the stage full of confidence.

I held her gaze for a moment. She nodded at me. Then she turned her attention to Gabriel.

'Do these people know who you really are?' she asked, her voice soft but carrying as if she were onstage in front of an audience. 'Do they know that you're nothing more than a glorified stalker? Do they know how you sat in that room upstairs, jerking off in front of a dumb horror film like a sad little boy?'

Gabriel's face turned pink.

'Do they know how fucking crazy you are?'

'You bitch!'

He lunged for her. He still had the cauterising pen in his hand, the tip glowing red-hot, and he aimed for her face.

I elbowed Brittany in the stomach, pulled free and threw myself into Gabriel's path. The pen connected with my cheek.

I had never felt pain like it, and I think I must have cried out, but I was momentarily blinded by the agony, the burn, and I was only dimly aware of Eden grabbing hold of Ruth and pushing her to the ground, and Gabriel shouting, 'Kill him', presumably meaning me.

I saw Emilio raise his gun towards me.

Behind him, a blur of motion. It was Eden, pulling a Glock from her bag.

Shooting Emilio in the head.

Chapter 42

For a second, nobody moved. Blood had sprayed from Emilio's head, coating Gabriel and Mona. Gabriel turned to Eden, his mouth hanging open, blood in his beard. At the same moment, the door to the room, which was about fifteen feet from where we stood, flew open and someone burst through it, holding aloft an assault rifle.

It was Callum.

'Everybody down!' he yelled.

Pandemonium broke out in the crowd. There was a surge away from the door, a scramble towards the windows at the back of the room. Somebody started screaming, and then it was a chorus of screams and yells as they pushed and shoved each other to get away from Callum. Somebody barged into me, sending me sprawling, but a pair of hands caught me. Ruth. When she pulled me up I saw the room had split into two groups. Most people were crowded around the windows. In the middle of the room: me, Ruth, Eden and Gabriel, with Emilio's body on the floor at our feet.

Eden had her arm around Gabriel's neck, pushing him down so he was bent over. She held the muzzle of the gun against his head. Callum was slightly to the side of our group, holding what I thought was an AK-47. Facing us, between our group and the huddled mass to their rear, stood Brittany, Nick and Mona. Nick had his rifle in his hands, aimed at Callum, who pointed his own gun back at the other man. Brittany held a handgun – presumably the Glock that Emilio had dropped – and had it trained on Eden.

'Come on!' Callum shouted, and Eden retreated backwards towards the door, dragging Gabriel with her. We followed. Callum kept his gun aimed at Nick.

Mona stood between Brittany and Nick, weaponless. She took a step towards us. 'Let him go,' she said.

Eden retreated another half-step and tightened her grip on Gabriel's neck. 'Don't come any closer.'

'Let Gabriel go,' Mona said, 'and we'll let you all walk out of here.'

'Liar.'

Slightly behind Mona, I watched Nick adjust his stance. He still had his rifle aimed at Callum and he looked jacked, his eyes wild, finger on the trigger.

'Kill them,' Mona said.

'But, Gabriel . . .' said Brittany.

'*Just do it.*'

Brittany still hesitated, but Nick didn't. Callum must have realised at the same time as me, and he squeezed the trigger.

He missed. The shot went wild, not striking anyone.

Nick shot Callum in the chest. The impact sent him crashing against the wall.

Eden cried out. She took her gun away from Gabriel's head and shot Nick. He went down. Then Eden turned the gun towards Mona – but Gabriel, now the gun was no longer against his temple, shoved Eden so she lurched to the left, and the bullet she fired missed Mona. There was a quick, desperate struggle, but somehow she managed to keep hold of Gabriel and put the gun against his head again.

'Shoot her!' Mona screamed at Brittany, but Brittany hesitated. There was no way she could get a shot off at Eden without there being a high chance she would kill Gabriel.

'Give it to me.' Mona snatched the gun off Brittany and pointed it at Eden and Gabriel.

I tried to catch Ruth's eye. We were six feet from the door. Mona had already demonstrated that she didn't care if she killed Gabriel. But she must have known that if her first shot hit Gabriel, not Eden, then Eden would surely shoot her. To win this, she would need to hit Eden in the head with her first shot. And if she managed that, Ruth and I would be her next targets.

There was the rifle lying on the floor beneath Nick's body. Brittany kept looking at it, then flicking her eyes towards Eden, measuring her chances of getting to it. Surely, any second now, she would decide to try it – because Eden couldn't risk removing the gun from Gabriel's head.

And then Gabriel said, 'Kill her, Mona', and that made up my mind.

I grabbed hold of Ruth and pulled her through the open door, slamming it shut behind us.

She pushed me away. 'What the hell are you doing? I need to help Eden.'

'No. We need to go. We'll call the police.' I tugged at her arm, pulling her to the lift and punching the button.

She struggled to free herself. 'Dammit, Adam, I can't just leave her.'

'What? Ruth, please, come on.' I stabbed at the button again. The 'Up' arrow was lit but there was no sign of the lift. 'Where the hell is it?'

'But I promised her,' Ruth said.

'What?'

'This evening. She came to see me. She told me what was going to happen, except she said Gabriel was going to brand me.' She shuddered. 'She said she was going to get me out, but I had to promise to help her afterwards.'

I stared at her. 'Help her? How?' The lift still wasn't coming. 'We're going to have to go down the stairs. There must be an exit here—'

A gunshot came from within the room.

At the same time, the lift doors pinged and slid open. Inside were half a dozen men, dressed head to toe in black, carrying guns.

Police.

'Oh, thank God, thank God,' I said.

Every gun in sight was pointed at us. More officers appeared from the end of the corridor; I guessed they had come up the stairs. They levelled their weapons at us as well.

'Get on the floor and—'

The door to the communal room burst open. It was Eden, still holding on to Gabriel. Blood was pouring from a wound on her shoulder. Mona must have taken her shot but only managed to wound her.

The cops had turned as one, and were all now aiming their guns at her.

Eden dropped the weapon she was holding and let go of Gabriel at the same time. Gabriel fell on to his hands and knees, next to the Glock, while Eden stood there with her hands in the air.

'Don't move!' one of the cops screamed at Gabriel.

He looked at the cop, then at the gun. Eden stood beside him, her hands still in the air.

'Move and I'll shoot,' yelled the cop.

Gabriel seemed to think about it. I still wonder, sometimes, what went through his head in that moment. If he thought about everything he'd built. If he remembered where he'd come from, the

271

boy he'd once been: the boy who liked the theatre and computers, who'd been bullied and humiliated. I wonder if he contemplated what life would be like for him in jail, all his power and wealth and influence taken away. Nobody to protect him anymore.

The cops continued to shout at him to leave the gun, to put his hands on his head, and then Gabriel locked eyes with Ruth.

He reached for the gun.

Chapter 43

I took my coffee out on to the front deck and, not for the first time, had to remind myself that this was real. We were actually staying here, in a house on Carbon Beach in Malibu. There were palm trees, a barbecue grill, five bedrooms, a beautiful pool, and every morning, after writing for an hour on the deck, I would take a walk along the white sand, down to the ocean, saying hi to the middle-aged rock star who lived in the next house along. Maybe take a drive, just cruising the canyons and hills of Los Angeles, nowhere to go or be.

I felt relatively safe on the beach and in my car.

The beach house belonged to the head of the network that was making the TV show Ruth was filming. It had a huge budget and ensemble cast of A-list stars, and was being hyped as the next *Stranger Things* or *American Horror Story*. It was adapted from a novel called *Sweetmeat*, by a fellow Brit. I'd met him and his wife at a party thrown by the network. All the cast were there, and the novelist had seemed starstruck. He kept pointing to well-known actors and saying, 'I can't believe he's going to be playing so-and-so.' He'd seemed a little drunk, while I was sticking to water. I was off alcohol. And so was Ruth.

Then Lucas, that was his name, started telling me how he'd finally finished his second novel after a long, agonising process. It was semi-autobiographical, about a missing child and the legend of a witch who lived in the woods. We talked about writer's block and the struggle to come up with new ideas.

'I was going to quit writing,' I told him.

'But now you've got something to write about?'

'Exactly.'

I sat at the little table on the deck, sipped my coffee and flipped open my laptop, reading over the pages I'd written the day before. I was working on my own TV show with the provisional title of *The Network*, a title that would have to change. It was about a shadowy cult that operated among the beautiful people of New York and Los Angeles, led by a reclusive billionaire with a tragic past. It was a high-octane thriller with a Shakespearian cast of characters, and they were currently in the process of hiring a cast to shoot a pilot.

During the days, I worked on the script. At night, I lay beside Ruth, unable to sleep, convinced that every creak was a footstep; that the gentle lap of the ocean beyond the walls was actually the sound of somebody breathing close by.

Because I kept remembering what Gabriel had said to me.

We're everywhere.

There had been ninety-three people present at the ceremony that night, including me and Ruth. The FBI had turned the entire building upside down, along with Gabriel's offices and other properties. They had searched his computers, his phones, everything. But there were no records. No list of who belonged to the cult. It appeared he had kept everything in his head. And when he'd reached for that gun and the cop had shot him, that knowledge had died with him. Because every surviving member, all the people who had been there – except Eden – swore there was no cult. No network. They had no idea what the police and the FBI were talking about. They were just associates of Gabriel's, that was all, and they had been invited to his place for a party.

It was as if they had been given a pre-prepared script. Deny, deny, deny. They didn't know Eden or Ruth or me. We were lying. Even with all the evidence against them, each one of them stuck to the story. No network. No secret club. No knowledge of murders or kidnappings. They had never heard the phrase 'Protect one, protect all'. They hadn't seen that poor boy get branded; it must have happened in a different room.

The day after the ceremony and our escape, I had spent an entire day in an interview room with two FBI agents, going through what I knew, over and over. For a while I wasn't sure if they believed me. I had to persuade them I wasn't a member of the cult, that I hadn't been involved in any criminal activity.

Apart from burying Krugman's body in the woods. They didn't like that. And they didn't like it when I told them I hadn't gone straight to the police because I didn't know if I could trust them. They'd had a lot of questions about Callum and how I had really met him. Did I know he had been a cop once, in California? A disgraced cop with a record of domestic violence and a wife who would never testify? I told them I knew some of it.

In the end, they let me go. Krugman was a crooked cop, a murderer, and the DA and the police didn't want a spotlight being shone on that aspect of the case.

And they were lucky. The press were far more interested in the reclusive billionaire, with his connections to most of the big, household-name tech companies. They unearthed photos of him at fundraising events chatting with prominent politicians and famous CEOs. They tracked down everyone he'd known at school and college and got them to tell all about the 'loner weirdo who loved Shakespeare and computer games'. *The Nerd Who Turned*, read one of the headlines.

They focused on Jade Thomson too, the only really famous person who had been there, and wrote various Beauty and the Beast–style exposés in which it was alleged she and Gabriel had had sex in his 'penthouse lair' on piles of hundred-dollar bills. She was denying everything else, so why not give her one more thing to refute?

There was also some interest in another survivor: Mona, the rich, privately educated WASP who ran a 'kooky' business separating bored and gullible millionaire housewives from their money. TMZ ran a story about how she and Krugman had been sleeping together, apparently leaked by the police. And now she was in custody, awaiting trial for sex trafficking: the trafficked person being Ruth – who, it was alleged, had been procured by Mona for Gabriel as a sex slave. Ruth was reluctant to go along with this at first, but the FBI convinced her it was a charge they could make stick. Mona was also charged with conspiracy to murder Jack. She had shot Eden in the shoulder, too, though that was a more minor offence.

'It's difficult to pin charges on any of the others,' one of the agents told us later. 'Pretty much everyone we have evidence against is dead.' He meant Krugman, Emilio, Nick and, of course, Gabriel. 'But we're trying. We're looking at every person who was there, everyone they associate with, any unsolved murders or missing persons cases near where they live. We're monitoring them too. Every phone call, every email.'

The only other person they had managed to charge was a guy called Tyler French, who Jesse had identified as the man who had stabbed his best friend after being shown photos of everyone who had been at the ceremony. The second man who had been in the park that day was Emilio. Tyler was denying everything, but the police were confident of a conviction.

Brittany was in jail too. It turned out she was really called Anya Simpson and she had gone missing three years ago, having jumped bail after being charged with assault.

I still heard from Wanda occasionally. It was thanks to her that I was still alive, and I would forever be grateful. Unknown to me at the time, she and Callum had an arrangement that, if Callum didn't contact Wanda every four hours, she should alert the authorities and tell them everything – including, as proof she wasn't making it up, the location of Krugman's body. Thankfully, Wanda was known to the FBI because of her previous crucial role in bringing down the sex-trafficking cult she'd told us about. They took her seriously.

Now she was, unofficially, helping the authorities with their inquiries. 'Some of my followers have accused me of selling out by helping the Feds,' she'd told me on the phone.

'Are there any signs of activity?' I'd asked. 'Do you think there are still a lot of them out there?'

'There must be. From everything we've found out, and from what Mona and Gabriel said to you and Ruth, it seems unbelievable that there were only ninety of them. It's possible that Gabriel was exaggerating. I mean, it seems like the kind of thing he'd do. Maybe he made it compulsory for every member of the cult to be there that night to witness the ceremony. But my gut tells me there are more of them.'

'And what do you think they're doing?'

She'd answered without hesitation. 'They're lying in wait. Sleeping. Waiting until they think it's safe to start up again, with a new leader. These people really believe, Adam, and from what you said, Gabriel had made it clear that he wanted his network to carry on his name after he died. He saw this as a forever thing. Like L. Ron Hubbard with Scientology. In the end, the founder isn't that important. And the Feds say they're monitoring everyone, but it's not hard to communicate in secret.'

Ever since that conversation, I'd had the feeling I was being watched. Because no matter how many times the police told Ruth and me that we were safe, I didn't believe it. We were the enemy.

We were going to testify against Mona when her trial eventually took place.

If I were them, I would try to stop us.

I worked on my screenplay for a little while, then watched the ocean, wondering if I would ever feel safe.

We're everywhere.

I went back inside, washed up my empty coffee cup and fixed lunch for myself. This was how my days went. In the afternoon, I swam a few lengths in the pool, then went online for a while. Did a little more work. Answered some emails. Went on to 4Chan and searched the boards for references to Gabriel and his followers. I thought about how by writing this TV show I was making the target on my head even bigger, before persuading myself it would all be okay.

Night fell. The moon shone on the ocean. I waited for Ruth to come home and told myself that this was what I'd always wanted.

We're everywhere.

Life was perfect.

And then, at 8.30 p.m., when I was two episodes into a new series on Netflix, there was a knock at the door.

Chapter 44

I peered out of the side window. It was a young woman with blonde hair. She had her head down but I knew instantly who it was. I removed the chains from the door and slid both bolts across, then opened it.

'Hi, Adam.'

'Hello, Eden.'

She smiled at me, just as she had that evening in Brooklyn, nine months ago. She wasn't dripping wet this time, though. She didn't look like she'd crawled out of the Pacific. And she wasn't a stranger. Not anymore.

'Are you going to invite me in?' she asked.

I stepped aside to let her enter, then closed the door after her, sliding the bolts back into place and re-applying the chains.

She watched me. 'Paranoid much?'

'Aren't you?'

I knew that she was in witness protection. She was the prosecution's most valuable asset, had done a deal with them whereby she would testify in return for immunity. She was the only member of the cult who had even admitted it existed. The only person willing and able to stand up in court and describe what Gabriel's organisation had been like, from the inside. She had already helped the authorities dig up two bodies and had, I knew, spent days – weeks – painstakingly telling them everything she knew.

This was the first time I had seen her in the flesh since the night of the ceremony. The first time I had spoken to her properly since we'd all got drunk on tequila, and whatever else she'd dosed it with.

She had helped us. But, unlike Wanda, I didn't feel that I owed her. Because I blamed her too.

I led her into the kitchen, which was huge and shiny, with a central island.

'Do you want a drink?' I asked. 'We don't have any booze in the house, I'm afraid.'

'Water's fine. Thanks.'

I pulled out a stool on one side and gestured for her to sit opposite me.

She looked around. 'What a place,' she said. Beyond the kitchen window, we could see the ocean shining in the moonlight.

'I know. I always thought of myself as an East Coast kind of person. Now I'm not so sure.'

'Planning on staying here?'

I shrugged. 'It's where the work is. I guess we'll go back to the UK at some point.' Despite the luxury of my surroundings, I missed London. I missed our cat, who was still being looked after by a neighbour. She had undoubtedly forgotten us. I'd been back at Christmas to see my family and pick up some stuff, shocked to feel cold for the first time in months. Then I'd returned to the never-ending sunshine.

'Is that where Ruth is now?' Eden asked, sipping her water. 'At work?'

'Yeah. She'll be another hour or so.'

'Good,' she said. 'That gives us plenty of time to talk.'

'What, do you want to reminisce about the good times? When you took my girlfriend into the clutches of a death cult and almost got us both killed?'

That brought a faint smile. 'I'm sorry, Adam. But if it hadn't been me it would have been someone else. And that person wouldn't have got you both out of there.'

I paused. There were so many things I wanted to ask her.

'Did Gabriel tell you how it all started? It was him and Mona together, right? At Columbia?' I said.

'You know how many times I've had to go through this with the Feds? But yeah, they started it – only it was a year or so after they left college. Mona had already given Gabriel the cash he needed to start playing the stock markets, and apparently they went out one night to celebrate his first big success. That's when they came up with the idea.'

She traced a pattern on the island with her finger as she continued.

'We all knew the origin story. It was part of our central mythology. One night, Mona got mugged, was convinced she was going to be murdered, except some passers-by happened to scare them off. That got her thinking about how even being wealthy couldn't protect her from all the bad shit in the world. At the same time, Jack was doing some study into the psychology of gangs and criminal networks. How people in those kinds of groups feel safe because they have the protection of their fellow gang members. That's what started it all. So they set out to recruit people. Gabriel and Mona had money and were starting to get influence. They needed muscle. It all grew from there.' She stared into space. 'It was simple, and seductive, you know? Being told no one will ever be able to hurt you again – and at the same time, they would teach you how to be confident, how to make money, how to walk through the world with your head held high.'

'What about Jack?' I asked. 'Was he never part of it?'

'No. Too wimpish,' Mona said. 'We had a long, drunken chat about him one afternoon in a bar near their house.'

That must have been where Jack had seen Eden, when he was spying on Mona to look for evidence of her affair. An encounter that had led to his death.

'She told me Jack was happy with his life, mostly. Too busy having tawdry affairs with students to worry too much about what Mona was up to. I asked her if Jack had any suspicions and she told me she thought he knew something, but preferred to stick his head in the sand. I could tell Mona got a kick out of it – having this massive secret from her husband. A much bigger secret than the affair she was having.'

I rubbed my face. 'It's my fault Jack's dead.'

'Mine too. But if it makes you feel any better, I think they were planning to kill him anyway. Mona knew Jack suspected she was cheating on him. If he'd found out it was Krugman – that would have posed a risk to the group. Gabriel was putting pressure on her to do something about it, and then when you turned up with my picture on your phone she was forced to act.'

'Wait. Did Mona kill Jack herself?'

'Um, hello? Didn't you realise that?'

'No, Krugman told me it was him.' But that, of course, had been before I knew Mona was part of the cult.

She had murdered her own husband. I should have been shocked, but my capacity for surprise had taken a severe beating lately. And knowing they had been planning to kill Jack anyway didn't make me feel any better about my role in it.

I decided to move on. 'The stuff with Callum. Did you plan it all along?'

'Yeah. Well . . . I hated him. I joined up to get away from him and everything he did to me and my mom. He was an asshole. And

I didn't go looking for him, but when I saw him at the convention, once I'd recovered from the shock, I made a decision. I let him follow me.'

'Why?'

'Because I was already disillusioned. Let's just say the scales had fallen away from my eyes. It was the way Gabriel treated women. His obsession with young actresses. You know Ruth wasn't the first, right?'

Emilio had said something about that, and the police were trying to link the disappearances of two young actresses to Gabriel.

'I'd been such a believer,' Eden continued. 'I thought Gabriel was my saviour. And there were parts of it I found hard to let go.'

'Like getting revenge on people who crossed you? Like Jesse and Brandon?'

'I'm not proud of that. I didn't actually want them killed, but I told Emilio about it and he took it into his own hands.' She sighed. 'I couldn't go to the authorities because I had no idea who I could trust. If Gabriel or any of the others suspected I was making plans against them, I would have ended up buried in those woods. So I had to pretend to go along with everything. It was hard. I couldn't even risk saying anything to Ruth at the hideaway because I didn't know if she'd slip up and tell Gabriel. Also, all the rooms, apart from the penthouse, were bugged. Gabriel was listening to us all the time.'

That didn't surprise me.

'I knew after I disappeared with Ruth that my dad would ask you to team up. And I had installed software on your phone so I knew where you were and could listen to your calls, read your messages.'

Seeing my face, she said, 'Sorry about that. But it was necessary. If I hadn't done it . . .'

I shook my head. What did it matter now?

'I needed my dad to get into the building. Once I'd discovered that you guys were getting help from Wanda, I sent information to one of her researchers that helped her connect Krugman to Gabriel. It was pretty straightforward. My dad was a former cop. I knew he'd make some arrangement with Wanda to call the Feds if he disappeared. Then all I had to do was wait for Emilio to bring you and my dad to the building. I knew they wanted to interrogate you. To be honest, I was kind of winging it after that. You obviously know that I pretended to kill Dad. When I talked to him and left him in a room with a gun, he wanted us to leave straight away. But I told him I wasn't leaving without Ruth. And I also wanted Gabriel dead. I wanted the cult destroyed so they wouldn't come after me. So I made a pact with him. If he did as I asked and came into the ceremony as soon as he heard a shot, we could talk about a reconciliation.'

I got up and refilled my water glass. This conversation was bringing it all back. I could really do with a proper drink.

'Were you upset?' I asked. 'When he was killed?'

'No. I hated him. I was using him.'

But she stared at the counter as she said this and I wasn't sure if I believed her.

'What about Gabriel?' I asked. 'Are you happy he's dead?'

'Oh yes. That gave me great pleasure.'

'Even though he never faced justice?'

She scoffed. 'There isn't enough justice in the world. I told you . . . the way he treated women. The things he made us do. All of us.' She stared out at the ocean. 'I hope he felt those bullets. I hope it hurt.'

My phone, which was lying on the counter, lit up. A message from Ruth. She was a little earlier than expected.

I'm home. Can you open Fort Knox?

I went to the door and let her in, and said, 'We've got a visitor.'

Eden had followed me out to the hallway. The two women stood facing each other for a moment, and then Ruth said, 'Is it time?'

'It is,' Eden replied.

Ruth nodded. She was acting like someone who had just been delivered news she'd been expecting for a long time. News that required action.

I looked from one of them to the other. 'What are you talking about?'

Ruth walked into the kitchen. She reached into a top cupboard and took down a bottle of gin. She poured some into a glass and knocked it back, then refilled the glass. She poured a glass for Eden too.

'Want some?' she said to me.

I stared at her.

'Suit yourself.'

'Ruth, what's going on?' I said.

She sat down at the counter, where Eden had been sitting. Eden stood close by, waiting expectantly. Ruth downed another mouthful of gin.

'I made her a promise,' she said to me. 'When I was tied to Gabriel's bed.'

I remembered what she'd said about promising to help Eden.

She swivelled on the stool towards Eden. 'And anyway, I want to do it.' Her eyes shone. 'I really want to do it.'

'Do what?' I asked.

'You tell him,' Ruth said to Eden.

Eden smiled. She was jiggling from foot to foot with barely suppressed excitement. 'We're starting our own network,' she said.

I waited for them to laugh.

I kept waiting.

'Very funny.'

'It's not a joke, Adam. I'm serious.'

'She's deadly serious,' said Ruth.

Eden came over to me. 'You don't understand because you only saw the bad stuff. But some of what Gabriel created was wonderful. People helping and supporting each other. Protecting one another. It only went wrong because Gabriel was a megalomaniac.'

'"Only",' I said.

'And they tried to expand too fast, got complacent. Drunk on power. Plus the whole branding thing . . .'

'Yeah, we won't do that,' said Ruth. 'And Eden's right. There were good things about it. Gabriel was right when he said it was like a family. Everyone looking out for each other. I was tempted to join, Adam. If they'd gone about it more slowly and subtly, I probably would have. The things he promised . . . That sense of belonging.'

'Oh my God. You want to start your own cult.' They were talking about it like they were planning to start their own business. Like, *Hey, why don't we open a café together?*

'It's not a cult,' Eden said. 'It's a network, and what's wrong with that? We'll keep some of Gabriel's central tenets. It will be secret. It won't have a name. We'll do everything we can to advance and protect other members . . .'

'Protect one, protect all?'

'I think so,' said Ruth.

'Definitely,' said Eden.

'You mean you'll kill people who threaten you?'

'No. We're not going to do that,' said Ruth, but seeing Eden's expression, I wasn't so sure.

'And what about me?' I asked, grabbing the bottle of gin and pouring myself a glass. I couldn't hold out any longer. 'You expect me to join too?'

'Oh no,' said Eden.

Ruth smiled. 'It's women only.'

Eden nodded. 'That's why it went wrong last time. Which means,' she said, turning to me, 'we have a problem. Because how can we keep it secret if you already know?'

I backed away, and Ruth got up from the stool and came over to me. She linked her arm with mine. 'I think we can trust him not to tell.'

'Can we?' Eden asked.

'I think we can,' Ruth said. 'Because he needs us to protect him from the remnants of Gabriel's network.' She whispered in my ear. 'They're *everywhere*.'

They both grinned, lips twitching with mirth.

I stared at them. 'Hang on. This *is* a joke, right?' I said. 'You're not really going to start your own women-only version of the cult, are you?'

They laughed together, clutching one another like they'd just pulled off a brilliant practical joke.

'Oh, thank God,' I said. 'You really had me worried there for a minute.'

'You should be, Adam,' said Eden, her face straight, and suddenly I didn't know if they were kidding or not. But then they both started laughing again, and Eden raised her glass and suggested a toast. *To freedom.* We all lifted our glasses and I told myself they were joking.

Definitely.

I was almost certain of it.

Acknowledgments

Warning: this letter contains spoilers so please don't read it until you've finished reading the novel.

I'm writing this on a dreary, damp afternoon in Wolverhampton, a long way from the streets of New York, where – in my head – I've been living for the past nine months, and where I spent a wonderful week with my family in the summer of 2018, researching this book.

Each day, I dragged my wife and our children around the sweltering, sun-blasted city, scouting locations and soaking up the atmosphere, and every evening we returned to the most important location of all: our Airbnb. The Cunninghams' house in Williamsburg is based on that house, a stone's throw from Bedford Avenue subway. It's where, during a thunderstorm that brought some respite from the insane heat, I first pictured Eden, standing on the front stoop, fist raised to knock on the door. The house had a vintage jukebox and erratic air conditioning, along with a garden that acted as a small oasis in the middle of the metropolis. I'm happy to say, though, that we didn't encounter any cults.

Long-term readers of my books will know that belief is a theme I return to repeatedly, and I have always been fascinated by cults (or new religious movements, as they are sometimes called). Halfway through writing this novel, by which point I had already created Gabriel and his network, I heard about NXIVM, a 'multi-level marketing' organisation based near Albany. Its leader, Keith Raniere, had been accused of operating a cult that contained a 'secret society' of women who were expected to have sex with him. Shortly before I completed this novel, in June 2019, he was convicted of sex trafficking and racketeering. The characters in *The House Guest* are not based on any real cults or cult leaders, but reading about the NXIVM case, and listening to the testimonies of women who escaped, provided inspiration and helped me get into the heads of the people who join such organisations – as well as those who start them.

If you want to find out more about Raniere and NXIVM, I highly recommend Season One of the *Uncover* podcast.

If you enjoyed this book and want to get in touch, you can email me at mark@markedwardsauthor.com or contact me on Facebook (www.facebook.com/markedwardsbooks) or on Twitter (@mredwards). You can also find me on Instagram (@markedwardsauthor).

And if this is your first Mark Edwards book and you'd like to read more, I've put together a guide for new readers, which you can find on my website: www.markedwardsauthor.com/new-readers-guide.

Time for some thanks:

My editors David Downing and Laura Deacon, who passed me the scalpels and mopped my brow as I performed critical surgery on this novel;

Everyone at Thomas & Mercer, including Hatty Stiles, Eoin Purcell, Sana Chebaro, Jack Butler, Nicole Wagner, Sarah Shaw and Gracie Doyle;

My agent Madeleine Milburn and everyone at the agency;

Sophie Ransom and Amber Choudhary at Midas PR for sterling work spreading the word;

Lisa Harrison for helping me make time to do the important stuff, i.e. writing.

Two readers won the dubious honour of having characters in this novel named after them: Niven Kyle and Cara Barker. I hope you enjoyed meeting your namesakes! Thanks also to everyone on my Facebook page and those in my street team, who are the best cheerleaders ever.

This book is dedicated to my children – Poppy, Ellie, Archie and Harry – and my amazing wife, Sara. Thanks for not complaining too much as I marched you around New York in the blazing August heat.

Finally, a big thank you to you, the reader, for taking the time to read this book and making it all the way through to the very last word. Hey, maybe we should get together and start a cult . . .

Only kidding.

Mark Edwards

Free *Short Sharp Shockers* Box Set

Join Mark Edwards' Readers' Club and immediately get a free box set of stories: 'Kissing Games', 'Consenting Adults' and 'Guardian Angel'.

You will also receive regular news and access to exclusive give-aways. It's 100 per cent free and you can opt out at any time.

Join here: www.markedwardsauthor.com/free.

About the Author

Mark Edwards writes psychological thrillers in which scary things happen to ordinary people.

He has sold 3 million books since his first novel, *The Magpies*, was published in 2013, and has topped the bestseller lists several times. His other novels include *Follow You Home*, *The Retreat*, *In Her Shadow*, *Because She Loves Me*, *The Devil's Work* and *Here To Stay*. He has also co-authored six books with Louise Voss.

Originally from Hastings in East Sussex, Mark now lives in Wolverhampton with his wife, their children, three cats and a golden retriever.

Mark loves hearing from readers and can be contacted through his website, www.markedwardsauthor.com, or you can find him on Facebook (@markedwardsbooks), Twitter (@mredwards) and Instagram (@markedwardsauthor).